The Key

Stephanie Turner

NEWMAN SPRINGS PUBLISHING
320 Broad Street
Red Bank, NJ 07701

First originally published by Newman Springs Publishing 2021

ISBN 978-1-63692-595-0 (Paperback)
ISBN 978-1-63692-596-7 (Digital)

Printed in the United States of America

Chapter 1

"Elizabeth?" Ethan sighs, trying to get my attention. Just like the other hundreds of times, I give no response. Why does he think this time is going to be different? It has been a horrible week, and I do not want to talk to anyone about it. I wish he would just leave me alone. It has been four days since I've talked to anyone, and today is going to be no different.

I know I sound like I am being an overdramatic teenager, but this week has been the worst week of my life. Mom and I were attacked on Saturday morning, and my mom was murdered. To make things worse, I could not get ahold of my dad until after the funeral yesterday, which is not like him. Although my parents are not together, they are best friends, and he would have wanted to be at her funeral.

There is one thing confusing me, and it's how my mom died. The police report said that her neck was sliced and she bled to death, but I do not know if I believe that. I have no reason to question the police, except right after I got free from my attacker, I turned around to see where my mom was. That was when I swear I saw her attacker bite her neck. I'm aware that does not make sense, and maybe my mind was playing tricks on me, but that was what I saw. Now, every time I close my eyes, that is what I see. Except why would anyone want to bite her neck? It wasn't like we were attacked by vampires. Ethan made all the funeral arrangements and

3

convinced me to have a closed-casket funeral, so I couldn't even confirm what I saw. I just feel like this whole thing is made up and my mom is going to jump out and say, "Just kidding!"

"Lizzy, please talk to me," Ethan begs, placing his hand on my shoulder.

I move from his touch and shake my head. Although I have known Ethan for a long time, he has always made me feel uncomfortable. The weird thing is, he has never done anything to make me feel that way around him. I should just be grateful he planned the whole funeral and has taken me in until my dad gets here, but the problem is, he is one of the cops that told me how my mom died, and I feel like he is covering something up. I know I should give him the benefit of the doubt, since he was dating my mom, but I can't. Something doesn't feel right.

He has been very emotional through all this. I have never seen a man cry so much in my life. Then there's me, who has not cried yet for the loss of my mom. I had been raised believing that crying shows weakness, and you never show weakness. Therefore, I am trying my best to stay strong. Even if that means I have to shut out the real world.

There is a loud knock on the door, and I jump. I was not expecting that. I glance over to the door and debate on getting it myself. I want to embrace my dad in a giant hug when he walks through that door, except I am also mad at him. I need an explanation on why he was not here yesterday.

"That must be your father," Ethan states, walking over to the door.

My eyes never leave the door. I need to see my dad right now. The door opens, and I roll my eyes, cross my arms, and slump down in the chair. I take a couple of calming breaths to stop the tears from escaping my eyes. At the door is not my dad; instead, it is some younger gentleman. He has short light-brown hair, is fit, and kind of gives off a "bad boy" vibe. He is wearing a leather jacket and looks a little annoyed.

"Hello, I'm Joe. I'm here on Jason's behalf. He is very sorry that he could not make it today. He wants me to assure you I will be able to handle whatever the situation might be," he says.

His voice is deep and manly. It almost reminds me of Dad's voice. *Why is he not here? He would want to be here if he knew what was going on. Something isn't right!*

"Hi, Joe. It's not that I don't trust you, but why isn't Jason here himself? Didn't he get the message saying this was an emergency?" Ethan pries.

Joe nods. "He did. He regrets that he was unable to come. He trusts that I will be able to help out in whatever way I am needed to."

I am a situation now? That does not sound like Dad. Joe has no idea what he is getting himself into being here today. Wait, what if he is working for the people who killed my mom and is actually after me? I cannot let my guard down.

"What did Jason tell you?" Ethan quizzes him, crossing his arms.

He is not letting him in the door. Good. I'm not ready to die today. Well, maybe if I did, I would not be feeling this emptiness anymore. Although I am curious what Joe has to say. Maybe I should tell Ethan to let him in for a minute.

Joe sighs. "I don't know much. All I know is Lizzy's mom died, and now you guys need our help. I'm going to be honest, he didn't even tell me how you guys knew each other."

I could feel Joe is getting annoyed. I suppose I would be, too, if I didn't know why I was at some stranger's house.

The more I study him, however, the more I feel comfortable with him. I do not think he is a threat to us.

"Well, I guess come on in. Take a seat wherever you feel comfortable." Ethan steps aside for Joe to walk in. "I'm Ethan, and Lizzy is on the couch. I'm surprised Jason did not come running himself when he heard Lizzy needed him."

I watch Joe carefully as he chooses to sit in the chair next to me. He looks over at me and gives me a friendly nod. I catch a glimpse of his golden-brown eyes and could feel how uncomfortable and scared he is. I want to know why he is scared. I should dip a little bit more into his emotions, I decide. I need to know if he is here for good or bad. I close my eyes and concentrate on his aura. I learn that the "tough boy" look is just a gimmick; he doesn't want people to see the real him. He is feeling a lot of grief, almost the same thing I'm feeling right now. He feels so empty, almost like he lost someone very close to him. Okay, I need to stop prying now and pay attention to what is going to happen to me.

"So can you explain to me what is going on?" Joe pushes.

Ethan looks over at me, and I shake my head. I'm still not ready to talk yet. Not to this total stranger.

Ethan rolls his eyes. "Elizabeth's mom, Alyssa, was murdered on Saturday morning. Luckily, Lizzy fought her way out and got to safety," he answers for me. "I need to know if Jason is planning on taking Lizzy in now, or does he have family she could stay with?"

I glance back over at Joe, and he makes quick eye contact with me. He is hiding something; I can feel it. He shifts his weight in the chair and looks down to the floor. That is when it all comes to me. Joe isn't Dad's man to do his errands; he is his older son. Except if Joe is here and doesn't know who I am...

"He is dead!" I gasp.

That was the only thing that would keep Dad from seeing me. That was why we couldn't get ahold of him.

Joe didn't know if he should have answered the messages. That is why he has the same grief I do—he lost a parent, just like me. Wait, that means...I lost both parents in one week. I don't know if I can handle this news. Please let me be wrong!

"Joe," I say, and he doesn't look back at me. "Be honest, is he dead?"

He glances over at me, and I look directly into his eyes. They give me the answer I do not want to hear. A lump forms in the back of my throat, and it is taking every bit of strength I have to fight back tears. Just when I thought this week couldn't get any worse! I need to know more.

"Are you his eldest son?" My voice is shaky.

Joe nods. "I am. How did you know?"

"I will answer any question you have, but first, I need you to say it out loud. Is...he...dead?" I stammer.

I don't want to hear it out loud, but I need to. I need to know what happened to my father.

My eyes stay glued on Joe. He closes his eyes and sighs. "Yes, he died last Thursday in a work accident. I found his phone yesterday and listened to all the voice mails Ethan left. I felt this was too urgent to ignore, so I thought I could show up, help, and leave without telling you that our father was dead."

Hearing him say *our* father really hurt. Especially knowing he is talking about him and his brother. I wish Dad had told them about me. At least we could have grieved together. I could have gone to the funeral, and then maybe my mom and I would not have been home when the attackers broke into our house. Now I have to be the one who tells them their father has a secret child, and it is me. Tears threaten to fall.

"So how did you know I was his son?" Joe pushes.

Maybe this could distract me from falling apart. "Weird fact about me, I can read people's emotions or tap into their aura. When I tapped into yours, I felt the same sadness and emptiness I feel about losing my mom. Therefore, I assumed you lost someone close to you. Then it all clicked: the only reason Jason would not be here personally is that something happened to him. He always talked so highly of you and your brother, so it all made sense. I was hoping I was wrong. You also sound like him, and you both have similar features," I explain.

I should have just said *Dad* instead of *Jason* to see his reaction. Except I'm too chicken to see what his reaction will be once he finds out about me. I do know, from just having met him fifteen minutes ago, I feel a lot safer with him than I have ever felt with Ethan.

"He talked to you about us?" Joe questions.

I give a weak smile. "Of course, all the time. Well, he talked to my mom more about you two than to me. He was proud of his boys. He hated that he lied to you about where he was going once a month. He always said how much respect he had for his older son. How he took on more responsibilities than he needed when he was little."

This is too much to take in for one week. Mom and Dad are both gone, and now I have to tell my brothers about myself. To top it off, what am I going to do now? Who is going to take me in? I'm going to end up in foster care.

"What do you mean he lied to us once a month about where he was going? He would come here? Was he dating your mom?" he asks.

I think he is starting to realize who I am. *This is it, Lizzy,* I think, *just tell him.*

"No, my mom and him were not dating. Ethan here was my mom's boyfriend." I chicken out.

"Wait a minute, let's go back to when I first got here. Ethan said something about finding out if Dad could take you in or if he has other family. Why would Dad take you in, Lizzy? Why would he care if they were not dating?" Joe is panicked.

Ding, ding, ding, we have a winner. It's all coming together for him now too.

"I think you just figured out the answer yourself," I whisper.

I could not actually say it. I do not want to see his reaction. I could not even look at him anymore; I just look down at the floor. Ethan has beautiful hardwood floors.

"I want you to say it. What I'm thinking cannot be true. He would never keep that kind of secret from us!" Joe's voice rises.

His emotions are high now. I can feel the anger radiating off him. I'm afraid to answer. What if he takes that anger out on me? I cannot handle any more right now. If he yells at me, I just might start crying. Well, either way, I better just say it. Then he will know, and we can just go on with our lives.

"Hello, Joe, my name is Elizabeth McCann." I stop and inhale deeply.

I glance back up at him, and he is shaking his head. I know this is hard for him, but this is hard for me too. How would he feel if the roles were reversed? I was the secret child, and I had to find out my dad died after the fact. Okay I should just keep talking. No going back now.

"I'm Jason's daughter, which would make me your sister," I finish.

"Liar!" Joe jumps to his feet. He starts to pace back and forth. "This has to be some kind of sick joke."

"Joe, Dad always told me he was going to tell you guys about me. When I would ask him about it, he always had an excuse why he could not do it at that time. At first, he would tell me he didn't want to rub it in that I had two loving parents and you only had one. Now that I'm older, I can see that he was guilt-tripping a little kid to stop asking. Then he said he felt like he messed up your and your brother's lives. He would always say how normal my life was compared to yours. I just believed I wasn't good enough to meet his two wonderful boys. He always talked so highly of you and your brother to us but never talked about me to you guys. I am sorry you found out this way, though," I explain.

I know this is big news to him, but so is finding out your father has been dead for almost a week. Joe stops pacing and looks me dead in the eyes. I feel like he is looking right into my soul.

"If you are really my sister, tell me something Dad would say," he demands.

Joe is making me nervous. If I do say something, is he going to attack me? I take a deep breath and exhale slowly before I say, "'Think of your family today and every day thereafter. Don't let the busy world of today keep you from showing how much you love and appreciate your family.' I don't know if he ever said that to you, but he always would state that quote by Josiah before he left."

Joe bows his head in defeat. "He heard that quote five years after our mother died. He told us since he was always on the road, he felt like that quote hit close to home."

I hate that I can feel the disappointment radiate off his body. I've never disappointed anyone a day in my life, and it does not feel good having done so now. Especially when none of this is really my doing. I need to get away from all this. Breathing is becoming difficult for me. I need to get some air.

"Excuse me," I whisper, getting up.

Rushing into the kitchen, I start hyperventilating as soon as the door closes. I do not know how much more I can handle before I fall apart. My mom and dad are dead, and now I have no one. I do not want to live in the foster care system. Can I somehow prove I am old enough to take care of myself? I am not afraid to work; I could get a full-time job to support myself.

Tears start to stream down my cheek. No, I cannot start crying now. If I do, I will never stop. What can I do to get my mind off all this for a second?

Glancing around the kitchen, I spot my house keys on the counter. That is it; I always feel safer at home.

Grabbing them, I rush out the back door. The sun is bright, but the warm summer air feels good on my skin. I take a moment to soak it all in. Closing my eyes, I take a few deep soothing breaths. Being outside helps calm me a little. Opening my eyes, I look around and see a squirrel running in the grass. I wish I were that squirrel. I would love to not have a care in the world right now. Fidgeting with my keys, I decide it's time to run home. Running always clears my mind; maybe it will help in this case.

Taking off, I scare the squirrel, and it runs in the opposite direction. Poor thing, it was just minding its own business, and then I spooked him. How could I be so selfish? Okay, now I know I am far from being okay—I am feeling bad for a squirrel!

My house is only two blocks away, but it feels like I just jogged ten miles. I normally run five miles a day, but these two blocks killed me. By the time I make it up the stairs to the porch, I am huffing and puffing. I bend over and put my hands on my knees, trying to catch my breath. Can I really be that out of shape after only a few days, or is grief really taking that much of a toll on my body?

After inhaling through my nose and exhaling out of my mouth a few times, I am finally breathing normally. I stand up straight and stare at the door. Anxiety starts to kick in again. My heart is racing to the point it almost feels like it is skipping beats, my breathing starts to get shallow, and my body starts to shake. Maybe once I am inside, I will feel better. I fumble with the key, struggling to get it in the keyhole. Finally, using my left arm to stabilize my right, I got it in and unlock the door. I cannot do anything without struggling lately.

Opening the door, I walk through the threshold and stop. Knowing it is not possible, I wish my mom were sitting on the couch, waiting for me. Instead, the room is eerily quiet and empty. Slowly I make my way through the living room into the kitchen, where everything happened that Saturday morning. There is police chalk outlining a person on the kitchen floor. Right there was where my mom died.

Tears start to fill my eyes.

Why did I leave her? Maybe I could have done something to save her. I close my eyes, and the memory starts to replay…

"Hey, Mom, what is going on?" I shout, walking into the kitchen.

A scrawny guy with shaggy blond hair is holding my mom. His eyes, I will always remember those eyes. His pupils are constricted and bloodred.

"Run!" she demands.

I turn around, and a bigger guy is behind me. Before I could react, he wraps his large arms around me. He has a little tattoo under his right eye. It almost looks like a dog.

"We just need to talk," he whispers.

"No!" I yell and headbutt him.

That hurts like hell, but it knocks him out for the time being. He falls to the ground, and I turn around to see how I could help my mom. She is fighting the best she could. Her black hair is flying everywhere.

"Mom!" I cry.

"Run away, Lizzy! Go get Ethan!" she demands.

I debate for a second what I should do. Then my decision is made for me when the guy I thought I knocked out grabs my arm.

"Please, let's just talk." It is almost a beg. His big brown eyes look directly into mine. It is almost a pleading look. What in the hell does this guy need to talk to me about?

"I said no," I sternly state while I kick him in the balls.

He drops, and I jump over him to make a run for it.

Before I leave, I turn around one last time just to watch my mom get bitten. Well, that's what I think happened.

I open my eyes, and I am standing alone in the kitchen. The tears threaten to fall again, and I take a few deep steady breaths to try to stop them. *Maybe my bedroom will make me feel better.* I walk out of the kitchen and head toward the stairs. I look up. Although there are only seven stairs, it seems like a long way. I take each step one at a time. A trip that normally takes me two seconds takes me two minutes this time.

Walking into my room, I notice everything looks exactly how I left it Saturday morning, the clothes I was going to wear after my run still folded on my bed. I never thought my life was going to change drastically that day. I was just planning to go for a run and come home and eat breakfast with my mom like I did every Saturday morning.

Seeing my full-length mirror, I walk up to it to see how pathetic I look right now. When I see my reflection, I become disappointed. Although I do not feel like myself, staring back at me is the same beautiful reflection I see every day. I was hoping all the things that happened in the last few days had uglified me just a little, but instead I'm still the same beautiful girl that everyone talks about.

I know that sounds vain, but unfortunately, it is true, and I hate every minute of it. My eyes are so bright they almost glow a unique turquoise color. I'm tall and slender and have curves in all the right areas. My hair is long, blond, wavy, and it never frizzes or strays. I'm also blessed to have never had to wear makeup, because my natural complexion is flawless. Many people tell me I look like a life-size Barbie doll.

With all my wonderful qualities, I do not look like either parent, and people always asked my mom if I was adopted. My mom had beautiful black hair, with green eyes. She was short and was bigger built but wasn't unhealthy. My dad, on the other hand, had dark-brown hair with brown eyes and was very fit. On occasions that I questioned where I got my looks from, my parents always changed the subject and never answered me.

Glancing down, I see my necklace dangling from my neck. It is a cross with a ruby in the middle. Personally, I don't remember a time I didn't have this necklace on. My dad gave it to me for my fifth birthday and made me promise to never take it off. I remember trying to take it off once, and I almost got grounded for it. When I asked why I couldn't wear a different one, my dad just told me it had sentimental value to him since he could not be with me at all times.

Today there is no one trying to stop me. I mean, both my parents are dead. What is the worst that is going to happen if I finally take it off?

I reach back and pull the magnetic latch apart. I let the necklace dangle in my hand, and I just stare at it. I feel different without it, but I cannot explain how. It almost feels freeing, but something does not feel right.

"Put that necklace back on now!" I hear someone shout.

I jump and look around my room, but I'm the only one here. That is weird; my mind is really playing tricks on me today.

"Elizabeth Samantha, put on your damn necklace, now!" I hear again.

This time I recognize the voice. "Dad?" I question, looking around my room.

"PUT ON YOUR FUCKING NECKLACE NOW!" he yells at me.

This time the stuff on my dresser rattles. If this is Dad, he is pissed at me for taking it off. To avoid getting yelled at again, I quickly put the necklace back around my neck. Is Dad so possessive about this necklace that he is haunting me about it? Why is it so important?

I need to get out of this room, before something creepy happens again.

I turn around and freeze. Standing in my doorway is Ethan. Well, I think it is him, though his face doesn't look anything like him right now. He looks like he has aged fifty years. His eyes look exactly like the attacker's eyes before he bit my mom. His pupils are constricted and bloodred.

"E-E-E-than?" I stutter.

He doesn't say anything; instead, he opens his mouth and hisses. I see his teeth, and they look like fangs. *What the hell is going on here?* He takes a step closer to me, and I back up against the wall. I look to my left to see if I can find an escape, but it is too late—Ethan has me pinned to the wall.

He grabs my hair and moves it to expose my neck. He puts his face closer to my neck and sniffs it.

"What are you doing?" I panic.

He doesn't say a word and doesn't move his face away from my neck. I can feel each breath he exhales, and it gives me goose bumps. Is this how I'm going to die? I wonder. Was Ethan in on the attack this whole time? His teeth pierce through my skin, and I scream. It takes me by surprise and hurts at the same time. I try fighting him off, but he lets go willingly and begins coughing.

"What is wrong with you?" He coughs right before he collapses.

"What is wrong with me? You just tried eating me!" I reply.

Ethan doesn't answer; he just lies there motionless. Part of me knows I should run, but the other part wants to know what is wrong with Ethan. I put my hand up to my neck and cautiously walk up to him. Blood is running down the side of his mouth. Is that mine or his? Kneeling down, I try to feel for a pulse. I sigh when I feel nothing. His face is looking normal again, except he is paler. His eyes are wide open and back to their normal blue color. A feeling of sickness comes over me when I realize Ethan is dead.

Chapter 2

"What the fuck just happened?" Joe asks.

Turning my head to face him, I see the inside of the barrel of a handgun. Although it is pointing right at me, I don't fear him. I do, however, fear what might happen to me now that I have been bitten by some kind of infected person.

"He bit me," I say, "and then died. He must have some kind of disease. I better go get checked out to make sure I don't get whatever he has."

I'm starting to panic now. The last thing I want to do is go around and bite people. We do not need an outbreak of whatever this is. Even if that means I have to be killed, I'm weirdly okay with that.

Joe walks closer with the gun still pointing at me. "You mean to tell me you do not know what Ethan is? Are you sure Jason was your dad?"

It almost sounds like he doesn't believe me. Does he know what Ethan is? Well, I'm assuming he does, since he is questioning me about it. Also, what does Dad have to do with this? Does he study weird diseases that I am not aware about?

"What does Dad have to do with this? Did he study this kind of stuff? Am I going to get whatever he had?" I indicate Ethan.

I am so confused.

"Don't worry, you will not get what he had. You were not infected the right way," Joe responds. "I am curious what is in your blood, though. You should have become paralyzed the second his teeth pierced through your skin. I also want to know why he died biting you. I've never seen such a thing, and I've been doing this for thirteen years. You have me stumped!" he admits, lowering the gun.

What the hell is he talking about? Why in the hell should I have become paralyzed as soon as Ethan bit me? Were these two planning something against me the whole time?

"Did you want me to die?" I finally ask.

He kneels down next to me, and his face looks serious. "I never want these monsters to hurt anyone. I was just about to shoot him when he attacked, except he died from biting you. So tell me who the hell you are," Joe demands, his tone serious, almost threatening.

What does he mean what I am? I thought I was a human, like everyone else.

"I'm Elizabeth Samantha McCann. I am the daughter of Alyssa Jones and Jason McCann," I say. "And until now my life has been very simple. I'm unaware if my blood kills people if they touch it, but if that were the case, my mom and dad would have been dead a long time ago. Now, can you please tell me what was wrong with Ethan? You act like you have seen this before!" By now I'm in a panic.

He does not look impressed with my answer. I can feel the frustration radiating off him.

"I don't understand how you don't know anything about this, especially if we share a dad," he accuses.

What is with this guy? He really doesn't want to believe that I'm his half sister.

"Did Dad specialize in Renfield's syndrome? Because I'm starting to believe that was what Ethan had. Why else would he want to drink someone else's blood? I mean, he could be a vampire, but those are just a myth...right?" I babble.

Honestly, I have no idea how I came up with Renfield's syndrome. I remember reading about it just once, but it is the only logical explanation at the moment. I study Joe, and he keeps glaring at me. I know he isn't happy with my answers, but I don't know what else to say.

"And that is what he meant by your life being normal compared to ours," Joe says, then sighs. "Elizabeth—"

"Lizzy," I interrupt.

"Okay, Lizzy, Ethan was a vampire. I do not understand why Dad kept that a secret from you. Vampires are everywhere. You would think he would want you to be aware of that. I do not remember a time I didn't know about vampires, and I always had to be aware of my surroundings. I know this sounds crazy coming from a complete stranger, but I am a vampire hunter. Well, actually, so is my brother, and so was our dad," he informs me.

I can't help but laugh. That is the most ridiculous thing I have heard. "Dad did not hunt vampires! He owned a furniture store," I tell him. "Now you are just humoring me."

Vampires cannot be real, right? They are just fictional characters you watch on TV or read about in a book. There is no way I went sixteen years without realizing there are vampires around. I'm not that gullible.

"Lizzy, stop laughing. I'm telling the truth," Joe continues. "Dad always told us he wanted a normal life for us too. But it just wasn't possible. He tried for years just to hunt himself and leave us at home. He would train us how to protect ourselves, but somehow it got to the point that he felt like he needed help, so he had to take us with him occasionally. Next thing you know, we were hunting right along with him every weekend." He pauses, albeit only slightly. "My mother and our father were killed by vampires. Which brings me to my next point: being bitten can be very dangerous. Although you are not showing any signs, you are going to die in eight hours. But I have the antidote here. Please eat one."

He pulls a pill bottle out of his pocket and hands it over to me. I smile, shake my head, and push it away. I'm not that crazy. He is talking nonsense, and I don't know if I should trust anything he is trying to give me.

"Lizzy, you are in danger. I know it sounds crazy to someone who knows nothing about vampires, but I am telling the truth!" He hands it over to me again.

I roll my eyes. "If vampires were real, shouldn't I be changing into one by now?" I reason. "Besides, Ethan was out in sunlight. Wouldn't he have turned to ash when the sun hit him?"

Everything I have heard about vampires does not add up to what Joe is saying. Vampires cannot walk in sunlight, they hate garlic, and they sleep in coffins. The only thing that Ethan did that fit the vampire credential was that he tried to drink my blood.

"I promise, if you take this berry, I will explain everything," he vows.

He dumps one in his hand and offers it to me. I grab it and examine it. The berry is round and red, and when I give it a gentle squeeze, it is firm. Is this even going to taste good? I wonder.

"What is it?" I have the right to know.

"Hawthorn berry," he answers.

I have heard that name before. I examine it a little closer and remember I was told to never eat one of these. Dad told me they were poisonous and could kill me in a matter of minutes. Then again, he never told me about vampires, so maybe he was lying to me about this too.

"Dad told me these berries would kill me within minutes if I ever ate one," I respond.

"Why in the hell would Dad tell you that?" He closes his eyes in frustration. "Although you are not acting like someone who has been bitten, it would make me feel better if you ate it, just to be safe."

I suppose, what is the worst that could happen? I die? Well, then, I wouldn't be feeling this pain anymore.

I pop it in my mouth and find it to be sweet. Honestly, it does not taste bad at all. I swallow it, and immediately a chill runs down my spine.

"Well, I ate it," I say, opening my mouth and sticking out my tongue. "Now, tell me what you know about vampires."

"I don't mean this to sound rude, but why are you not sleeping? The cure is supposed to knock you out for four to eight hours, then you wake up feeling better," he explains. "Nothing about this situation is normal!"

Was he trying to drug me, then? Would that explain why my heart is starting to race, with a lump forming in the back of my throat? *No, Lizzy, you are just getting worked up with this whole situation,* I muse. *Just hear him out.*

"Becoming a vampire is a little different from what people think. There is the theory that you have to die with vampire blood in your system. I don't know where people got that idea from, but it is completely bogus. The other theory is that they have to bite you. That one is closer to the truth, except they have to bite you while being intimate," Joe continues.

"What! Who would have sex with a vampire?" I choke.

My throat feels like it is swelling, and swallowing and breathing are becoming difficult. Am I about to have another anxiety attack?

"Lizzy, are you okay?" Joe asks. "Your face is starting to swell."

I can't answer. My airway is starting to close completely. I glance down at my arms, and I'm breaking out in a rash. My vision is becoming tunnel, and I am getting very dizzy. Maybe if I lie down on the floor and relax, it will pass in a few minutes? I close my eyes to take a few deep breaths.

To my surprise, when I open my eyes, I am not in my room anymore. What did Joe do to me? I wonder. Did he actually drug me and take me out to the middle of nowhere to let me die? I stand up, dust myself off, and try to figure out my surroundings. The sun is bright, so I guess it must be the middle of the afternoon now. Before I closed my eyes, I felt so empty and lost, but now I feel at peace. I do not want to leave this area, but I should find out where I'm at.

Maybe I should walk down this road and see if anyone is around. I'm cute; I should be a great hitchhiker.

"Lizzy, dear," I hear behind me.

The voice gives me goose bumps. I turn around, and my mouth drops. Standing in front of me are my mom, my dad, and Ethan. Does this mean I'm dead too? To be honest, I do not care at the moment; I am just happy to see Mom and Dad again.

"Mom!" I cry, running up to her. I wrap my arms around her tight and start to sob on her shoulder. She kisses my head and squeezes me tighter. I do not want to let go. "Mommy, I miss you so much!"

"I know, baby. I miss you too," she says, letting go.

Why is she letting go of me?

I back up, and she wipes my tears away with her thumb. "Am I dead?" I ask her.

She smiles. "Not yet, baby. It isn't your time yet." Her smile is so bright and beautiful it feels like an angel is smiling at me.

Is she an angel? Is she even real, or is this just a dream? Are any of them real? I do not care if they aren't; I'm just happy to be with them right now.

"Daddy, why did you keep a secret like this from me? I feel like this is too big a secret to hide!" I scold, crossing my arms.

"Peaches, your mother and I wanted to keep you safe. We were afraid you might tell the wrong person and put yourself in danger. You are very special to the vampire world," he explains. "Which reminds me, why did you take off that necklace?"

I couldn't stay mad at him; I am just happy to see him. "I'm sorry, Daddy, I'm just confused."

"Come here," he says, putting his arms out.

I run up to him, and he embraces me in a giant hug. I start to sob on his chest even harder. I know I'm going to get in trouble for crying, but I don't care. I miss them so much.

"What do you mean I'm special to the vampire world?" I sniffle.

He squeezes me tighter. "Unfortunately, my dear, I cannot tell you in this world, and now I wish I had told you sooner. I'm also aware I should have told my boys about you too. I'm sorry I left that up to you. I thought I would have more time on earth. It just never felt like the right time then. I went to tell them a million times and couldn't do it!" He sighs. "But I can tell you this: as long as you never take that necklace off, you will be safe from any bite. Also, never eat that berry again with the necklace on. I told you it would kill you." Then he smiles. "I love you, Peaches, but I do not want to see you for a long time."

"I love you too, Daddy," I say, sobbing. "Except I want to stay!"

He pushes me out of the hug and grabs my forearms. I look into his eyes and believe he secretly wants me to stay too.

"Peaches, you don't know how much your mother and I would love to be with you again. The problem is, you still have so much good to do in this world. Now, do you remember what I used to tell you when you would get upset?" Dad questions.

I sniffle. "I'm a McCann, I need to be tough. There is never a need for tears."

He wipes my tears away from my face. "Do not listen to me with this situation. You have every right to break down. I don't want you to get lost in your emotions."

"But, Daddy, I *am* lost. Where am I going to go now?" I tremble.

"Baby girl, we have that all figured out," Mom says to comfort me, putting her hand on my face.

How could they have it all figured out? Before you go to heaven or hell, do you get to fill out paperwork?

"I know Joe. He will take you in. Especially now that he just witnessed Ethan biting you and him dying. He is going to want to know more about you. He will help you figure out what you are. He is also a protector, so he will protect you from anything that comes after you. John is so sweet. He will love you. It will be weird at first, but I think you will all grow to like each other," Dad explains.

How can he know for sure? What if he doesn't know his boys as well as he thinks he does? Joe might be keeping secrets from Dad, just like Dad kept secrets from Joe. I mean, it is one thing to ask him to accept me as his sister, but asking him to take custody of me might be too much.

"Speaking of Ethan biting Lizzy, what kind of true vampire hunter are you? You let me date a vampire knowing what Lizzy is!" my mom scolds him, placing her hands on her hips.

My dad is in trouble. Wait, what is a true vampire hunter? Is there a difference between a true and a regular vampire hunter?

"Don't blame him, Alyssa," Ethan butts in. I forgot he is here. "Weirdly, Jason did know at one point. Oh, Lizzy, I'm sorry for biting you. I don't know what came over me. I haven't hunted a human in over three years. There was a delicious scent, and my instincts took over. I had no control over myself. Otherwise, I would have never hurt Lizzy on purpose."

What did he eat if he didn't eat humans? Can vampires survive off normal food too?

"It's because Lizzy took off her damn necklace," Dad scolds.

I don't understand how a necklace has anything to do with this. It will save my life; I won't die if I get bitten while I am wearing it. But if I eat the berry while wearing it, I will die. I want to know what is so special about this necklace, but I'm sure if I ask now, he will not tell me.

"What are people going to think when they find your body?" I panic.

If Joe was nice enough to call an ambulance, it would look suspicious to see a dead body and me lying there when they show up. How do you explain that one?

"That he died of a massive heart attack. When you kill a vampire, they turn to dust. Except if a vampire bites you, it will look like they died of a heart attack. Don't ask me why, because I do not have any idea," Dad explains.

"Wait a second. Let us go back to how you knew my boyfriend was a vampire," Mom says, stepping in front of Dad. "How did that just slip your mind, Jason?"

"To be honest, I do not remember finding out that he was one. If I knew, I would have told you right away," Dad admits.

I have never seen my parents fight before. It is weird seeing Mom mad at Dad.

"I can explain," Ethan states. "Jason and I met four years ago. He came down to visit Lizzy and ran to the store for you. Jason caught me feeding in an alley. I don't know how, but I somehow compelled him into believing he didn't see anything."

Vampires can compel?

"How in the hell did you get compelled? I didn't even know that was possible. If it were, wouldn't more vampires be taking over the world?" Mom snarls.

"I didn't know it was a thing either!" Dad shrugs.

"Honestly, you are the only person I have done it to. I was completing my change, so it was my first kill. Can vampires compel if they are in the middle of the transformation?" Ethan asks.

"Maybe," Dad replies.

I want this conversation to stop. "Mom, Dad, I have so many questions."

"I know, baby, but we cannot answer any questions about that world here," Mom states.

Of course, I knew that was going to be the answer.

"You can ask your brothers anything. They have been doing this forever. They will fill you in about the vampire world. The only thing is, they don't know how special you are to that world. You will have to figure that out together, I guess. They will keep you safe, I promise," Dad explains.

"I am so scared!" I admit.

Both Mom and Dad wrap me in a big hug. It has been a while since we have had a family hug.

"Well, baby girl, it is time for us to go. You behave and stay safe." Mom kisses my head.

"Remember, Peaches, keep that necklace on, and keep up with your self-defense and nothing will stop you!" Dad hugs me tighter.

"I don't want you to go!" I hold on to them.

"We have to," my mom says, peeling me off her.

"Bye, Peaches." Dad kisses my head before letting go.

"Please don't leave!" I cry.

"Bye, Lizzy." Ethan waves.

"No!" I sob.

They all walk away, and none of them turn around. I run after them, but a bright light stops and blinds me. I couldn't help but close my eyes.

When I open them up, I am not outside anymore. I don't move; instead, I glance around the room with just my eyes. I see a monitor, IV pole, and side rails.

Crap, I'm in the hospital now.

I turn my head to look to my left and see an empty chair. "Well, Lizzy, it looks like you're alone again," I say out loud.

"Alone? Not really, but I'm glad you are awake," someone says.

I jump and look in the direction of the voice. To my surprise, Joe is sitting in the recliner.

"What are you still doing here? I thought you would have run away by now," I mutter.

My voice is hoarse, and my throat is sore. What happened to me? I recall talking to Mom and Dad, and everything floods back.

I ate that berry.

"What do you remember?" Joe asks, walking closer to the bed.

What did Joe and I talk about before I went to whatever that was? Oh yeah. "I remember you telling me about..." I pause to whisper, "Vampires."

He starts to chuckle. What is he laughing at? Does everyone in the world know about vampires but me?

"While you were talking to me, I remember I started feeling like crap. I thought I was just having an anxiety attack. I lay down and closed my eyes to try to relax, except when I open my eyes..."

I pause again. I don't know if I should trust him completely yet. Would he think I'm crazy to say that I was talking to my dead parents while I was out? If someone told me that, I don't know if I would believe them. Except some of the things that Mom and Dad were telling me made a lot of sense. I mean, I did almost die after eating the berry with my necklace on, and Ethan did die by biting me with it on. Maybe I was in the in-between and they could have visiting hours for a few minutes.

"What happened when you opened your eyes? You were here?" he questions.

What the heck! The worst that could happen is he doesn't believe me. "When I opened them, I was outside. I first thought you poisoned me and left me in the middle of nowhere to die. Then when I turned around, I saw my mom, our dad, and Ethan. They told me they were sorry they did not tell me about vampires. Dad also told me I must keep this necklace on at all times. If I have this on, I will always be safe from being bitten. He also told me to stay away from the berries while wearing it—it could kill me!"

Joe nods. "That would explain why you almost died earlier. It all happened so fast. I was afraid the ambulance wasn't going to get there on time. They pumped you up with something to help with an allergic reaction, and the doctor told me everything was reacting well. She said it could take a while for you to wake up because the med can cause drowsiness. Then I was told that if I waited any longer, you would have been dead."

Does he actually believe I talked to my dead parents? Then again, anything is possible. I mean, vampires are real, so I guess ghosts could be too.

"Thanks for saving me." I smile. "Wait, what about Ethan's body?"

How did Joe explain one dead body and me almost dying?

"That was tricky, but I managed to come up with a plan," he whispers.

"What did you tell them?" I rush out.

I'm sure I'm going to have to go along with the lie. I just hope I can sound believable and not mess it up. I've never lied in my life.

"I sneaked Ethan's body back to his house." He shrugs.

"How?" I quiz.

When did he have time to do all this? Won't his fingerprints be all over him? I feel like Joe implicated himself in a murder he did not commit!

"After I hung up with 911, I threw him over my shoulders, put him in my car, drove him back to his house, and laid him down in the living room. I made it back to your house and inside right before the ambulance showed up. Believe me, when you are a vampire hunter, you learn how to think quickly," he explains.

I lie back down and close my eyes. I am not looking forward to following that lie. I would never have thought of that if I were in his shoes. How am I going to lie? Mom and I always had an open relationship, so I never felt like I had to lie to her. Though I guess now she didn't feel the same way.

The door opens, and I open my eyes. Walking in is Dr. Stone and her nurse, Lisa.

"Lizzy, honey, I'm so happy you are finally awake. You gave us quite a scare!" Dr. Stone states.

"Hi, Dr. Stone and Lisa." I give a fake smile.

"Lizzy, you know you can call me Maggie. We have known each other for a long time," Dr. Stone replies.

"Sorry, Maggie," I sigh.

Maggie and my mom were best friends. Maggie was just finishing med school when they met. I was even the flower girl in her wedding! But I still feel like I have to call her Dr. Stone when I'm at the hospital or clinic.

"Lizzy, Joe here told us everything," she says, sitting next to me.

"He did?" I gasp.

Well, if Joe told her everything, maybe then I don't have to lie. That would be the best thing that has happened today.

"Yeah, I'm sorry about your father. Joe said he came up today after he got Ethan's voice mails. Joe said he wanted to meet you since your father didn't tell him about you. He explained that you told him to meet you at your house because you wanted to meet alone. Except I have some horrible news for you. Nathan went over to tell Ethan where you were, and unfortunately, he was found dead. They are thinking heart attack," Maggie explains, putting a comforting hand on my shoulder.

"What?" I clap my hand over my mouth. "I should have never left him! He told me he wasn't feeling well. Why is everyone around me dying? If I were there…"

"There is nothing you could have done. You would have been there to call 911, but you would have just witnessed another death," she says to placate me. "It probably was a good thing you were not there. Not only do you have to now deal with another death in your life, but also, do you really think you could have witnessed it without going over the deep end?"

Only if I could tell the truth. I am so far in the deep end I am drowning, and there is no lifeguard on duty. At least I know now why I didn't feel comfortable around Ethan.

"Now, Lizzy, I have to ask, What happened?" Lisa asks.

Shit, it is my turn to lie. I hope I can stick with the same story.

"Well, Joe and I were awkwardly sitting in the living room. Neither of us knew what to say. We would look at each other to say something but then give up. He pulled out a bag of berries and started to eat them. I broke the silence by asking him what they were. He told me they were hawthorn berries and offered me one. Since I have never heard of them before, I accepted. They were good, except I started to feel weird. I asked him to excuse me for a minute and went up to my room," I lie.

Joe picks up. "That was when I heard a crash coming from upstairs. I yelled up to her, but there was no answer. So I ran up there and found her on the floor, unconscious. Her face was swollen, and she had hives everywhere. I called for help as soon as I could. Her breathing was eerie. She was wheezing and struggling, and there was nothing I could do but watch. I know we just met, but it was one of the scariest things I have ever witnessed."

Weirdly, this lying thing seems so easy. It feels like it almost comes natural to me.

"Well, now that you know you are allergic to them, I hope you stay away from them for good!" Maggie scolds me.

"I didn't know I was allergic to them. Why are you getting upset with me?" I question.

I don't understand. Maybe my lying capabilities are not as good as I thought.

"Because you have hawthorn berries listed under your allergies," Maggie states. She rolls the computer over to me, and sure enough, in red it reads, "Allergies: penicillin and hawthorn berries." She then continues, "Now, Lizzy, I need to know, did you try to kill yourself?"

I gasp. I did not realize Mom put those in my allergy list. Now it does look bad. "Maggie, I swear I didn't know. I knew I had heard the name before, but I couldn't place why. I don't recall ever trying them before. I promise you, I am not ready to die."

Well, after feeling at peace five minutes ago, I figure dying isn't a horrible choice. Especially if that means I get to see Mom and Dad again.

"Okay," she finally says, watching me. "I want to keep you here for another couple of hours for observation. Then I will discharge you."

"How? I'm a minor and have no place to go. Is child services coming to pick me up?" I start to panic.

I don't want to go into the system; I'm too old for that. And I still think I might be able to figure it out myself. My life will be a living hell in foster care.

Joe starts, "Lizzy, I know we just met, but..." He pushes his hair back and shifts his weight. "John and I are your only living relatives, correct?"

"Yes," I answer. "Unless Dad has family I don't know about."

"Well, if you would like, you can come live with us. I am your next living relative, and I am capable of watching over you," he offers.

Dad was right about Joe taking me in. I hope Dad is right about John loving me. Especially because I haven't met him yet. What if this does not work out? Will they just kick me out and make me live on the streets?

But I shouldn't worry about that right now. This is the only offer I have, and I'm desperate.

"If you don't mind. I promise I will get a job and pay for my share of everything," I vow.

It is the least I can do. I cannot just go live with them and expect them to give me money for the things I need.

"You will not be getting a job. Your only job will be to go to school and be the first of us to graduate high school. We have more than enough money to raise you. You don't have to worry about a thing," he replies.

They didn't graduate high school? No wonder Dad has always been onto me about getting good grades and getting into college. He wanted one kid to brag about when he decided to tell people about me. I don't understand how they have more than enough money, though. Do they sell fangs for money? So many questions that I cannot ask right now.

"Okay, can I ask, Where exactly do you live?" I question. I feel like it's a legit question. Dad never told me what his boys did after they left the house.

"Dad never told you where he lived?" he quizzes.

"He did, but he never told me where you lived," I answer.

He walks closer to the bed. "John and I still live with Dad. So we live in his house still."

That would explain why I was never told where they moved to. Wait, that means…

"I'm going to be moving to Colorado?" I ask rhetorically. It upsets me more after I say it out loud. Mom and Dad die, and now I'm expected to move away from all the memories and the only home I know. We lived somewhere else before, but I do not remember it at all. I have lived in Centennial for thirteen years.

"We live on an acreage near the town of Olathe, Colorado, to be exact. It is about a six-hour drive from here. If you like, I can go to your house and pack some things, and we can head straight there after you are discharged," Joe offers.

"Leave so soon?" I choke out.

I don't know if I can just have him pack my things and leave; he won't know what is important to me or not. I need to do it myself. If I have to pack up and move, I think I should have the right to choose what I bring.

I look at the clock, and it says it's 5:38 p.m. By the time I'm discharged, it will be around sevenish, then a six-hour drive. That would get us there around one.

I'm not ready to leave.

The tears threaten to escape again. And this time, I don't know if I can control them.

"Can we stay in town for this one night?" I ask. "It will give me the chance to pack the things that are important to me. I know it is asking a lot, but so is packing up and moving away. I need to figure out what I'm supposed to do with the house. I'm sure my mom has legal papers put away somewhere. I can look for them tonight. Maybe I'm supposed to end up with someone else, and then you will not be stuck with me. I know you want to leave and get home, but this is my home. I just need to stay one more night."

To me nothing has ever felt as important as this. I have to stay one more night for closure. It will be like saying goodbye to a lifelong friend. If he says no, I will beg, and that is not like me. Mom always told me she didn't know how I was her child. I never acted like she did when she was younger. She was an only child, too, and she knew she was spoiled. I'm spoiled, too, but I don't ask for much. She always told me I was the perfect daughter.

"Only if we leave early tomorrow morning," he counteroffers.

"Deal!" I smile.

I'm so happy he is letting this happen. I think he realizes more than anything how important it is to me.

"Well, I will let you guys talk it out, and I'll be back soon. If you need anything, let Lisa know," Maggie tells me. "Joe, it was nice meeting you. You shouldn't have any problems with this one. I've known her since she was six, and she has always been well-behaved. I always told Alyssa I hope my children are as good as she is."

She and Lisa then walk out of the room. Immediately, Joe comes and sits at the foot of my bed. He tilts his head and smiles. "Well-behaved or just know how not to get caught?"

I grin. "I am well-behaved. To be honest, today was the first time I have lied in my life. I don't party, because I don't have any desire. I don't like going out much. I think I don't go out because of the curse of being beautiful. I don't say it to be full of myself, I say it because I know it is true. The boys drool all over me at school, I would hate to know what would happen if alcohol was involved."

He raises his eyebrow and chuckles. "You think it's a curse, being beautiful?"

"I'm not?" I question.

He quits laughing. "You are my sister. That is inappropriate."

I love how he is avoiding my question. "You have known I was your sister for a couple of hours. Before you knew, and if I were closer to your age, wouldn't you try to hit on me?"

"Okay, fine. Yes, my first thought was, damn, I've never seen anyone who looks like that in my life. You almost look like a life-size Barbie doll," he admits.

"I get that a lot. I wake up looking like this. I could never brush my hair, and it would stay the same. I know, because I've tried. I cannot gain weight. I am cursed," I explain. "But once people get to know me, they learn I'm a socially awkward girl just trying to make it through life like everyone else."

"So you are not going to be like my brother and me and get in trouble in school. I think Dad had a parking spot reserved for him for how often he was called to the school." Joe smiles. "When you pack tonight, I ask you pack as little as possible. I don't think I can fit everything in the car. Besides, I can buy you everything you need when we get there tomorrow afternoon. Just pack the necessities. Also, I called John to get your room ready."

He is leaving something out. I can feel it. I know exactly what it is too. "You haven't told John about me yet, have you?"

He shakes his head. "I feel like this is a conversation to have in person. I'm going to need his help figuring out why Ethan died after he bit you. I don't need him to be panicking all night long. He still has to go to work in the morning."

"I feel like it has something to do with this," I say, grabbing my necklace.

"Maybe Dad has papers or something at home we can look for. If your blood kills vampires, then you are a special kind of special. I have never seen that before in my life of vampire hunting. It would have been nice if Dad had mentioned it. Instead, I find out Dad is a liar and doesn't tell anyone anything. Doesn't tell us about you, and doesn't tell you about vampires. Who knows what else he has lied about?" Joe snarls.

"I'm sorry you are stuck with me. I will help do my share, I promise," I repeat.

I do not want to look at him now. I know this is hard for him. If I were in his shoes, I would be furious about the whole situation. I would take me in too, but I wouldn't be happy about it. I just hope, after a few months, we will be okay.

"Not your fault. It isn't like you asked for any of this," he answers.

"That is true, but you never asked to take in your orphaned sister either. I do appreciate everything you are willing to do. I promise to help out," I repeat.

"Neither of us asked for this," he says. "And like I said before, you do not have to worry about helping out with your share. Maybe just help out around the house, but you do not have to help with bills."

Again, he states I do not have to help with bills. How do they have all this money?

"I have a weird question. Do you sell vampire fangs for money?" I ask.

He bursts out in laughter. I do not appreciate him laughing at me; I think it is a fair question. It isn't like I was raised to hunt vampires.

"No, we don't sell fangs for money. Dad does own a furniture company. John and I took over about a year ago. Dad also put enough money away for us to live comfortably if we chose to get away from hunting," he explains.

Well, that makes me feel a little better, that they do work hard for their money. Although I'm sure vampire hunting is not easy and would be an even harder job.

"How long have you been hunting? How long had Dad been hunting?" I ask.

"How about you get some rest for now? Once you get discharged, we can talk more. I do not want people to overhear our conversation," he states.

He does have a point. We do not want people to think we are crazy. With my luck, someone would overhear us, think Joe isn't fit to raise me, and I would end up in the foster care system. Joe might regret having me wait with all my questions, though. I feel like once I start asking, I will not be able to stop.

"Okay," I say, lying down.

The blood pressure cuff tightens on my arm, and I look at the monitor. It beeps once, and numbers pop up on the screen. I don't know what any of those mean, but I do hope they are good. I yawn and realize how exhausted I still am. I decide to close my eyes and drift off into sleep.

Chapter 3

Although I'm sitting in the car with my brother, the ride is still awkward. We are total strangers, and now I'm going to be living with him for at least two years. I glance over at him, and his aura is giving off uncertainty, which makes a lot of sense in this situation. I have a lot of questions, but I do not know where to start. So right now, I'm just going to sit here in silence until we get to my house for the last time. I do fear something bad is going to happen, since every time I've been to the house this week, something has happened.

Joe pulls into the driveway, and I have mixed emotions. I am scared, my heart is racing, and I feel like I could start crying. He shuts off the engine, and I do not move; I just stare at the orange house in front of me. Joe places his hand on my shoulder, and it startles me. For a brief moment I forgot he was here.

"Are you ready?" he asks.

He sounds sincere. I wonder if this was how he and John felt after they buried Dad. If they pulled up to their house and just sat there for a moment, thinking about how everything is changing. How did they manage to get through it so quickly? The only difference between my situation and theirs is, they didn't have to pack up and move away from their memories.

"Ready or not, I have to go in." I sniffle. "I cannot believe this will be the last time I'd walk through the house. I have so many memories."

I cannot start crying now.

I unbuckle my seat belt and slowly get out of the car. Standing outside, I try to step toward the house but cannot get my feet to move. All I can do is stare at the house and reminisce about the first time we moved in.

Flashback
Thirteen Years Ago

"Lizzy, dear, can you open the door for Mama?" Mom asks.

"Okay, Mommy!" I cheer.

I run up the four steps of the porch and trip over the last one. I fall down and scrape my knee. It hurts, but I stand right up and open the door. I am a big girl, and I will not cry.

"Are you okay, Peaches?" Dad questions, coming behind me.

"Me strong, Daddy!" I smile.

"That's my girl!" Dad praises me.

"Daddy, will you stay with us?" I ask when he walks by me. I hope Daddy says yes this time. I miss him so much.

"I'm sorry, Peaches, but you know I have to work. I am going to stay an extra couple of days this time, though. I have a surprise for you," he expresses.

"What?" I jump in excitement.

"Tomorrow, while Mommy unpacks some boxes, you and I are going to paint the house," he tells me.

"Just me and you?" I am hopeful.

Mom states, "Yes, baby, just you and Daddy. I want you to spend time with him while he is here."

I could not smile any bigger. "What color?"

"*Well, that is the last two boxes. This house is so big, and I do not have anything!*" Mom sighs.

"*Don't worry, darling, when the furniture shows up and you and Lizzy have lived here a few months, it will fill up. Soon you will feel like you have no space!*" Dad laughs.

"*What color!*" I ask impatiently.

Mom shakes her head and chuckles. "*Here is the surprise: we are going to let you pick the color.*"

"*Really?*" I cheer.

"*Yes, so you better think long and hard. The color is going to be on for a long time,*" Dad advises.

Present

The color I picked was orange. Now that I'm older, I wonder why my parents were okay with this god-awful color. It is so bright! But we never had time to repaint it. I think secretly Mom never wanted to repaint it because it was something Dad and I did together. Well, Dad did most of it—I made a mess.

"It is going to be hard. I will not sugarcoat it. The first few nights were hard for John and me after Dad died. If you do decide spending the night will be too hard, just let me know. We can leave at any time. I know I probably will not sleep, and it being your last night here, I'm sure you will not either," Joe states.

I close my eyes and take a calming breath. After I exhale the air out of my lungs, I take the first step forward. I manage to get to the door and grab the knob. When I open the door, I just stand in the doorway, staring at the empty living room.

"Joe, can I tell you something?" I whisper.

"Sure." He shrugs.

I sigh. "When we moved into this house, I was three. We literally moved in with nothing but a few clothes for my mom and me, and some toys for me too. For a week my mom and I had no bed or furniture because the place she ordered from was late on delivery. I think it was from Dad's store."

"What did you guys do?" he questions.

I give a weak smile and look up at him. "I played with my toys, and Mom and I would cuddle on the floor in sleeping bags. This house used to seem so big when I was little. Now with everything that has happened, I feel so small and this house seems huge again." I sigh, then pause. "We better go find those papers."

I walk in and wipe my tears before they fall from my eyes. I don't want to hear Joe's reply; I just want to find the papers. I quickly head up the stairs and walk past my bedroom. My mom's room is across the hall. When I open the door, my heart shatters even more. It is hard to see my mom's room empty. And now it is getting harder to hold back the tears.

I take tiny steps inside and shuffle toward her bed. I get down on my knees and look underneath, where I find a lockbox. I pull it out and realize it is coded. Rats, Mom never told me what the code is! I stare at the numbers and decide to try 2-2-2-0-0-0. To my surprise, the green light lights up. I open it and notice it is fuller than I expected.

I pull out a handful of papers and start to organize them on the floor. Mom was such a hoarder of everything—some of these papers are receipts from when we first moved in.

Halfway through the papers, I spot three envelopes, each one with my, Joe's, and John's names on it.

Why would Mom have envelopes for John and Joe?

Although I want to just read what theirs say, I decide against it. Maybe Joe will tell me what his says, anyway.

"Hey, Joe!" I shout.

"Yeah!" he yells back from the other room.

"I found something," I reply. "Can you come here?"
Right away, he walks in the door.

"I found three envelopes, each one bearing each of our names on them. Here is yours, and here's John's." I hand them to him.

He sits on the bed, opens his letter, and starts to read. I watch him for a moment, then glance down at my envelope. I am kind of afraid to open it and find out what it says. But I inhale and exhale and decidedly open it. Unfolding the letter, I start to read:

Peaches,

If you are reading this, then it means I'm dead. Also, if you are reading this, I want you to know there are a few things your mom and I neglected to tell you. One, I haven't always been honest about what I did for a living. I do own a furniture company, but I handed that over a year ago to my sons. (I update this letter when needed every month when I come see you.) What I kept you from is, I'm a vampire hunter. Yes, honey, vampires are real. Your mother and I kept you sheltered from this life for important reasons. We needed to make sure you were mature enough to understand. Your mother knows a lot about this world and is able to answer any questions you might have now.

Now, the reason we kept you sheltered from this life is that you are very special in the supernatural world. I'm not going to tell you what you are in this letter, but your mom can answer that question. I just wish I could be there when she tells you. Now, because you are special, you do have to follow a couple of rules.

Rule number 1: Never—and I mean never—take that necklace off! It protects you from all vampires. If a vampire bites you with the necklace on, they will instantly die, and you will not. If your necklace comes off, you will give off a scent that only vampires can smell. Your blood is like a drug to them. Once they get a whiff, they will hunt you down. So again, never take off your necklace! If, for some reason, your necklace does come off, you get bitten, but don't die from getting sucked dry, you will die quickly. Most people have eight hours without the cure. You, on the other hand, will die a lot faster than that.

Rule number 2: Do not eat the hawthorn berries. They will kill you if you eat them with the necklace on.

Along with being special, you also have some powers. You have a sixth sense to danger. If you are in any danger, you will feel it. So always listen to your gut. If a vampire is near, you will know. They will make you feel uneasy.

You can also feel what people are feeling. I know you already know how to do that, since you have told me a lot that you can tell I'm hiding something. Well, you are right. This is what I've been hiding. Be careful whom you use it on.

One thing you've always been right about is your beauty. You are right, you are cursed with beauty. You are beautiful due to your gift.

Any other questions you have, feel free to ask your mother. She will be able to answer them all. Also, don't worry, the letters to my sons will explain they have a sister. I also have money put away for your college. So do not worry about that. You can still go to medical school, if that is what you want to do.

I love you, Peaches!

Love always,
Dad

"What am I?" I question out loud.

I glance over at Joe, and he is still reading his letter.

"It doesn't say in yours either?" he asks, never taking his eyes off the paper.

"No." I roll my eyes. "It just tells me I am special, I have some powers, my beauty is a curse, and to not take off my necklace. It also says not to eat the berry with the necklace on, or I will die. If I get bitten with the necklace on, a vampire will die, but if they bite me without it on, I will die quicker than eight hours. If my necklace does come off, I will give off a scent only a vampire can smell," I tell Joe. "What does yours say?"

He glances up at me. "Most of it is about the furniture store. The last part is about you. It states we have a sister named Elizabeth who knows nothing about the vampire world. He isn't asking us to befriend you but is asking we keep an eye on you. He says you are special to this world, but is afraid the letter would get in the wrong hand. It explains I could ask your mother if I want to know more. If something happens to your mother and him, I become your legal guardian. It also explains you are good at self-defense and with a gun." Then he asks, "If you are so good with self-defense, why didn't you defend yourself with Ethan?"

"Ethan got the upper hand. Normally, I'm better at defending myself, but Ethan caught me off guard. While I was growing up, Dad used to sneak up on me all the time, and I would have to fight him off. If he got the upper hand, he would scold me. Then in front of my friends he would point out what I did wrong. It was super embarrassing." I smile despite the memory. "So I'm special to the vampire world, and neither of us knows why. Of course, Dad didn't think my mom was going to be dead too," I finish.

Joe doesn't reply; he just goes back to his letter.

I then get off the floor and walk out of the room. Heading to my room, I stop in the doorway. Just a few short hours ago, in this room, I went from thinking I was normal to finding out I was nowhere close to being normal.

I don't think I can stay in here tonight.

Walking in, I head toward my closet and grab my going-away bag. Joe wants me to pack light, so I will do that. As I place the bag on my bed, the first things I grab are the photo albums under my bed. I put them inside the bag and grab the couple of picture frames on my table, carefully packing them. There is no way I'm moving away without these. I can replace clothes, but I cannot replace pictures.

After packing a few items of clothing, I sit on my bed and look around the room. This used to be my safe place, yet now I am terrified being in here. Knowing it will be hard, I need to leave. I know it is the right thing to do.

Standing up, I shuffle to the door. Then I turn around one last time for one final look. I grab the doorknob.

"Goodbye, old friend," I whisper as I close the door.

I stroll down the stairs and find Joe sitting on the couch. He has a bunch of papers on his lap he is going through.

"Let's go," I demand.

"Are you sure? I don't want you to think I'm forcing you to leave," he states.

I sigh. "Yeah, I'm sure. I cannot be in this house anymore. After everything that has happened in here this week, it just doesn't feel like home anymore."

I walk over to the dining room table and grab the house keys. Turning around, I see Joe walking out the front door.

Okay, Lizzy, this is it. Your last time in this house. It is time to start your new life.

I drag my feet across the hardwood floor to the entryway. I walk over the threshold, then turn around to close and lock the door. Each step I take away from the house makes me feel sadder. When I get to the car, I put my bag in the back and get in the passenger's side. I buckle my seat belt and just stare at the house.

"Well, we have a six-hour drive. Any music preference?" Joe asks.

I don't answer; instead, I just keep staring at the house. I feel so empty. I am thankful Joe offered to take me in before he found out he had no choice.

He drives off, and in ten seconds, the house disappears. Needing to get my mind off everything, I turn to face Joe.

"Joe, can we talk? I know that is asking a lot, but I need to get out of my head," I say.

Please say yes, please say yes.

He turns down the music. "Sure. I guess we have to get to know each other somehow. We are stuck with each other for a couple of years, after all," he says. "Okay, I'm aware that sounds bad, and I don't mean it like it sounds. If I had known about you since day 1, this would be different: I would be welcoming you with open arms. Right now, my arms are not quite open yet, what with all these secrets. It's hard."

I nod. "Completely understandable. If I were in your shoes, I wouldn't open my arms up for me either."

After a brief silence, I ask, "So…when is your birthday?"

"May 7. How about you?" he answers.

"February 2," I respond. "How old are you?"

"Twenty-six, and you are sixteen, right?" Joe says.

"Yes, I am. How old is your brother?" I counter.

"He is twenty-two. His birthday is April 18. His name is John," he tells me. Then Joe asks, What is your full name?"

"Elizabeth Samantha McCann. Yours?"

"Joseph Jason McCann. John's is Johnathan Alexander McCann. Your middle name is Samantha?" he quizzes.

I smile. "Yup. I was named after a woman that Dad loved very much. A woman that died way before her time. If she were still alive, I wouldn't be here. That woman is your mother."

Part of me wishes their mom never died. If she were still here, I wouldn't have been, and then I wouldn't be special to the vampire world. It would be so much better than the pain I am feeling now.

Joe looks at me and raises an eyebrow. "Dad told you this?"

"Dad loved your mother. Said her life was taken far too soon. My mom and dad never dated. I was an accident child, but I never felt that way. They loved each other, but just as friends. He told me stories about your mom, and he would tell my mom stories about you guys. I would just overhear things. I envy you guys since he was so proud of his boys, but he kept me a secret from everyone. I felt like he was embarrassed of me." I could feel the tears start to fill up my eyes again. But I cannot start crying now.

"Are you married, or have a girlfriend?" I choke out.

"Nope on both," he answers. "Do you?"

"No. I'm a little young to be married, and I don't have a girlfriend. I don't swing that way." I giggle, then add, "I do not have a boyfriend."

Joe lets out a small chuckle. "I should have thought about that question before asking."

"Tell me about vampires," I say.

Joe sighs. "So vampires are not immortal. They do die of old age, but they just age slower. So instead of dying at the age of seventy to one hundred, they can live up to two-hundred-plus years. Like I said, you have to be bitten while being intimate with them to be changed. If they bite you, normal people become paralyzed for five minutes, and if they don't suck you dry, you have eight hours to live without the cure. Those eight hours are the worst eight hours of your life. You will just wish they sucked you dry. Luckily, we have the cure with us at all times. Not that you ever have to worry about that."

That is weird, that vampires do die. I realize then that every stereotype about vampires is a lie. "So how do you kill them?"

"Wooden stake or bullets. Although they do die, that is the only thing that will kill them. That or starvation."

The rest of the trip, I find out more about vampires, and we, Joe and I, learn a little more about each other. It doesn't help keep my mind off things like I hoped, but it does keep me from having a meltdown.

The next thing I know, it is four in the morning, and we pull into the driveway of a beautiful white house with black trim. The front yard has a nice-size porch with a porch swing, a table, and chairs. The outside of this house looks beautiful. Excitedly, at least a bit, I wonder what the inside looks like.

Wait, there have been three men living in this house—the inside is probably a mess! Am I going to have to pick up when they are at work? Is that going to be my job, picking up after them? But then again, I guess it is the least I can do for their taking me in. I just hope the house doesn't smell bad.

"I'm sure John is asleep. So I'll show you around a little, then I think we should try to get some sleep as well. I'm sure later today you will meet John," he explains.

"Sounds good." I nod.

Anxiety is setting in again. I've never had anxiety in my life, and this week, I feel like I'm going absolutely crazy. I'm about to move into my new home and start my new life. My heart is racing. I hope this is going to go well.

I get out of the car and grab my bag. Joe waits for me and then leads me to the porch. I notice in the yard there is a huge tree with berries.

"You guys grow your own hawthorn berries?" I ask.

"Yes," he answers. "The cure is hawthorn berries soaked in holy water all night. It is easier to grow our own berries than scramble to find one when needed. When we need the holy water, we talk to our good friend Father Foreman."

Day 1 and I already know what the cure is. It isn't like I can eat it, anyway, without dying, but it is good to know.

We walk up to the door, and he unlocks it. "Welcome home," he states before walking in.

I follow him in, and I am surprised that it isn't dirty at all. Actually, it is very clean. I glance in the living room. It has two chairs, a couch, and a huge television. I've never seen a TV that big before. I don't watch a lot of TV, but I might have to start now.

"I'll give you a little tour." He smiles. "You are welcome to anything. This is your home now, so please don't feel like you have to ask for permission for food or something to drink. If you do need something we do not have, ask for it. If it isn't too unreasonable, we can get it after work or give you the money to go buy it," he explains.

"Okay," I whisper.

But that is going to be hard for me. I will feel bad asking them for money. It is going to take time for me to realize I live here now too.

"So through this door is the kitchen," he states, walking in.

Following him, I am in awe. The kitchen appliances are all stainless steel, and the cabinets have black trim with glass doors. This is the most beautiful kitchen I have ever laid eyes on. It almost looks like it has never been used.

"We don't cook much, as we are either at work or on the road. I will admit, we eat out for almost every meal. Since you are going to be living here now, though, I guess we will have to start buying more food," he says.

That explains why it looks so spotless. "I can cook. If you tell me what you guys like, maybe I could cook it."

"That would be great!" He smiles. "Now we will go back out to the living room." He holds the door open for me. "Down that hallway is a guest bedroom and a bathroom. You can investigate that when you want to. I'm not going to show you now. Now we will go up the stairs, and that is where our bedrooms are."

We go up the stairs, and when we get to the top, I'm surprised how big and roomy it is up here.

"To the right here you see three doors. The first door is my room, the second room is John's, and the third is a bathroom. To your left, there are only two doors. The first door is your new bedroom, and the last is a staircase to the attic. Are you ready to see your new room?" he asks.

Before I could answer, he opens the door. He waits for me to go first. I slowly walk in and gasp. This room is huge. It has a king-size bed, and I get my own bathroom. I walk to the closet, and it is a huge walk-in. I'm going to need more clothes.

"This was Dad's room. I called John and told him to put new sheets on the bed. It was a hard decision, but with everything going on, I figure this would be good for you. Instead of sticking you in the small guest bedroom downstairs. This way, you have privacy *and* your own bathroom," he explains, smiling a bit wearily. "I'm exhausted, so I think I'm going to try to get a little sleep. I'll wake up around noon. After we both wake up, I'll take you downtown to get you more clothes and whatever you might need to make this room feel homier to you. I don't know if John is going to work today or not, but I will introduce you to him whenever he is home. I would wake him up now, but he can sleep through anything and is a bear to wake up. I prefer him refreshed when we break the news about Dad's secret."

I nod. "I hope you sleep well."

I watch him walk out the door and close it on his way out.

I glance around the room, not knowing what I should do. I have spent years imagining what Dad's house would look like. Now that I'm living here, it is a lot nicer than I imagined.

I put my bag down on the bed and open it. I pull out my clothes, which are only three shirts, shorts, three pairs of jeans, two sets of socks, and three pairs of underwear. I realize I didn't pack another bra or pajamas. I guess I'll have to buy some tomorrow. I grab my pants, socks, and underwear and go to the dresser. I put my socks and underwear in the first drawer, and the pants in the second. Grabbing my shirts, I hang them up in the closet. It is so bare in here now. I turn around and see my black shorts lying there. I guess those and the camisole I'm wearing are going to be my pajamas tonight.

I take off my pants, then put on my shorts. They could almost be underwear themselves. My mom would never let me out of the house with them, which was how they ended up as "bedwear." I take off my shirt and slip off my bra from under my cami. I put my dirty clothes by the wall between the bathroom and closet until I get a hamper. I should write down the things I need.

I sit on the bed, and it is soft. My beds have always been firm; I hope a soft bed will be comfortable. I grab the photo albums and put them under the bed. Afterward, I glance around the room to find the perfect spot for the frames. On top of the dresser should be a great spot. Getting up, I see a frame lying down on the dresser. I put mine down and pick that one up. In the photo is Dad's family. Standing in front of Dad are John and Joe, but they are really small. I'm guessing Joe has to be five, and John maybe one, in the picture. Next to Dad is a gorgeous lady, who, if I have to guess, is Samantha. She is wearing a stunning red dress. Her hair is long and black, and the closer I look, the more I could tell she has blue eyes. They all look happy in this photo.

I smile and stand the photo back up. I put my pictures around it, leaving Dad's in the middle.

Walking back to the bed, I grab the last frame. Just one glance at it and the sadness sets in again. It is a picture of Mom, Dad, and me. I hug it before putting it on the bedside table. Throwing my bag on the floor, I hit the light switch and crawl into bed.

This bed is super comfortable. I feel like I'm lying on top of a cloud! I pull the blankets up and feel they are so soft as well. With the bed and blankets combined, I instantly relax. I liked my blankets at home, but I think I've just fallen in love with these. Dad sure knows how to sleep like royalty!

I roll over to my left side to glance back up at the photo.

"Good night, Mom and Dad. Please be with me," I whisper.

I roll over to my right side and wrap the blankets around me. The tears start to roll down my cheeks, and now, instead of stopping them, I silently cry myself to sleep.

Chapter 4

A chill suddenly wakes me up. I roll over and pull my blankets closer, snuggling into them more. A feeling of uneasiness suddenly comes over me. Something isn't right. I peek one eye open and pull the blanket away to look around the room. I jump, scream, and sit up quickly.

"Who are you?" I shout.

Breathing heavily, I feel like my heart is about to beat out of my chest. I hope this guy isn't dangerous; I do not feel like protecting myself now.

"I'm sorry, I didn't mean to scare you. I was just seeing if I could get a glance at the person staying with us while I was getting ready for work. I'm John, Joe's brother," he explains.

I give him a look-over. He looks legit. I don't have any reason I shouldn't believe him; he does look a little like Dad. He is tall and slender, with shaggy brown hair.

"I'm…Lizzy," I stammer out.

I'm not sure what else to say. I mean, I don't know if Joe wants to be there when I break the news to John. But perhaps I should just tell him now. I mean, what's the worst that could happen? He reacts just like Joe?

"What is going on here?" Joe asks sleepily.

Well, I guess I can tell him now, since Joe is here.

"My bad. I peeked in to see if I could see who is here. I scared her," John replies. "I was just about to ask how she knew our dad, and why it was important she came. What kind of danger is she in? I mean, she looks a little young to be Dad's girlfriend." He turns to me. "You are very attractive, but you probably are more interested in a guy my age."

I roll my eyes. It never fails; I meet a guy for the first time, and they start to flirt with me. I wonder how he is going to react when he finds out I'm his sister.

I glance over at Joe, and he shrugs. That is when I notice he has nothing on but his boxers. I suppose that is something I'm going to have to get used to living with two guys. I don't have much room to talk, especially since I'm in shorts and a camisole.

"I don't believe she is in any danger at this moment," Joe states. "She is going to be living with us for a while, though."

John raises an eyebrow. "How long?"

"Minimum of two years," Joe answers.

John focuses his attention on me again. "Why?"

"Lizzy, do you mind if we come in and sit on the foot of your bed?" Joe asks. "I have a feeling this is not a chat for standing up."

I nod. "Yeah. If I weren't living it, I wouldn't believe it either." I sit up straighter in bed so they both have room by my feet.

They sit down, and John looks at me. I give him a weak smile. I'm not quite sure if I'm ready for his reaction to all this.

"Lizzy, do you want to start?" Joe asks.

"From where?" I shrug.

"I think the beginning of this week would be good," Joe answers.

I sigh. "So Saturday morning, my house was broken into. The intruder decided to fight us to get the upper hand. I was fortunate and fought off my attacker, and instead, I got the upper hand. I escaped, but my mom was not so lucky, and she was murdered. I tried to get ahold of my dad all week, but there was no answer. I emotionally shut down and did not talk to anyone in the last couple of days. My mom's boyfriend, Ethan, took me in and got the funeral arrangements all set up. The problem was, I never liked Ethan, and I was hoping I could get ahold of my dad or any other family."

I cannot keep the tears from coming now; they start to roll down my cheeks.

"Sorry," I say as I wipe them away.

"What are you sorry for? You just told us your mom died. We get that. Our mom died many years ago, and at times it still feels fresh. Unfortunately, I do not know if Joe told you, but our dad died last week too. So if you are waiting to see him, you won't," John states.

"I know," I sob.

I hide my face in my hands and start to cry harder. John telling me I cannot see him just breaks my heart even more.

"John, Lizzy is our sister," Joe whispers. "And I have custody of her."

I'm crying so hard now I'm shaking. I feel so stupid for crying, but I cannot stop.

"She is what?" John gasps.

I need to finish talking. I look back up and take a few calming breaths. "Ethan kept trying to call Jason, because he is also my dad. Once a month he would come spend time with me. He was supposed to show up last Friday, but he didn't. My mom kept telling me he was probably just busy and would call me soon. Now I wonder if deep down she knew he was dead. Unfortunately, I didn't grow up knowing about vampires. I didn't know they were a thing until after I was attacked yesterday."

"And we don't know what kind of danger she is in, because I don't know what she is," Joe interrupts.

John gives us a puzzled look. "She is a female if she is our sister. What do you mean you don't know what she is? Hell, why didn't Dad tell us we have a sister?"

I finally wipe the tears away from my eyes and get my crying under control. *Lizzy, you need to be tougher,* I think, *especially if you are going to be raised by your brothers now.*

"Dad left you a letter. I placed it on the refrigerator door. But I'm sure it is similar to mine. Mine basically told me how much he loved us, and telling me I get custody of Lizzy if something happened to her mother and him. It also states that Lizzy is very important to the vampire world. The only thing it didn't tell me was what she is. He didn't want to go into detail in case the letter got into the wrong hands," Joe explains.

"In my letter, it told me to never take off my necklace. If I do, my blood is like a drug to vampires," I say, picking up Joe's explanation. "I also cannot eat the berry if I am wearing the necklace—it will kill me. Which Joe and I found out the hard way last night. Luckily, if we treat it like an allergic reaction, I can be saved. If a vampire bites me while I'm wearing the necklace, they will die. Which Joe saw firsthand yesterday and was how I found out vampires are real."

"It was fucked up to see. I was about to shoot, but then he dropped dead before I could pull the trigger," Joe states. "And here stood Lizzy, acting perfectly fine, as if she were never bitten. I still made her eat the berry, though, and then she almost died on me. It has been a very eventful twenty-four hours, to say the least."

"Oh," I say, remembering. "My letter also states that if my necklace does come off and I do get bitten but don't get sucked dry, I will die quicker than normal people. I can eat the berry if the necklace is off. Dad also said my mom could tell me why I was special, but I'm sure he wasn't expecting her to be dead too. Since I am special, I do have some 'superpowers.' I can sense when I'm in danger and can tap into people's feelings. The only reason I woke up now was that I felt like I was in danger. Since it was just John standing in the doorway, I'm guessing it was just paranoia from life events in the last few days. I hope John isn't going to hurt me."

John chuckles. "I will not hurt you," he promises. "I think it is to be expected for you to be a little jumpy." A pause. "So you are our little sister. Tell me about yourself."

I hate that question. "What do you want to know?"

"Let's start with your full name, I guess." He shrugs.

"Elizabeth Samantha McCann. My birthday is on February 2, 2000. And I'm sixteen years old," I reply. "Oh, before you ask, yes, my middle name is after your mom. Dad loved her so much my mom was okay naming me after her. My mom and Dad loved each other, but just as friends. She was seventeen when she had me."

"Dad rocked the cradle a little?" John raises his eyebrow.

I giggle and nod. I wonder why I was feeling uneasy at first when he peeked in. I feel very comfortable with him now. I need to just start to woman up and stop being so jumpy.

"So you are special. Did Dad give you any hints growing up how special you are?" John asks.

I sigh. "Nope. He only pounded it in my head to keep my necklace on. He never told me about vampires or anything about the supernatural world. Dad would always tell me my life was normal compared to yours and he didn't want to rub that in your faces. That was why he kept me a secret from you two. My life was pretty normal. I went to school, and the only thing I had to worry about was which boy was going to flirt with me today. I didn't have many friends because I'm cursed with beauty. A lot of girls would get mad when their boyfriends would turn to look at me. My attractiveness is part of how I'm special, I guess." I pause. "I know he didn't want to rub my normal life in your face, but maybe if he were honest with all of us, we wouldn't have been in the boat we are in now. Maybe we would have already had a relationship as brothers and sister. Maybe we would even know what I am."

"What kind of person are you?" John queries. "Do you get in trouble a lot?"

"I've never been in trouble. I have never lied to my mom either. I never felt like I needed too. I just try to stay low-key. Go to school, come home, and work out is about all I do. Dad was very adamant about me working out and keeping up with self-defense," I reply.

"So, Joe, now, what do we do? When we are gone on the weekends, are we just going to leave her home alone?" John asks Joe.

"She is sixteen. I mean, Dad left us alone at a younger age. She should be okay." Joe shrugs.

"I want to hunt," I whisper.

"We will need to do some research to find out how special she is. What if she gets attacked while we are gone?" John continues, either ignoring me or just not hearing me.

"I want to hunt," I say again, louder this time.

Joe chuckles. "Lizzy, that is nice, but it takes a lot of practice."

I roll my eyes. Of course, they are going to doubt me. I know I've never done it before, but I also know I can do this.

"I'm a fast learner, and Dad taught me things that might help. I'm a black belt in karate and tae kwon do. I also have a purple belt in jujitsu and had to take self-defense classes. I know it sounds like a lot, but Dad enrolled me early in life. I haven't done karate, tae kwon do, and jujitsu in a while, but

I kept up with my self-defense moves," I explain. "I'm sure I can kick your asses. Shooting a vampire shouldn't be a problem either. I think I learned how to shoot when I was five, and Dad took me shooting every month. It was something I always looked forward to."

It is hard talking about going to the gun range, since Dad and I never got a chance to go one last time.

"Get out of bed," John demands as he stands up.

I look at him funny but do what he's asked me. As soon as I am on my feet, he grabs me and pins me against the wall. He puts his arm up to my throat, catching me off guard.

"If you beat me, Joe and I will talk about you coming on the road with us. So you're pinned. What are you going to do now?" John smiles.

"Don't be easy on me—choke me," I say arrogantly.

He grins and does as I ask.

My airway is cut off, and I start to struggle to breathe. There is no way I'm going to let him win, though. I take my knee and jab it into his groin as hard as I can. It works; he lets me go and bends over. I push him out of the way and try to escape, except he grabs my arm.

Now that I know what he is doing, I start to fight harder. He takes a few swings at me, and I dodge them, and he dodges mine. You could tell we practiced with the same guy. Still, I cannot let him think I am a weak little girl. He goes to swing at me, but instead I duck and get behind him. I jump on his back and put him in a choke hold. He starts to move around and slams me into the wall. The first couple of times, it hurts, but I do not let go. He does it a third time, and I let go and slide down the wall and land on my butt.

"Give up?" he huffs.

"Never!" I stand back up.

He grabs my arm and turns me around to put me in a choke hold again. I couldn't slam him into the wall, because he is bigger than me. So I put my foot around his and get my head free and his hand pinned behind his back. I kick him and give him a dead leg. He is now on one knee. I make a gun gesture with my fingers and put it onto his back.

"Boom," I say.

"The only thing I would change is, if you're shooting him, the gun goes here," Joe explains, moving my hand over. "Or stabbing him with wood works too."

I feel good knowing I just beat him. "So what do you say? Can I go hunting?"

I am eager. I need to do this. It will be nice to help others that do not know about this world.

"Lizzy, I don't know," Joe states. "But later, we will take you out to see how accurate your shooting skills are. There is a lot you don't know about hunting. Right now, why don't we get ready and I'll take you shopping? I'm guessing you are going to need more than the couple of items you brought with you."

I huff. I knew it was a long shot for them to say yes right away, but I was hoping. "Okay, will I have time to shower?"

"Yeah. I have no plans today," Joe replies. "John is going to work soon, and it is only eight in the morning,"

"If you both work, then when do you go hunting?" I ask.

"The weekends. We don't normally work on Fridays, so we travel Thursday night when we have long distances to drive," John answers.

"I guess that makes sense," I reply.

"Well, we will let you get ready," Joe says, "and, John, we will see you later."

"Yeah, I'll get to know you better when I get home."
John smiles.

"It was nice to meet you, John!" I wave.

"Same, Lizzy," he said, and they both leave my room.

Closing the door behind them, I head into the bathroom. I look in the mirror and remember what I am wearing. I'm surprised I didn't lose a boob while fighting. I take my cami off, and when I raise my arms over my head, my back spasms. It has been a while since I have been in a good fight. I spin around and look at the shower. I guess I'm going to use Dad's bodywash and shampoo right now. It's the only thing I have.

I take my bottoms off and turn toward the mirror again. This time my reflection disappoints me. The person looking back still is not me. My eyes are paler than normal, and I look sad. I tip my head sideways and look at the bright-red bite marks on my neck. They are still very noticeable. I decide to worry about them later. I turn on the water and get into the shower. As soon as the hot water hits me, my body instantly relaxes.

Chapter 5

We pull into a parking spot next to a small store called Clothes and More. I'm going to assume this place is a local store and not a chain store, since I've never heard of it before. Although I'm not that into fashion. So maybe this is a chain store.

"A family friend owns this store. I don't know if you will find anything that is your style, but it will have to do for now." Then Joe goes on to explain, "Todd and Gertie used to babysit John and me when our parents went out hunting. Yes, our mom was a hunter too. Weirdly, it was how our parents met. They were hunting the same vampire. Todd and Gertie are like a second set of parents to us. They would watch us after school and on weekends. They are the sweetest couple you will meet."

Well, now at least I know this is a local store and I'm not out of the loop when it comes to different stores.

"I cannot wait to meet them!" I smile. "Also, I'm not picky about my clothes."

That isn't completely true, since every girl *is* picky about what she wears. I, on the other hand, don't dress for style; I dress for comfort. So I'm sure there will be something I like.

We get out of the car, and I follow Joe to the store's door. He holds it open for me, and we walk in.

I glance around and notice it is a decent-size store. Movement in the corner of my eye catches my attention, and

I turn my head. Walking out of the back room is an older gentleman. He is dressed in a black button-down shirt and blue jeans. He has wild gray hair that goes a little past his shoulders, and he has a long gray beard that goes down to his chest.

"Joe, it is great to see you, son," he says, coming to embrace Joe in a hug.

"Hey, Todd!" Joe hugs him back.

So this is Todd. He is nothing like I imagined.

"What brings you by? Do you need new clothes already? I swore I just sold you some a few weeks ago!" Todd smiles, getting out of the hug.

"Nope, I'm not here for me. We are here for her," Joe says, pointing at me.

Now I become a little nervous when Todd's attention turns to me. He gives me a glance-over. "Hi, I'm Todd. I'm the owner of this beautiful establishment. Please excuse my asking, but have we met before?"

He puts his hand out, and I shake it. "I don't believe so, but I'm Lizzy."

"Lizzy here is John's and my sister. We just found out yesterday. Unfortunately, her mother died earlier this week, and Dad died last week, so I get custody of her," Joe explains.

"That is how I know you. I've seen pictures of you. Your dad was very proud of his little girl," Todd states.

A big smile comes across my face. Turns out I wasn't a secret to everyone like I thought. Dad *did* talk about me every once in a while.

"Dad talked about me?" I gush.

"And you didn't tell us. Why?" Joe questions.

"Well, I haven't seen you since Jason died. I also didn't know how to tell you that you had a secret sister. I always told him that he had to tell you at some point, but he just ignored me," Todd explains. "Now, why don't we let Lizzy look around? You can come to the back with me and talk. Also, I need help moving some boxes."

"Okay," Joe sighs. "Would ten outfits be reasonable for right now?"

"Yes, that is perfect," I answer.

Ten is a lot more than I planned on picking out, but who am I to argue?

I watch while they disappear to the back. Part of me wants to follow to see what they are going to talk about, but with my luck, I would get caught.

I turn around and glance at the shop, looking for the women's section. Over to my right is the kids' section, and to the left is the men's. Did Joe think I was going to find something I like with these options? I walk in a little farther, and that is when I spot the women's section. Thank God I didn't have to dress in men's clothes for the time being! I venture through the men's section to get to the section I need to be at.

The first rack I come across has a top I just have to have. Then searching the racks, I find a few more tops. After collecting three shirts, I decide to wander to the dressing room before grabbing any more.

The first shirt I try on is a tight-fitting black V-neck. I turn to gaze in the mirror and love how it looks on me. It shows off all my curves. This one is for sure a keeper. I take off the top and fold it back up and place it on the empty chair. I glance in the full-length mirror, and the bite marks are still noticeable. Maybe I should get some scarves to hide them. I grab a purple shirt, and this one hugs my body perfectly too.

After picking out tops that I adore, I find four pairs of jeans. I have started to fold them and add them to my pile when a sudden chill and feeling of uneasiness come over me.

Knowing there could be some kind of danger, but not wanting to make it a big deal, I think maybe I'm just overreacting. I grab my clothes and walk out of the dressing room. I then glance around, but I don't see anyone in the store. Okay, this paranoia is getting ridiculous.

I start to walk up front and someone grabs my arm, quickly putting me in a choke hold. I drop my items and try to pull his arms off my throat. When I realize that isn't going to work, I figure I need to come up with a different plan, and quick. I am running out of time as I'm gasping for air. Reaching behind me, I grab the guy in the groin and twist. He lets go of me, and I turn to face him. The guy looks exactly like Ethan did right before he attacked me. Which only means one thing: he is a vampire. Time to prove to Joe that I'm capable of hunting.

"You bitch!" he yells, lunging at me.

I dodge to the left to avoid his attack, but I do not take my eyes off him. I turn around quickly so he could not get ahead. I get into a fighting stance, and he starts to laugh.

"Do you really think a little girl like you can take me?" he mocks.

"Bring it!" I smile.

He starts to swing, and thankfully, I dodge them all. After a few more swings from him, I decide it is my turn to fight back. My first right hook is not successful. Instead of my fist making contact with his face, he grabs it and pushes me into a shelf. Instead of catching me, the shelf collapses underneath me. The pain is almost unbearable, but I have to keep fighting. I take too long to get up, and the vampire climbs on top of me and pins my arms above my head.

"Now it is time for me to have some breakfast!" he hisses.

I bend one of my legs, and with all my strength, I roll over and get on top of him. I smile down at him. "Not today."

I grab a piece of wood from the broken shelf, but before I could stab him, he pushes me off. I unsteadily get back to my feet. My back is spasming, but I cannot let that slow me down. He is back to his feet now and staring me dead in the eye. I feel like he is looking into my soul. While our eyes are locked with each other, I slowly place the wooden piece in my pocket. He comes at me, and I move out of the way. When I turn to face him, he is already charging at me again. This time I don't have a chance to get out of the way; he slams me into the wall. If it weren't for the fact that he is holding me up, I probably would have fallen to the ground. He raises my arms and pins them over my head. Leaning into me, he smells my neck.

Another feeling of uneasiness comes over me. This time, I know it is because I'm screwed. Except I am not going to give him the satisfaction that he wants. He licks my neck, and that grosses me out. His tongue is wet and rough and gives me goose bumps.

"There is nothing you can do now," he hisses in my ear.

I am terrified. I cannot die. Not now. I move my legs a little and notice they are free. With all my might, I kick him in the groin.

He lets go of me and bends over. I use my knee and high-knee him in the stomach. This time he drops to his knees.

"And you said there was nothing I could do!" I chuckle.

I grab the piece of wood from the shelf out of my pocket and raise it high. I glance at the spot Joe told me about this morning and stab him. It surprises me when he turns to dust and disappears before my eyes. Once it is over, I lean against the wall and slide down to my butt. My heart is racing, and I am visibly shaking. I couldn't tell if I enjoyed the high or if I am terrified. Honestly, it is probably a little of both.

"Lizzy, are you okay?" Joe asks.

I nod. "That was awesome! Scary, but the high of it is kind of enjoyable. Does that make me weird?"

"No." He chuckles. "All hunters get that high after a good hunt." He pauses. "After seeing what I just saw, I don't understand why Dad kept you out of this world. You are a natural hunter. Later, if you prove to us you have good aim with a gun, I don't see why you couldn't hunt. I mean, if you still want to."

I stand up, and if my back weren't hurting, I would have been jumping for joy right now. "Yes, I do! I want to find the person who killed my mother and kill him."

"That is not a good reason to go hunting. Revenge can blind you," Joe explains.

I sigh. "I understand that. I also know that I will probably never see that bastard again. But I would also like to keep people safe from these monsters. I couldn't save my mom, but maybe I could save someone else." Then I quickly add, "Wait, how do you know I'm a natural hunter? You were in the back."

Joe looks down. I can feel guilt coming from him, but what does he have to feel guilty about? "We came out after we heard some commotion. When we got to the door, you were in your fighting stance. I told Todd I wanted to watch you fight. When you got pushed into the shelf, Todd really wanted to help you, but I told him no. You want to hunt? You need to prove you can protect yourself. Besides, I knew if he bit you, he would have died. Of course, if it got out of hand, I would have stepped in," he says. "I will be honest, when he had you pinned against the wall, I had doubts. I thought he was going to bite you and die. I wasn't going to call that hunting. Then you surprised me and kept fighting. I'm glad you killed him and he didn't just bite you. I am very impressed. Especially since you have never done this before."

I am feeling really good about myself. There is nothing that is going to bring this day down. To make it better, it's only day one, and I already have Joe's approval. I couldn't even be mad that he decided to watch instead of help; it was the only way I was going to prove myself. I'm also glad I stabbed him in the right spot. Which leads me to my next question. "Why do they turn to dust, but when Ethan bit me, he looked like he had a heart attack?"

"When you kill a vampire, they are supposed to turn to dust. The only guess I have is, you didn't technically kill Ethan. Your blood is a whole new weapon that kills them differently." Joe shrugs. "But I cannot give you an honest answer, because I don't know."

Why did I expect him to know that answer? It was just one of those questions I had to ask, hoping maybe there was an answer.

"So now what?" I question.

"We will help Todd clean up this mess, buy your clothes, and do some more shopping throughout the day. We don't have much food in the house, so I'm sure you will need to eat at some point today." He smiles.

"I do love to cook. Like I said before, I could cook every night," I offer.

Joe's smile grows bigger. I'm going to guess he doesn't remember me saying that earlier. "Home-cooked meals? That will be awesome! I don't remember the last time I had one of those. Probably when we stayed with Todd. His wife cooked for us all the time. Once we got old enough to stay home alone or go with Dad, we always just ate out."

My heart aches for Joe and John. Mom and I hardly ever ate out. When Dad came to visit, he always had a home-cooked meal from Mom. How could Dad do that to his kids? He should have at least attempted to cook. Now I am seeing again how my life was different from theirs.

"Tonight I can make tossed salad, tacos, and tater tots," I offer.

"That sounds great," Joe says, licking his lips. "Todd, do you have a broom?"

I turn my head, and Todd is standing right there. I now feel bad that I didn't even notice he is here. I watch while he heads to the back. How did I not notice him? He probably thinks I'm a snob. He walks to the back and comes back with three brooms in his hands.

"I'm sorry I made such a mess," I apologize while he hands me a broom.

"It isn't like you planned on being attacked." Todd smiles. "I'll close the store for a couple of minutes so we can clean up."

Todd walks toward the door, and before I am told to do anything, I head toward the broken shelf. I start to pick up the broken pieces of wood, and my mind starts to replay everything that happened. I close my eyes and shake my head, but that doesn't help. Every time I blink, I see images of the vampire attacking me. I find it weird that this time is the time that is going to haunt me. Especially after everything that has happened.

"It's normal," Joe states, and I jump.

"What is?" I question.

My heart is racing. Joe must have scared me more than I thought.

"To replay your first kill in your head. Go outside and take a few minutes to collect yourself. I'll clean this up," he offers.

"But I'm the one who made the mess," I say.

I think I am fighting this because I do not want to be alone with my thoughts.

"Go," he demands.

I put the broom down and head toward the door. "It only locks from the outside. You can get out!" Todd shouts.

I nod and walk out the door. Outside there are many people strolling about the area. I realize we are right in the middle of Main Street. I don't know or trust any of these people, so I need to find a place to hide. I study my surroundings, and finally to my left I spot an alley. That should be a perfect spot to hide.

I walk up to the opening of the alley and notice the end of it is blocked off by a wooden fence. So this is just a one-way street. I continue to walk down the alley and stop when I get about three feet from the fence. Staring at it makes me feel emotional. I feel like this roadblock represents my life at the moment. It's like I hit a dead end in my life's journey, and now I don't know where to go. I could turn around, but I was always told to never live in the past. I'm starting to feel really anxious. I need to move. I start to pace back and forth like a caged animal. There is so much going on in my life I could scream. That is what I do; I scream and start hitting the fence, all while I let the tears roll down my face. If anyone would see me, they would think I am crazy. Who am I kidding? I *am* crazy!

A few minutes pass, and I realize I need to get ahold of myself. I need to stop this self-pity party. Wiping the tears away from my eyes, I step back a few feet from the fence. I glance up to the top and smile.

"What am I doing? I am a McCann. When I'm at a dead end, I make my own path," I whisper to myself.

I start to inspect the area, and to my right is a trash can. I walk over to it and drag it to the middle of the fence. Carefully I climb on the top and stand up straight. The trash can wobbles under me, but I grab the top of the fence and steady myself. I hop over the fence and smile when I land on the sidewalk on the other side. There is nothing great waiting for me, just another road. I sometimes forget, when life gives you a dead end, you just have to make your own path. Weirdly, I am feeling a lot better.

The back of the store is to my right, and I decide to see if the door is unlocked.

I yank the handle, and it opens. Todd doesn't worry about strangers coming into his building? Walking in, I am surprised how big the back of the store is. There are boxes and clothes everywhere. I now need to find my way to the front. I decide the best bet is to walk straight. After walking around a few boxes and other items, I finally find the door to the front of the store. Before I walk through, I hear Joe and Tod talking. I decide to wait to see what they are talking about.

"Are you sure?" Joe asks.

I close my eyes to tap into his aura. He is feeling uneasy about something. Now I really want to know what they are talking about.

"Joe, you know you will do great at this. She will be a little more emotional than John and yourself. You already did one thing right today. You saw she was needing time with her thoughts, and you made her face them. Which is something you have issues doing yourself. I can tell all she wants is your approval, which will take time. I know that, because when you told her she did a great job at killing that vamp, her smile was huge. From what you have told me, she has gone through a lot, but so have you. You all need one another. I know you're still upset your dad didn't tell you about her, but that doesn't matter. If you knew about her and your dad and her mom died, what would you do?" Todd says.

"I would have taken her in like I did. The only difference is, I would already have known about her. I don't know her," Joe replies.

"Then get to know her. She is your sister, and from what I heard from your dad, she is a good kid. It will take time to make this big adjustment for you and for her. But I know you will be a great guardian for her. I couldn't think of anyone better. Look at John—he turned out great. Remember, you basically raised him yourself," Todd says, praising Joe.

Joe shifts his body and pushes his hair back. "So does that mean I'm responsible for his mistakes?"

"No. He is responsible for his own actions," Todd reassures him, putting his hand on Joe's shoulder.

"What if I mess this up?" Joe asks.

"We will learn together," I answer, walking in. "Sorry I was listening to your conversation." I smile sheepishly. "Joe, Todd is right, I am just wanting your approval. Sending me outside to collect my thoughts helped out a lot, thanks. I feel a lot better now. I'm not going to be optimistic saying you are going to be the best guardian, because I'm sure you will mess up, but I'm also sure there are going to be things I will mess up too. You, John, and I are in this together. We will adjust."

Joe smiles at me, and I couldn't help but grin back. "If you heard anything negative, I didn't mean anything by it."

"What I overheard was not negative. It is just you being unsure about this. To be honest, I'm unsure too. No one prepared us for this. It will just be an adventure," I assure him.

"You are right. It is an adventure we will take together," Joe agrees. "Well, Lizzy, why don't you pick up the clothes you wanted? I'll pay, and we will head out."

I nod and head to the pile of clothes on the floor. This is going to be a challenge for us. I just hope we're up to it.

Chapter 6

This has been one of the best days I have had in a long time. Joe has bought me not only new clothes but also a new cell phone and some toiletries I will need, and we go out for lunch. I think it is safe to say we are getting along well. With how things started today, with my being attacked at the store, I'm surprised I'm having such a wonderful time. All this running around today has also helped keep my mind off how tired I am.

Supper is also a success, with both Joe and John saying they are going to keep me around for a while. They eat the tacos like they have never eaten food before. I don't even think they are chewing! Normally, I would have found that disgusting, except this time it hurts my heart seeing them eat that way. It is sad they never got to enjoy home-cooked meals growing up. So I vow, with me in their lives, they can experience it every day.

I am going to pick up afterward, but John stops me and offers to do the dishes. He collects the plates and head into the kitchen. In a panic, I look at Joe and ask if John even knows how to do dishes. This causes Joe to laugh and tell me I should see the look of horror on my face.

Right on cue, John comes back and asks if there is a certain way dishes are supposed to go in the dishwasher. I am happy to show him the right way to do it.

With supper all cleaned up, Joe, John, and I go out to test my shooting abilities. I still don't understand why we have to wait until dark. But I do not want to ask them; I am determined to figure it out myself. The more I think about it, however, the more I realize nothing comes to my mind except that they want me to fail. The ride is quiet. Instead of paying attention to the music, I stare out the window at the sky. It is beautiful. There is no moon, but the stars sparkle high. I start to think about the times my parents and I would go out stargazing.

Before I reminisce too deeply, Joe pulls into a patch of trees. It frustrates me that I can't see the sky anymore. Joe parks, and I glance around our surroundings. We are literally in the middle of trees. Now I really feel like they are setting me up to fail. How am I going to hit anything if I cannot see my target?

"Are you ready?" Joe asks.

"Um, no. How am I going to hit my target if I cannot see where I'm shooting?" I complain.

John turns to face me. "We hunt at night, so we need to see if you can aim and hit a target in the dark. Sometimes all you will have is a flashlight and a pistol. This gives you practice to see if you can handle little light. This took us a couple of years of practice, so don't feel bad if you do not succeed on the first try."

I guess that makes sense, except I am still confused. Why do we only hunt in the dark? I have been attacked twice now, and both times have been in the daylight.

"Why do you only hunt at night?" I finally ask. "I mean, I've only known about vampires for about twenty-four hours, and both times I have been attacked have been during daytime hours."

"You were, but they are more likely to hunt at night, when fewer people are around. That way, no one sees them take their prey," Joe explains.

Everything he is saying is making sense; I just don't want to hunt in the dark.

I get out of the car, and the warm summer breeze dances around me. I close the door and take a moment to be one with my surroundings. I close my eyes and start to listen to everything. I can hear the leaves dancing to the songs of the crickets. From a distance, I can hear a hoot from a lonely owl. I never got to enjoy the country life growing up. We lived in town, and my mom was very adamant about my being home before dark. Now I know why.

"Let's get started," Joe says, interrupting my inner peace.

I open my eyes and see they are standing in front of the car. I join them and instantly notice John laying out three different kinds of guns. Although he has his flashlight shining on them, it is still too dark to see what kind they are.

"Here is the first gun. It is an AMT AutoMag III. It holds eight bullets. We make our own wooden bullets, so if you ever notice us running low, just say something. Now, to shoot, you hold the gun and flashlight like this." John demonstrates.

He holds the handgun in his right hand while holding the flashlight with his left underneath the gun. I don't know if I'm going to be able to do this. John hands me the gun and flashlight, and I swallow hard. I have never been so nervous to shoot a gun in my life.

"There is a target down there." He points.

I shine the flashlight in the direction of the target, and even when squinting, I can barely see it. If I cannot hit it, they are going to leave me home, and I'm never going to be able to hunt. *Okay, Lizzy, this is it.*

"Okay, show us what you got," Joe states.

They shut off their flashlights, and now only mine is shining. I point the gun and light toward the target. To me it seems like it is the smallest target in the world and they are just setting me up to fail. I swallow while I get my hands adjusted on the gun and flashlight. I aim, cock the hammer, and pull the trigger.

"You have seven more bullets. Shoot them all," John tells me.

I have to do this seven more times? At least it gives me a better chance at hitting the target at least once.

I aim and let the next seven go one after another. After the seventh time, I turn around and place the gun on the hood and exhale. Joe leans in the car and flips the headlights on. I groan and cover my eyes from the bright light. A little warning would have been nice.

"Let's go see how you did," Joe states.

"I probably missed them all," I mutter under my breath.

I follow behind, nervous to see how I did. Joe takes my flashlight and shines it onto the target. "Well, I'll be damned! Johnny, look at this!" Joe says in awe.

What did I do?

"Damn, she has an eye on her," John replies.

"What? What is it?" I'm starting to panic.

"Take a look for yourself," John says, stepping aside.

I walk up to the target and gasp. All eight holes are right in the middle. I know I have good aim, but I never realized how good.

"I don't even think I could be that accurate," Joe admits.

"Beginner's luck?" I shrug.

"I want you to do it one more time. John, get another target out of the trunk. Lizzy, we will reload the gun and see if you can do it again," Joe directs.

I could not believe I just did that. It has to beginner's luck, but I'm willing to try again. I feel so giddy that I just did that. I feel like I can do anything right now. We get back to the car, and Joe hands me eight more bullets. I load them one by one while I watch John hang up a new target. When we are all ready, Joe shuts off the lights, and it is my time to shine again. Lining up my target, I start to shoot again.

After shooting off the seventh round, I stop for a second. A cold chill with a feeling of uneasiness comes over me again. There is a vampire around.

"Lizzy, you still have one more bullet," Joe states.

"Shush," I whisper. "Flip on the lights."

Joe doesn't say anything but does what I ask. When the headlights turn on, I don't see anyone but the three of us. Am I wrong about this feeling? Am I becoming paranoid now?

"Sorry, I thought…" I turn to face Joe, and there she is, sneaking up on him. "Joe, duck!"

I point the gun at him, and he turns to face her and then ducks. I shoot, and she turns to dust a few inches from Joe. Good to know in a hurry, I can still shoot accurately.

"What the hell? How did you know?" John comments.

"I felt danger was near. When I turned around, there she was. I'm sorry, Joe, for shooting so close to you," I respond, breathing out.

"Don't apologize. I should be thanking you instead, for saving me from being bitten," he explains.

I'm glad Joe is happy I did that. I'm also very proud of myself for hitting the vampire in the right spot. Two vampires in one day? I am on fire! Especially for someone who has never been trained to do any of this stuff. I feel like it comes so naturally to me.

"As long as you are around, we will be unstoppable!" John cheers.

I nod and smile. I feel like they are accepting me a little more with each passing minute. I notice Joe and John looking at each other, and I want to know what they are thinking. I did prove to them I am capable of hunting, and Joe saw earlier I can fight. I hope they approve and let me join them on their hunts.

"Joe, I think she has proved to us that she can do this," John states.

Yes, I have.

"We leave for Walden tomorrow night. She proved to me twice now she can kill a vampire," Joe says. "I know it is only ten thirty, but I'm exhausted. Why don't we go back home and relax?" He then turns to me. "Lizzy, John and I are going to work tomorrow. So that means we are leaving you home alone. Just make sure your bags are packed. We will leave tomorrow after we get off work." Joe yawns.

I freeze in place. I don't know if I am ready to be left alone yet. I haven't been alone since before the death of my mom. What am I supposed to do in a town I'm not familiar with? Tomorrow is going to be the biggest challenge yet. I take a deep breath and walk to the back passenger side of the car.

"Well, I'll be damned," John says, walking back to the car. I didn't even notice he went down to get the target. "She hit the middle seven more times!"

"That's it, I'm convinced she is a natural," Joe states, getting into the car.

I don't say anything; instead, I am still too busy obsessing about whether I'll be okay tomorrow by myself. I guess ready or not, it has to happen.

Chapter 7

Today has been a decent day. It is a little rocky when I first wake up. All I want to do is hide under my blanket and let depression take over me. Unfortunately, for the first hour I am awake, all I do is lie in bed and cry and feel sorry for myself. The longer I lie there, the more I start to feel lost, and I know I need to get up and start doing something to get my mind off things. Slowly I crawl out of bed, put on some jogging clothes, and go for a five-mile run. On my run, I start to feel better and am glad I decided to do this. The mountains in the distance make everything look pretty and peaceful. Although it is summer, the temperature is only fifty degrees, which makes the run more enjoyable.

When I get home, I attempt to make myself a veggie omelet. Like always, the end result turns out to be ultimate scrambled eggs. For some reason, an omelet is very difficult for me, but I never give up trying. One day I will master the craft of an omelet.

After eating, I clean up and get my stuff packed for the weekend. I don't know what I will need, so I pack a little of everything. I've never been on a hunt before.

While I wait for Joe and John to get home, I decide to veg out on the couch and watch TV. This is something I have never done in my life. Back home, I always stayed busy; I only watched maybe an hour of TV a day. I flip through the channels until I land on a reality show called *Hannah Knows*

Best. It is really stupid, but I end up watching a marathon of it.

It surprises me when the front door opens—the guys are already home.

Now we are on our way to Walden, and I am excited but nervous about my first hunt. I keep admiring the view out my window. The sun setting behind the mountains tonight is the most beautiful sunset I ever have seen. This makes me really miss my mom. Every clear night, she would sit on the porch and watch the sunset. She always told me that even though her parents kicked her out, the sunset always reminded her of home.

The tears start to threaten to fall, but I decide I will not break down now. I take a couple of deep breaths until I calm myself. Joe and John are up front, talking business, but I feel like I need some interaction.

"So are we going hunting as soon as we get there?" I interrupt.

"No. We will scope the area out during the day tomorrow and go out hunting tomorrow night. Tonight, we will just get things organized for tomorrow," John explains.

Okay, good. I have a day to prepare myself for this hunt.

"Are you having second thoughts?" Joe asks.

Where did he get that idea from?

"No. Why?" I inquire.

"Your voice sounded a little shaky when you asked," he answers.

I sigh. "I'm not having second thoughts. Honestly, I'm just trying to stay strong after everything that has happened in the last week," I say. "I was watching the sunset, and it reminded me of my mom. I'm sorry, I'm trying to be strong, but it is just hard when everything reminds me of them."

Tears start to build up in my eyes again. *Please don't escape,* I silently pray. I do not want to start crying. Especially when I have to have a clear mind for the hunt tomorrow.

"Let me guess, Dad would tell you tears are a sign of weakness. You are a McCann, you are stronger than whatever is hurting you," Joe tells me, mocking Dad.

That is weird and creepy at the same time. Joe sounded just like Dad when he said that. I couldn't help but smile. "You sound just like him."

Joe lets out a sigh. "I should. I've had to imitate his voice enough growing up."

Is he talking about Dad negatively? Was Dad never there for them? Dad had to have been there for them! What kind of dad wouldn't be there for his kids? He was always there for me, and I would only see him once a month! Dad called or texted me every day, so I knew he was there for me. Was that what Todd meant when he said Joe basically raised John?

"Although we were raised the same way, I don't believe that crying is a sign of weakness. I think it just means you've been strong for too long. I also believe in talking, so if you ever need a listening ear, do not hesitate to come to us. Not all of Dad's rules were the greatest, but some of them were necessary.

"I thought I knew better when I was seventeen and ran away. Unfortunately, I got into some trouble the two years I was gone. Luckily, Dad found me and bailed me out. I don't want to talk about what I did, but Dad did forgive me. But at that time, I was not allowed to talk about what I did, and to this day, it still haunts me. If I had only listened to some of his rules, I probably wouldn't have gotten in trouble," John explains.

I wonder what he did. "Did you kill a man?" I joke.

"Four men, five women, ten kids, and a dog." He chuckles.

"Not the dog!" I laugh.

I notice Joe shoot a look of concern to John, but he doesn't seem to notice. John keeps looking straight in front of him. I wonder what he actually did. Whatever it was, he is feeling super guilty about it. I don't even need to tap into his emotions—it is so strong it overwhelms me.

"John, I know you said you don't want to talk about it, but you need to turn the guilt down a little. It hurts!" I moan.

His guilt is so overwhelming it physically hurts me. Just when I didn't think my depression could get any worse, I start feeling even more empty and the most guilt I have ever felt. All I want to do is lie down and never get back up. The guilt is almost driving me to feel suicidal. I need to get out of the car.

"Joe, I need you to stop now," I cry.

I start to hyperventilate and feel sick from all the anxiety that is hitting me. Joe pulls over, and as soon as I open the door, I fall out of the car and start to throw up. I am on my knees, physically shaking. My heart is racing, and I feel like I'm going to pass out. I need to get away from John.

With every ounce of energy I have left, I run down the road. When there is enough distance between John and me, I gasp and fall to my knees. I can finally breathe again. That is new; I have never experienced someone else's pain that strongly before. I stand back up and spot Joe walking toward me. Boy, these guys need to cool their emotions, because I can feel the anger radiating off him.

"Why are you tapping into his feelings?" he scolds.

I sigh. "I can promise you, I was not tapping into him," I say. "When someone is feeling strongly about one emotion, it radiates off them. Like right now, I can feel your anger and annoyance without tapping into your emotions. Except yours is not strong enough that I am actually physically feeling them. I do not know what happened back there. One minute I was feeling his guilt, and the next I was actually experiencing it. Whatever he did, he is feeling super guilty. Joe, I had so much pain mentally I was feeling suicidal. Now, I know I have a lot going on, but I have never contemplated suicide until his feelings set in. That is something he is feeling."

John really needs help, and I don't know how to help him. I don't want to tell him I know he is thinking about suicide, but at the same time, I worry for his well-being.

"He has a past that haunts him, and I'm aware that he feels that way. We do talk about it sometimes when he gets really down and starts thinking he needs to end the pain," Joe informs me.

Well, at least he *does* talk about it. That gives me some relief. "I want to go back to the car, but to be honest, if he is still feeling that way, I can't."

Joe nods. "I will go talk to him. Are you okay right here for a minute?"

Before I could respond, Joe starts walking back to the car. More secrets, but at least John is letting me know he does have a past. He could have kept that from me and just let things leak out like everything else is. I hope whatever he did, it does not come back to bite him in the butt. One day I hope John feels comfortable enough to talk to me about it. Except until then, I need to just focus on tomorrow. I need to make sure my first hunt goes smoothly and I do not get caught.

Nerves start to set in about tomorrow. Pacing back and forth, I start to worry. What if I am not as good as they think I am? I mean, I know I hit the middle multiple times yesterday, but what if it is just beginner's luck? A vampire could sneak up behind me and bite me. Oh, wait, I cannot die from their bites, unless my necklace does come off. Oh my, what am I getting myself into tomorrow?

"Hey, Lizzy, I'm sorry. I didn't mean to hurt you," John apologizes, and I jump. I did not hear them pull up.

"I didn't even know it was possible to experience someone else's emotions that strongly. Are you okay?" I counter.

"I'm better." He smiles.

Cautiously I get back into the car, and I do not feel anything overpowering. This is a good start.

Joe drives off, and the first couple of minutes are quiet. Tonight is the first night we are all sleeping in the same hotel room. What if they snore and I cannot sleep? Will I be focused on tomorrow's hunt with no sleep? Wait, am I sleeping on the floor? That will really put a damper on my night if I have to sleep on a hard motel floor. Especially for three days—my back will not stand for that!

"Hey, guys, am I sleeping on the floor tonight? I don't have a problem with it, just want to know," I lie.

"Do you think we are that mean?" Joe asks.

I panic for a second. "I would never think you were mean. I was the one who crashed your party this weekend. I just thought it would be fair if I sleep on the floor."

I am not going to be happy about sleeping on the dirty floor, but I am not going to argue if they make me. I am just happy we are getting along. I do not want them to think I am a privileged teenager. I am capable of sleeping anywhere they need me to.

"Don't worry, you will always have a bed to sleep on. John and I are going to take turns each weekend sleeping on a rollaway bed. We talked about it last night," Joe explains.

That does not seem fair if they always have to sleep on the rollaway. "Shouldn't I have a turn?"

"No," John states.

"I'm in charge of you now, so that means I have to put you first," Joe states.

That is the last thing I want him to do. I do not want him to feel like he has to put me first for everything. He can do things without thinking of me. "You know, Joe, I don't want you to have to change your life because of me. You don't have to put me first."

"Joe always puts people first," John explains.

That is interesting. Not many guys that I have met put others first. I bet whatever girl he is with just loves him. Especially if he puts others first and likes to listen. This thought leads me to the next question. I think I asked Joe earlier, but I don't remember what he said.

"Do either of you have girlfriends? Am I going to be home and be surprised by someone coming in?" I pry.

"Nope. I've been single for a while now. To be honest, I'm more of a friends-with-benefits type of guy. I have too much going on in my life to settle down with just one person," John states.

Well, at least he is honest. I wonder if Joe is the same way. Does that mean if you are a hunter you will never have a normal homelife? I mean, one day I would like to grow up and have a family of my own. Then again, if I am special to the vampire world, maybe it will be smart to not have kids. I do not know if this is hereditary, since I don't know what I am.

"No, I don't either. I was in a serious relationship a while ago. Unfortunately, it ended really badly. Since then I haven't found the right person," Joe answers. "Why don't we just listen to music and be quiet for a bit?"

Joe turns up the radio, and it is playing rap. I grew up listening to country, so listening to rap is weird for me.

I can tell I hit a sore spot with Joe; he is feeling sad and guilty now too. I just hope it does not get to the point of my physically feeling it again. If it ended badly, does that mean she broke up with him? With the guilt, did he cheat on her? I guess this is something I will never know unless he tells me about it one day.

I decide to download a book on my phone. It is a book I attempted to read a couple of weeks ago before this all happened. I do not remember what I read before, so I start over. Minus the rap music blaring, the rest of the ride is quiet. While the boys stew over their emotions, I get lost in my book.

Chapter 8

I finish the book as we pull into the motel parking lot. My heart hurts that it was over. It was such a great love story that I didn't want it to end. I can only hope that one day my life can be as perfect as a book. Fall in love and live happily ever after. Of course, I know that cannot happen, because that is fiction and this is real life, but I can always hope. I thought I would have time to process the book more, but fifteen minutes after we get here, Joe decides it is early enough for a short hunt. It is midnight, and Joe sees a bar at the edge of town. I guess that is a perfect feeding ground for vampires.

I see the bar that he is talking about, but instead of pulling into the parking lot, he keeps driving. That is weird. I swore he said we were going to this bar. "Where are we going?"

Joe takes a deep breath. "I'm going to drop you and John off two miles north from the bar. Then I'm going to park the car two miles south. We will meet up at the bar. Afterward, we will all walk back to the car. It will be a short hunt, but maybe we will get lucky."

I guess we cover more ground that way if we split up. Do they always split up, or is it because of me? I could ask, but I better not. I do not need them annoyed at all my questions again. Maybe I will ask tomorrow.

Joe pulls over, and John and I get out. He walks to the trunk of the car, and I follow close. My heart is starting to race, and I feel like I'm physically shaking. Maybe I'm not ready for this?

John hands me a flashlight and a gun, then one each for himself. He grabs a wooden stake and hands it to me. "Put this in your sock."

I give it a good look-over. This thing is sharp at the end of it. What if I stab myself with it or, worse, give myself a splinter? I swallow to try to make the lump in my throat go away. It doesn't, but I bend over and carefully place the stake in my sock. When I stand back up straight, it feels so weird having it there. Weirdly, the wood is smooth and not as rough as I thought a wooden stake would feel.

John closes the trunk and hits it twice, and Joe drive off. That must be a code for goodbye.

The streetlights are giving off a little light, but standing on the side of the road is very eerie. John starts to walk down the ditch, and that is my cue to follow. The first step is hard for me to take. I do not know if I'm actually ready to hunt. I know I was acting all confident before, but I think it was all talk.

I follow him into some trees, and now it is pitch-dark. I've never been afraid of the dark before, but now I feel like a little child who needs a night-light. How are we supposed to see where we are going? John turns on his flashlight, which reminds me I have one too. I turn mine on and shake my head at myself. I am just working myself up. Tonight will go fine. Besides, if something happens, John is here to back me up, and I have killed three vampires already. Then again, I never went looking for them; all three of them found me. I just hope now that I'm the hunter and they are the prey, I'm able to do this.

"Lizzy, you are supposed to be leading this hunt." John stops.

I almost run right into him. Although I have my flashlight, it is still hard to see anything. Wait, is he waiting for me to walk around him to lead him through the darkness? I'm not ready for this; I'm just here to observe. He isn't moving, so I finally sigh and walk around him. Walking slowly, I come upon a tree. Should I walk around it on the left or right side? Will it make a difference? If I choose the wrong way, will John yell at me? Oh my god, I'm going to freak out!

"Lizzy, you proved to us you can do this. There is no need to be nervous," John whispers.

"I know, but I've never led a hunt, so how do I know if I'm doing it right?" I am panicking.

He smiles. "That is why I'm here. If I see you doing something wrong, I will correct you."

He is right; I shouldn't worry. I take a deep breath and confidently go around the tree to the right. Nothing is happening, so I'm assuming it doesn't matter which way I go around the tree. I take a few more steps before I stop. I need a minute to listen to our surroundings. The air is still; I hear absolutely nothing except for the music coming from the bar. We must be close.

I start walking again, and when I spot the bar, I become very disappointed.

"I didn't feel anything," I sigh.

I hope Joe found something so this hunt tonight isn't a waste.

"Do you want to see if they will let you in and you get a soda or something?" John offers.

"Sure." I shrug.

We walk up to the door, and of course, there is a sign that reads, "No minors." That's okay, I didn't need anything.

"I guess we wait out here?" John smiles.

I'm guessing he wants a beer. I have no problem waiting out here for Joe while he goes gets one. "Go in, I'll wait for Joe."

John chuckles. "Do you think I'm going to let someone who looks like you stand outside a bar by yourself? Not only would I be stupid, but Joe would also kill me if anything happened to you."

Well, if something happens to me, their lives would go back to being normal. They wouldn't have to worry about their little orphaned sister anymore. Wait a second, why am I thinking this way? I do not want anything to happen to me; that is a very scary thought. Okay, Lizzy, you have every right to be depressed, but no reason to start thinking like this. I can't even blame John for that one.

"Don't you think…"

I stop. A chill and a feeling of uneasiness come over me. "Something is near."

I glance around; no one looks like a threat. Everyone outside doesn't look like a vampire. I don't let my guard down; I keep my eye on everyone when all of a sudden a sharp pain hits me. It feels like teeth piercing through my flesh. I turn around, and no one is behind me, biting me. "Joe is in trouble!"

Not waiting for John's response, I dart south of the bar. I need to find Joe to make sure he is all right. Half a mile from the bar, I see a vampire feeding.

"Hey, mosquito!" I shout.

I have no idea why I shout that, but it works. The vamp stops feeding and stares directly at me. I shine my flashlight at her face, and she hisses. Her face is old and has blood running down the side of her mouth. I feel like I'm in a horror movie and I am the dumb blonde that goes toward the danger. I pull my gun up to shoot, but she disappears. She is the quickest vampire I have seen yet. I look around, but I cannot find her.

Where did she go?

Somehow, she sneaks up on me and grabs my hair. I gasp. Everything happens so fast. She pulls my head back and bites me. It isn't long after that she just drops dead.

"Ha, bitch!" I say, stepping over her.

Running up to the body, I see it is Joe. He isn't moving. Am I too late?

"That was fucked up," John says, running up to me.

"Is he dead? Are we too late?" I panic.

"No. His eyes are blinking. You saved him. Not only did you know he was in trouble, but you also got the vampire to stop feeding on him," John explains. "I must say, it is weird seeing a vampire die from biting someone. I need to know, though, how did you know he was in trouble?"

Why is he asking me this? I feel like we should have more concern for Joe. He is just lying there so lifeless. Why isn't he moving? He might be blinking, but what if he is hurt more?

"Shouldn't we be worried about him right now?" I bark.

I don't mean to sound angry, but John is acting like nothing is happening.

"Lizzy, he will be okay," John says, putting a comforting hand on my shoulder. "He will be paralyzed for another few minutes, though," he adds. "So how did you know?"

I could not keep my eyes off Joe. I know John says he will be okay, but part of me doesn't believe him. How can someone lie there so still and be okay?

"I don't know. I felt danger, then felt like someone was biting me. When I realized I wasn't getting bitten, I figured someone close had to be in trouble. Then it hit me, it had to be Joe," I explain.

"Interesting." He shakes his head. "I'm going to go to the car and get the berries. I'll be right back."

John runs off, and I stand here over Joe. You are just going to leave me here? I want to ask him. What am I supposed to do in this situation? I kneel down next to Joe, and his eyes glance over to me. This is so weird; he looks dead, but his eyes are moving. This is one of the creepiest things I have experienced so far in these last few days. Can he hear me? I guess I can talk to him and find out.

"I don't know how I lost track of her. One minute she was in front of me, the next she was behind me. After she died, I feared I was too late," I whisper.

Maybe hunting isn't for me. I cannot handle seeing Joe like this. How is it fair that when I get bitten, the vampire dies, but when Joe and John get bitten, they become paralyzed? Joe sits up and gasps, and I jump. I feel instant relief when I hear him coughing. I know now he will be okay.

"Help me up," he requests, coughing.

I stand up and help him to his feet. He is a little wobbly, but I'm sure that is to be expected. I'm sure having blood sucked out of you will make you feel a little weak.

"By the way, Lizzy, that is what is supposed to happen after you get bitten," Joe explains. "So if I heard right, you could feel that I was being attacked?"

"Yes, but what happened?" I ask.

"Let's head to the car and I'll explain to you and John what happened at the same time," he replies.

Why doesn't he just tell me first? I will probably have many questions that he could answer on the way to car. I do have one question already. He looks normal. Shouldn't he be dying, since he hasn't eaten the berry yet?

He starts to walk toward the car, and I follow closely. I notice that with every step he takes, he is growing a little weaker.

"Joe, are you okay?" I ask.

He doesn't say anything; instead, he turns to face me. I shine my light on him, and he is sweating and is very pale. Now this is worrying me. "Are you going to die?" I whisper.

He shakes his head. "No, I'm not going to die. But being bitten does not feel pretty. Be thankful you do not have to go through this. I do have berries in my pocket, but if I eat them now, you and John would have to carry me back to the car. Personally, I don't want that to happen."

I give him a puzzled look. "Why would we have to carry you to the car?"

"When you eat the berry, you fall into a coma for six to eight hours," he explains.

He takes a few more steps and stops to lean against a tree. I feel like he is dying faster than he is letting on. He takes another step and falls to his knees. I cannot watch this anymore.

"Please eat the berry now. I cannot stand seeing you like this. I have no problem dragging you back," I insist.

"I'm fine," he groans. He grabs his stomach and bends over into a ball.

"No, you are not. Please, Joe, I cannot watch another person die. Not this week," I beg.

He sits back up straight. He has beads of sweat on his forehead and is starting to look gray. He needs help, and he needs it now. I try to tap into his emotions, but I feel nothing. Is this what death feels like?

He pulls a plastic baggie out of his pocket. I shine my light up to it, and it is full of the berries. He opens it and pulls one out. "Before I eat this, I need you to pass a message to John," he says. "That vampire was a newborn. He will know what that means."

He pops the berry in his mouth. While he chews it, I notice nothing different. Isn't it supposed to work right away? As he swallows it, he suddenly falls face-first onto the ground.

"Joe!" I shout.

I roll him over and stare at his chest. Thankfully, he is still breathing. So he wasn't lying when he said he would fall into a coma after he eats the berry. Okay, now I need to get him to the car. The only problem is, I don't know where the car is. Maybe if I pull him closer to the road, I will just drag him in the ditch until I find the car.

Grabbing both of his arms, I begin to drag him. He is a lot heavier than I thought he was. Then again, he is nothing but deadweight. Where is John? He is supposed to run to the car and come straight back. He should be back already.

After what feels like a lifetime, I finally make it to the car. I drop Joe and start to search his pockets for the keys. "Wait, how was John planning to get in the car without keys?" I ponder out loud.

To be honest, I don't even know why I said that out loud. It isn't like Joe is going to answer me anytime soon.

I find the keys and unlock the door. I look at Joe, and then at the car. How am I going to get him in? My muscles are so fatigued I don't think I can lift him in. My best luck of getting him in is to pull him into the back seat.

I open the one door and pull him up to it and sit him up. His head is dangling, but he is staying upright. I walk around to the other side and crawl through the back seat. Grabbing under his arms, I use every fiber of muscle in my body to lift him in. Once his butt is on the seat, I then lay his torso down on it. I get out and walk around the car again.

After this, I will surely not have to do a workout for a week! I swing his legs into the car and look at him. If he isn't sore after this, I will be surprised. I grab under his arms and lift his upper body up to make him sit upright. I put his seat belt on and call it good.

"Where the fuck are you, John?" I breathe out.

I get in the front seat and pull down the visor. I sigh when I see blood still running down my neck. There is a bloodstain on the collar of my shirt. This is a brand-new shirt too. Opening the glove department in hope to find some napkins, I am disappointed when there are none. I then slam it shut in frustration, then turn the light on to look at Joe. The blood on his neck is already dry. I pull off my shirt and use it to hold pressure to the bite. Good thing I decided to wear a cami today.

"Where is John?" I ask myself again.

Maybe he is hurt, or worse. I really should go look for him. I roll my eyes and make sure I have my gun, stake, and flashlight.

"First hunt and I'm the one who is watching over everyone," I mutter.

Throwing my shirt on the other side of Joe, I get out of the car and lock it. I don't need anyone finding Joe and doing anything with his body. Sticking the keys in my front pocket, I head back into the trees. Just as I walk into the complete darkness, a feeling of uneasiness comes over me.

"Okay, I'm not in the mood. I know you're here. Show yourself!" I shout.

If I'm lucky, the vampire will just walk out with their hands up to surrender. Highly doubtful, just wishful thinking. I look around and see nothing. Do we have to play hide-and-seek? I'm exhausted. I take a step forward, and someone fires a gun. The blast causes me to jump back. Thankfully, they were not shooting at me, but still, I wasn't expecting it. I put my hand on my chest and take a few slow, steady deep breaths to calm myself.

"Lizzy, what are you doing?" I hear.

I shine the flashlight to my left and see John walking toward me.

"What am I doing? Where in the hell have you been? I had to drag Joe back because he had a berry in his pocket. Now I am out looking for you. As soon as I walked out here, I could feel another vampire near," I explain.

"I'm sorry, I got lost trying to find you two again. I decided it would be best if I just went back to the car and waited. That was when I caught a vampire sneaking up on me. He is dead now," he states. "I'm sorry I wasn't there to help you. I'm surprised you were able to drag him by yourself."

He is lying, but I don't know what he is lying about and why. I decide I have had enough for one night and I'm not going to push it. He probably wouldn't tell me what he is lying about anyway.

"I didn't have a choice but to drag him back. I even got him loaded into the car by myself," I say bitterly.

I am not impressed with John right now. He doesn't say anything; instead, he walks past me. I shake my head and follow. When I get closer to him, I notice three tears in the back of his shirt. It almost looks like an animal ripped it.

"What happened to your shirt?" I pry.

"What happened to yours?" he counters.

"I needed to stop the bleeding from my neck somehow," I say, fuming.

I don't know why, but tonight he is pissing me off. First, he just leaves me with Joe, and then he doesn't come back like he said he would. What is he keeping from me?

"Calm down. I got my shirt caught on a tree. When I tried to get free, I ripped it," he explains.

Did he just tell me to calm down? Does he really think I have no reason to be upset right now? I also do not believe that was what happened to his shirt. How could a tree do that? Did it get caught on three branches? I am not going to ask, though, because I know he isn't going to tell me. The important thing is, we are all safe. I also do not want to make John mad, because I have lots of questions and want him to answer them.

"I'm sorry for being snappy. I'm just worried about Joe," I admit.

"Understandable. Let's get back to the car. Afterward, I can answer any of your questions." He smiles.

I nod, and we head up the ditch to the car. I look in the back seat, and Joe is still out cold. I would think he is dead if his chest wasn't moving. I'm just happy he is breathing normally. I get into the passenger side and hand John the keys when he gets in. He starts the car and takes off right away.

"John, Joe said she was a newborn. What does that mean?" I ask.

John answers, "So newborn vampires are different. It means they are still in their first three months. They are stronger and a lot quicker than older vampires. I'm sure you noticed her speed."

"Yeah, I did. One minute she was in front of me, the next minute she was behind me. It was all in the blink of an eye," I recall.

"That is one of their advantages. Speed is a great gift to a vampire. Especially during the changing period. After you get infected, you only have two hours to get blood or you die. During the first three months, the bloodlust is extremely high, and there is nothing that can stop them. Well, except for you, you're the only thing that can stop them. That new-born surely didn't know what happened to her when she bit you!" John chuckles. "They are the hardest vampires to hunt. We have been bitten by so many newborns it is ridiculous."

So newborns are stronger than older vampires. I guess that is one thing the movies and books got right. I look back at Joe and frown. I wish I had gotten there sooner.

"How have you guys survived before?" I inquire.

"We always hunt together. This is the first time we split up," he replies.

So they did split up because of me. Maybe next time all three of us should hunt together, or maybe I could go myself. Besides, it isn't like I could die from them biting me.

I look back at Joe again. I feel guilty. This is all my fault.

"So he will be out for eight hours?" I ask.

"Yes. Oh, I should warn you, when he wakes up, he will be a complete ass," John warns. "When people wake up from a bite, one emotion is always heightened. For me, I'm always happy, like, overly happy, to the point it is annoying. Joe, on the other hand, is mean. He will not be able to filter himself. So he might say some things but always feels so guilty after he snaps out of it."

That is good to know.

I realize I have learned more about this world in the last three days than I could have ever imagined. I'm sure I'm going to be learning things for a long time. Maybe I should start writing everything down.

I glance out of the window and we are already pulling up to the motel.

"Go open the door. I got him," John directs.

I get out of the car and run up to the door. John follows slowly with Joe over his left shoulder. He is carrying him like it is no big deal.

"It is 1:30 a.m. Why don't we try to get some sleep? Once he wakes up, no one will get any sleep," John suggests, throwing Joe onto the bed.

"How long will he be angry for?" I ask.

"Between two and four hours." John smiles.

I walk over to my bed and sit down. Staring at Joe, I start to slightly fear him. I wonder, when he wakes up, is he going to tell me exactly what he thinks of me? Will I be ready for this? Too much has gone on in the last week, and I feel this will just be another layer to the cake.

Chapter 9

Looking at the clock for the hundredth time, I realize it is still only five in the morning. I think I have checked the clock every five minutes. I'm so exhausted, but I'm too nervous to sleep. John, on the other hand, has no problem. He is in his bed, snoring away. Personally, I am afraid that if I fall asleep, something bad will happen to Joe. The other part of me is also anxious to see what happens when he wakes up. Am I going to find out that he actually hates me?

Grabbing my flashlight, I shine it in his face again. He looks like he is sleeping peacefully, and the color in his face is beginning to look normal again.

I lie on my back, and the light shines on the ceiling. Right above me is a little spider, but the way the light shines on it makes it look huge. I am terrified of spiders, so I jump out of bed quickly. I want to wake John up to kill it, but I know I cannot do that. I can hear it now: "You want to hunt, but you cannot handle a spider."

"Okay, Lizzy, you just need to relax," I whisper. "Go shower. You know showers always make you feel better."

Grabbing my bag, I walk into the bathroom. I glance at Joe one more time before closing the door all the way. To find my bodywash and shampoo, I place my bag on the sink and search through it. When I find the bottles, I place them on the edge of the tub and start the water. While I wait for it to warm up, I strip out of my pajamas and study myself in the mirror. The only thing I notice are the two sets of bite marks on my neck. Of course I would have a set, one on each side. Luckily, Ethan's marks are already starting to fade.

I turn back to the shower and step under the hot water. It is too hot and makes me jump back into the corner. Turning it cooler, I place my hand underneath the water. Of course it is ice-cold now. Ugh, is there going to be a happy medium? Finally, after fidgeting with it, I find a comfortable setting.

Stepping back into the water, I let the perfect warmth run down my body. I put my head under the water and start to think about everything. Is this life going to be for me? I knew hunting would be difficult; I just didn't realize how much energy it would take, physically and mentally. Seeing Joe get bitten tonight is one of the top ten scariest things I have witnessed. I know I can do it; I just don't know if I can mentally handle it.

Stepping away from the water, I grab my bodywash and squirt a bunch into my washcloth and get a good lather. As I wipe around my neck, I wince a little. The old bite spot is still a little tender. This gets me thinking, What if a vampire gets my necklace off and bites me? I will be dead. Am I ready for that possibility? What if once Joe wakes up, he will not allow me to go hunting again? All because I freaked out at him. I don't think I could handle watching him die.

I decide the shower is not going to relax me after all. I quickly rinse off and get out. Wrapping the towel around me, I wipe the steam away from the mirror. My reflection reminds me of a terrified little girl who got caught in a rain-storm. I dig through my bag to find my booty shorts and cami. I put them on as I walk out of the bathroom to find John still sound asleep.

I set my bag on my bed and decide to go outside for some fresh air. Grabbing the motel key from the table, I walk out. The morning breeze against my wet hair gives me a little chill, but it isn't cold out. The sun is starting to rise, and it is beautiful. The sky is full of different oranges and some purples. I sit down against the rail and wrap my arms around my knees.

"God, I know it has been a while. I just need strength. Please help me," I whisper.

I put my face in the crease between my legs. If anyone sees me right now, they probably would think I need help. Admittedly, I do, but there is nothing anyone could do to help me.

"What the fuck are you doing out here? Get your ass in here!" someone shouts.

I glance up, and Joe is in the doorway. I am so happy to see him awake, but I kind of fear him at the same time. I have never seen him look so upset before. John was not lying when he said he will be angry when he wakes up. I stand up and hurry back into the room. Last thing I need is to make him angrier.

"What makes you think you can just stand outside dressed like that? You are barely wearing anything!" he yells.

He sounds just like a parent; my mom would have never let me go out of the house dressed like this.

"I'm sorry, I didn't think about it. I just needed a place to think," I answer.

"That is just it, you didn't think about it. To make matters worse, John didn't even know you were outside. What if something happened to you?" he expresses.

His hands are flying everywhere. I never realized how much he talks with his hands. I almost could not concentrate on what he is saying, because they are so distracting.

"I'm sorry." I bow my head.

I am feeling super guilty. I know I am not supposed to take this personally, but it really is hard not to.

"God, how am I going to handle all this? I don't know how to raise a girl. You are fine now, but I'm sure you will change later. Will you become a spoiled bitch? I sometimes wish I didn't go and see why Ethan kept calling. Then I wouldn't have to deal with this stress," he admits.

My heart shatters. I know it is an adjustment, but hearing him wish he never came really hurt. Fine, if he wants nothing to do with me, I'll manage on my own. I walk over to my bed and zip my bag up.

"You want me gone? Fine. I'm sixteen, I'll manage on my own. You don't need to take responsibility of me any longer," I scold, putting my bag over my shoulder.

"You will not leave!" he yells, stepping in front of me. "I'm stuck with you."

"Not anymore," I whisper.

I push him out of the way and walk out the door. I do not know where I am going, but I have to get away from him. I know what I have to do for right now, though. I walk across the parking lot to the lobby. An elderly gentleman smiles at me as I stroll up to the desk.

"Do you have a room?" I ask.

"How old are you?" he counters.

"Eighteen," I lie.

"Do you have your license?" he asks, frowning.

Okay, I know he doesn't believe me. I need to step up my game.

"Will you please help me? I am far away from my family and lived with an abusive boyfriend. Last night he tried to kill me and I finally got out. I forgot my wallet, but I do have cash. Please, I just need a place to shower and crash for a couple of hours. Please help me!" I cry.

Tears roll down my cheeks. With everything that is going on, I didn't have to fake-cry.

"Fine," he sighs. "I get off at three. If you want, I can drive you somewhere," he offers.

"Thanks. I might have to take you up on that offer. How much do I owe you?" I ask, wiping my eyes.

"I'll worry about paying. We will wait until three to figure that out." He smiles and hands me the key. "Your room is 199, just two rooms away from the office."

"Thank you." I smile.

I am a little grossed out about what the payment might have to be. Except maybe I can get out of here before that.

I walk down to my room and unlock the door. When entering, I look behind me before closing the door. I want to make sure no one is watching me. After I lock the door with every lock it has, I go straight to the bed. I lie down face-first and start to sob in my pillow. Just when I think my life couldn't get any worse, it does. Now I need to figure out how I am going to make it on my own. I lie here and cry myself to sleep.

The sound of someone pounding on the door makes me jump. I glance at the clock, and it is already ten. Wow, I feel like I just fell asleep! The pounding starts again, and I slowly crawl out of bed. I look through the peephole, and Joe is standing on the other side. Oh great, I get to listen to him again. Didn't he say enough earlier?

I unlock and open the door.

"Hi," I say, turning around. I do not want to look at him right now.

"Lizzy, we need to talk," he states, walking in behind me.

I sit back down on my bed and glance up at him. He doesn't look angry this time, but I don't know if I'm ready to hear what he has to say. Except I'm sure he isn't going to give me a choice.

"Lizzy, you should have been warned better on what happens after a bite. John said he told you I would be angry, but he didn't give you a good-enough warning. Everything I said has been something I have thought of. Yes, at one point, I did wish I never went to see why Ethan kept calling Dad. Except, I promise you now, I do not hate having you around. To be honest, it's nice to have a danger sensor with us. If you were not with us, I would have died last night. I am grateful you came into our lives. Except it has only been three days, so we are still making adjustments," Joe explains. "Now I want to ask you something, and I want you to be completely honest. Do you ever wish your life would go back to normal? Go back to when you never knew us?"

"I have, but there is one difference. I have always known about you two. I was the secret sibling, not you guys. And I've always wanted to meet you guys," I answer. "So though I want to go back to when my mom and our dad were still alive, I would never take back meeting you and John."

Joe comes and sits by me, and I look away. I don't want him to see how hurt I am. "I would never take back not knowing you," he whispers. "Lizzy, I am sorry."

I roll my eyes and cross my arms. What am I going to do? It isn't like I can live on my own. I have no money, and I have no place to go.

I inhale and exhale sharply before I turn to face him.

"Hi, Joe, my name is Elizabeth, but everyone calls me Lizzy. I know we haven't met before, but I have some weird news for you. Your dad is also my dad. Does Dad have any family? My mom died a week ago, and I don't have anywhere to go. I could raise myself, but I don't know if I'm ready for that responsibility yet. I just recently learned vampires are real, and I don't know anything about that world. I'm afraid I might run into the wrong person. Could you help?" I ask.

"Wow, this is surprising. I cannot believe Dad kept this a secret from us. Unfortunately, my brother and I are the only family left. But you are welcome to stay with us. We have more than enough money to help you out. What do you say? Should we start over?" he asks.

"I'm willing to try, if you are," I answer.

"I am. I think we should go back to the room and plan the next hunt." He stands up.

I grab my bag and stand up. This makes me nervous, but I'm willing to give it another try. "I need to check out. Care to pay for it?" I smile.

I feel guilty asking, but he chuckles and nods. "Come on." He wraps his arm around my shoulder and leads me out the door.

Chapter 10

It has been a month since everything happened, and not surprisingly, all three of us have been getting along well. Ever since Joe was attacked, we decided that if we have an issue with something, we are just going to let one another know right away instead of keeping it bottled inside. There have only been a couple of times when I did something they didn't like, or vice versa. Our system seems to be working, and none of us is sick of one another yet.

The major fight we had was that I want to go hunting alone when we split up. I felt super guilty that I was the reason Joe was attacked and almost died. Although he keeps trying to tell me it wasn't my fault, that it was his for going alone. Emotions got high every time I brought up the idea. I made good points on why I should be the one who hunts alone: I can sense when I'm near danger, and I cannot die if one of them bites me. But the next three weekends, Joe always went with me and John always went alone. Of course, I was afraid for John's well-being. I don't know why they thought if Joe went with me, it would make me feel better.

Finally, today they are letting me go on my own. I don't know if it is because they trust me or if they just got tired of me asking. Either way, I'm happy they've decided to let me. It gives me peace of mind that they will have each other's backs. In the last month, I have killed a handful of vampires and haven't been bitten since that newborn. Maybe Joe just wanted to make sure I could actually hunt and not let them bite me. Although that would be the easiest way to kill them. I have so many bruises I don't know how I'm going to explain them when I go to school. I know people are going to think I'm abused at home.

Although it is dark, the moon and stars are bright enough to light up my path. I do not need my flashlight at all. I stop for a moment to admire the sky. The moon isn't full, but it is close, with only a corner missing. There are a lot of stars twinkling in the night sky. I wish I had a minute to lie down and admire them more.

A chill strikes me, and I raise my gun. I glance around and see nothing. I take a couple of steps forward, and a twig snaps behind me. I spin around and there he is. Before I could pull the trigger, he kicks me in the stomach. I bend over but smile up at him.

"So you want to play?" I say.

I stand back up straight, and we start to fight. He tries to punch me, but I'm able to dodge. Instead of trying to punch back, I go low and spin-kick him in the ankles. He falls, and I do not waste any time getting on top of him to pin him to the ground. Grabbing the stake out of my sock, I raise it in the air. He reaches up to grab my neck, but I move, and in the process he grabs my necklace. He yanks, and it comes off. Quickly I stab him in the heart, before he could get a whiff of my blood. I smile when he turns to dust underneath me. I grab my necklace and put it on before I stand back up.

Today is one of the days I'm happy it is a magnetic clip. If not, I would be in a lot of trouble, since the necklace chain would have broken.

I need to get back on my path to meet up with John and Joe. I turn around, but I freeze in place. Another vampire is creeping up on me, except I know this one. Standing in front of me is John. My eyes widen while I watch John slowly turn into the thing we are hunting.

"John," I say, shuddering.

"Lizzy, you need to run, now!" he growls.

"John?" I say again.

"Elizabeth, I cannot resist much longer. Run!" he hisses.

But I can't get my feet to move. The longer I stand here, the more his face changes. His fangs are now starting to show, and he is looking a lot older. I take a few steps back before I turn around and run. I need to find a safe place. I do not want to die in the hands of my brother. Except I do not want to kill him either. It would have been nice to be included in this family secret. Wait, what if Joe doesn't know and John has kept this from everyone? This would explain why the first time I was around him, I had an uneasy feeling. I should have put it together.

I turn my head to see if he is still following me, and to my fear, he is right on my heels. I fear one of us is going to die tonight. I turn back to face forward just in time for a tree to meet my face. As I fall to the ground, pain strikes me. I grab my face and could feel my nose gushing blood. Great, I just broke my nose. I try to stand up, but I fall down from the dizziness that hits me.

I look at John, who is trying to sneak up on me.

"Johnny, please, I'm your sister!" I plead.

He jumps on top of me and pins me the ground. I try to fight, but I feel too weak. Apparently, the tree did more damage to me than I thought. He bends down and sniffs me, and waves of fear come over me.

"Lizzy, I'm trying to fight my instincts, but you smell so good. I cannot stop thinking of the scent you give off. It is like a drug I have to have. I cannot explain it!" he hisses.

I want to cry. If my own brother cannot fight his vampire instincts when the necklace is off, that means I'm screwed if it ever comes off again. If I survive this, I need to find out what I am, and quick.

"Joe!" I scream, hoping he is near.

John bends down and licks my face, and I grimace. This is the most disgusting thing that could happen to me.

"Joe! Anyone!" I shout again, except this time John covers my mouth.

I scream, as the pressure of his hand is hurting my nose. He gets closer to my ear and growls, "Quiet, little girl. It will only hurt for a second."

He is no longer John. His vampire has taken full control. He takes his hand off my face, and my blood covers it. He licks his hand, and I start shaking in fear. I never thought I would die at the hands of my brother.

"Oh, you are the best thing I've ever tasted!" he says as he licks his hand clean.

He takes my necklace off and sniffs my neck. I close my eyes, hoping this does not last much longer. I also wish Joe were somewhere near and could help me. John licks my neck this time. His tongue is rough and dry. I am terrified, and the tears are now streaming down my face. I know I should try to fight or even kill him, but I can't. I would feel guilty for killing him, and Joe might hate me. He is close with John; if anything happens to him and it is my doing, I would never hear the end of it.

I do hope once he bites me it is quick and painless. I close my eyes, waiting for the piercing pain. Instead, a gun goes off, and I scream. I open my eyes, and John is on the ground next to me. Is he dead? I sit up quickly, grab my necklace, and back away from him. I put my necklace back on, hoping no one else smells me.

"Oh fuck, Lizzy, what happened?" Joe asks, taking his shirt off and handing it to me.

"Joe, John is a vampire, and he was going to eat me! He licked the blood off my face. I should have attacked him, but I just couldn't do it. I'm sorry," I babble.

I start to bawl, and I hate it. I'm so overwhelmed right now. Luckily, I didn't have to pee, or I probably would have peed myself.

Joe kneels next to me and grabs my chin to check out my face. "We need to get you looked at. I'll take you to the hospital and hope you are far enough away from him when he wakes up."

I give him a confused look. "You mean he isn't dead?"

Joe stands up and places his hand out in front of him. I grab it, and he pulls me to my feet.

"No,. I tranquilized him. We were by the car, waiting for you, when suddenly he hissed and took off in a dead sprint. I grabbed the tranquilizer and followed him. When I finally caught up to him, I did not see you at first. All I saw was John attacking someone, so I shot. He should be awake in a couple of hours. That should give me enough time to drop you off at the hospital and then lock him up in the basement," he explains.

I wipe my eyes and glance down at John. Fear strikes me. I back away and bump into Joe. Wait, what if Joe is a vampire too? What if I have been living with vampires all this time? What if they actually know what I am and are plotting my death?

I back away from Joe and ask, "Are you a vampire too?"

He rolls his eyes. "The first time you met John, did you feel uneasy around him?"

"Yes," I answer honestly.

"The first time you met me, did I make you feel uneasy?" he asks.

"No, I felt comfortable." I nod.

Okay, he is right. I would know if he was one. I just wasn't listening to my gut when it came to John.

"Okay, then, let's get to your car, and I'll explain everything on the way to the hospital," he says.

"Okay." I nod.

I wipe my eyes, and Joe starts to walk. I follow close since I'm afraid someone else may have caught my scent. I am not in the mood to fight again. My face is killing me! We walk past a few trees, and the car comes into sight. I feel like running to it because I want to leave now. I get in, pull down the visor, and see bruising around my eyes. *Thank you, John.*

"So what happened? Why did John try to bite you?" Joe asks, pulling onto the road. "He has been clean for three years."

Clean for three years? So he did once attack people?

"I was fighting a vampire and had him pinned down. Before I could kill him, he pulled off my necklace. I put the necklace back on as soon as I killed him. It just wasn't fast enough, apparently. I turned around and there was John. He was fighting his vampire and told me to run. I did, but while running, I made the mistake of turning around to see where he was, and my face met a tree. I didn't know what I should do. I knew I had to fight, but it was like I forgot how. He is my brother, and I didn't want to kill him. I knew he wasn't trying to kill me, but at the same time, he was." I pause, thinking. "Now I have a question for you: What happened to no more secrets? Did that one just slip your mind?"

I'm angry they kept this from me. I understand I've only been here for a month, but still, you'd think this would be something to pass on to someone that lives with you.

"We were going to tell you. We just wanted you to get settled here first. We didn't want you to see him as a threat," he answers.

"Little late for that." I roll my eyes. "How long has he been one?"

"Five years. He ran away from us when he turned seventeen. We found him while hunting two years later. Although Dad is all for 'kill first and ask questions later,' he didn't have the heart to kill his own son. So he tranquilized him and locked him up in the cellar. It was weird seeing him like that. We detoxed him, and it took him about a year to be satisfied with just animal blood. I just don't know what came over him tonight," Joe shares.

"My necklace came off. Dad did say if it did, any vampire near will be attracted to me. Unfortunately, John was one of them. I'm going to be honest, I've never been so afraid before. Especially when he licked my face and told me I was the best thing he has ever tasted. He said he was trying to fight it but the vampire was stronger. I just wish I knew why I was special to this world," I admit.

"So do I," he whispers.

We pull into the ER parking lot, and he parks. When we walk in, there is one other person in the waiting room. We go to the check in, and a lady smiles at us.

"My sister needs to be seen. I believe her nose is broken," Joe states.

"What is your name and date of birth, honey?" the nurse asks.

"Elizabeth McCann. February 2, 2000," I answer.

"We will need a parent's signature to treat her. Can we have you call them?" she asks.

"Do you have a Ouija board?" I ask.

"Elizabeth!" Joe snaps.

I shrug and smile. I am just trying to lighten the mood.

"Her parents have both passed on. I'm her legal guardian," Joe finishes.

"Okay, have you been here before?" the nurse inquires.

"No," both Joe and I answer.

"Okay, once we get her back, we will have someone come and ask you both a bunch of questions. Please have a seat and we will get her back as soon as we can," she explains.

"I have to leave for a few minutes to get something. I am hoping to get back before she gets called back. Is that okay?" Joe asks.

"If you are not back before, do you give us permission for testing and other things we may have to do?" the nurse asks.

"Yes." Joe smiles.

"Can you sign this?" she says, placing a sheet on the table.

Joe signs his name and runs out the door after.

I smile at the nurse. "Can I get an ice pack while I wait?"

"Yeah. I'll bring one out for you," she states and leaves her spot.

I go take a chair. As soon as I am sitting, she brings me the ice pack. I thank her and watch her go back to her seat. I decide, since I have a while to wait, I should see what is going on in the cyberworld.

While I log in, it dawns on me that I haven't been on since I have moved out here. The page pops up, and I start to scroll through the timeline. I start to feel homesick seeing all my old classmates posting things about their summer. Then it hits me: none of my friends have even messaged me to see how I am doing. I do see I have a couple of messages in my inbox and decide to read them.

Lizzy,

OMG! It has been, like, forever and a half since I have talked to you! Is everything okay? Why is your phone always off? Did those brothers kidnap you? Like, seriously, message one of us back.

—Sarah

What do they mean I haven't been answering any of their phone calls or texts? I haven't been receiving—oh, crap, I had to change my number.

Sarah!

OMG, I'm so, so, so, so, so, so sorry. I have been so busy adjusting to this new life I lost track of time. I haven't even checked my messages in forever. I had to get a new phone and number and lost all my contacts. But so much has gone on in my life. Please forgive me. I love you all. Please give everyone my new number. My brothers have been great. They are making me feel like I'm part of the family. It is really just a big adjustment for all of us. Right now, I'm in the ER, so I decided to check this while I'm waiting to be seen.

With love,
Lizzy

I decide I should at least update my status so no one thinks I'm dead. After a lot of consideration, I take a picture of my face, post it with this caption:

> *Hey, everyone! Sorry I haven't gotten ahold of any of you lately. I have been super busy getting adjusted to everything that I forgot to let you all know my number has changed. If it weren't for the fact that I ended up going to the ER, I wouldn't be on here tonight. I hope everyone is doing well. My brothers and I are getting along well. Just to let you know, never run into a tree roller blading. Tree, 1; Lizzy, 0.*

I hit Post, and a feeling of uneasiness comes over me. Is it because I posted that online? I sure hope so, because I know I have no weapon to fight with otherwise.

My phone chimes with a message from Joe:

> *We have a problem. I don't know where John is. He isn't where we left him. That should have knocked him out for hours, not half an hour.*

"Hey, Lizzy," I hear John say as he sits next to me.

> *Found him.*

I send the message while my heart starts to speed up. I can feel my breathing become shallower. I look up and put on a fake smile on my face.

"Hi, John," I whisper.

"Lizzy, I'm sorry for what happened. I tried to control myself, but I couldn't. Even after you put your necklace back on, all I could think about was your blood. Although the vampire in me wanted to bite you, the brother was fighting all that I could," he states. "Joe and I should have told you right up front that I am a vampire, but I haven't hunted people in a long time, so we decided against it. I was telling the truth when you asked me a month ago if I have killed anyone. I knew you would take it as a joke, but in reality, I wasn't joking. Right now your blood smells like everyone else's, so I'm fine. I will admit, your blood was the best blood I have ever tasted. So I'm happy Joe got me when he did. When I woke up, I drained two deer and a raccoon, and now I'm feeling better."

My stomach turns, and I want to throw up. It is really disgusting to hear John talk about my blood that way. He is acting so nonchalant about everything it makes me feel really nervous around him. Wait, how did he not die when he licked my face? My necklace was on. Maybe because he didn't bite me? I'm sure he doesn't know the answer either, so there is no point in asking.

"John, you almost killed me," I whisper.

"I know, and I regret it," he replies, looking away.

I don't know what to do. I could tell him to leave me alone, but then it would make living with him very awkward. I was finally starting to feel halfway normal again. *Thanks, John, for ruining that.* Maybe if I mask my fear, one day I would not be afraid.

"It's okay, Johnny. It might have scared me a bit, but I will forgive you. You are my brother, after all." I force a smile.

He gives me a weak smile. "Can I see your nose?"

My eyes widen, and my fake smile disappears. Why does he want to look at my nose? Does he want to lick it again? That would look so weird in the ER waiting room. If I refuse, he will know I don't trust him. Carefully, I pull the ice away from my face, and he frowns.

"Fuck, I'm sorry. If it weren't for the fact you were running away from me, this would have never happened," he whispers.

"Well, the story is I was skating and lost control and ran into a tree. So that is what happened. I don't know why I would have been running away from you," I reply.

He nods and gets up and walks to the desk. I pull out my phone to see if Joe has texted back.

I'm on my way. Be careful.

"My sister needs to be seen, now! Did you see her face? She is in a horrific amount of pain, and all you guys are doing is sitting on your phones. Help her *now!*" he demands.

I didn't realize how much pain I was actually in until now. With everything going on, it was the last thing on my mind. I get up and walk up to him.

"I'm fine. I'm sorry," I say, grabbing his arm.

We sit back down, and he glances at me.

"If I did this to you, at least I can try to get you called back quicker," he states.

"Making a scene might get us kicked out," I scold him.

I glance out the window, and a feeling of relief comes over me when I see Joe walking in. Although I know I am not in any trouble right now, I still do not feel safe. Joe walks up to us and scowls at John.

"John, you shouldn't be here," Joe mutters. "Go home."

"I needed to make sure she is okay," John states.

"After what happened in the forest, do you think she is okay? She might say she is, but I know you know she isn't.

Just give her time to breathe and she will come around. You scared her. Hell, you scared me!" Joe scolds him. "It has been years since I have last seen you like that. Did you know she was just going to let you kill her? She knew she should have done something, but she couldn't bear the thought of killing her own brother. Even if he is a vampire. So please go home. Once she gets checked out, we will come home, and we will talk, where there is more privacy. I don't think this is a conversation to have a public."

Yes, thank you, Joe.

"I think this should be up to Lizzy. If she wants me to leave, then I will." John is fighting back.

Crap, I don't want to be the one that tells him to leave. I cross my arms and shift in my chair uncomfortably. I don't know what to say. I want him to leave, but I don't want to hurt his feelings too.

"No, I'm putting my foot down on this one. You are going to leave right now. Think about it, John. She was going to let you kill her. Do you think she is going to have the decency to tell you to leave? She is scared and hurt. So I'm going to be the guardian and tell you, please go home," Joe says firmly.

Toward the end, I could hear the hurt in his voice. Joe didn't want to have to tell John to leave. They are best friends, and I am getting between them.

"Okay, fine, I'll see you at home." John sighs.

As John walks away, I say, "I'm sorry."

"For what?" Joe asks.

"Elizabeth!" a nurse yells.

Saved by the nurse! I don't feel like explaining what I'm sorry for. He doesn't need to know I blame myself for John attacking me. Walking up to the nurse, I give her a glance over. Her skin is dark, shiny, and it looks really soft. Her eyes are dark brown, and her hair is black with red highlights. She is a very attractive lady. I adore her outfit, too, as her top has Piglet all over it.

We step in a room, and she smiles at me. "We need to get your weight. Go ahead and step on the scale."

I step up, and the number 110 pops up. That doesn't surprise me; I've been 110 for a while now. She writes it down and leads me to a different room. She hands me a gown and walks over to the computer.

"I need you to strip your top half. Bra and shirt off, but you can keep your bottoms on," she states.

I look over at Joe, and he turns around. I strip my top off quickly, but I feel uncomfortable doing it. I don't know if it is because there is a stranger in the room or because my brother is here. I guess it could be worse. I put my clothes on the chair and sit on the bed. The nurse turns, and I glance over at her.

"My name is Tasha. I will be your nurse tonight. So, Elizabeth, what happened?" she asks.

I better keep my story straight. "I was out roller blading earlier tonight, and I ran into a tree."

"This late?" she pushes.

I look up at the clock and realize it is 11:30 p.m.!

"It happened around nine. The problem was, my brothers didn't get home until ten, so I waited. I didn't want to bother them at work," I lie.

She starts to type something. What is she typing? I hope it is just what I'm telling her. Although I can feel she has some doubts about my story.

"Why didn't you just come here yourself?" she quizzes.

I know she has to ask these questions, but I feel like I'm being interrogated.

"Honestly, I thought I just bruised my face. I still think it might just be bruised, but Joe is making me come in to make sure it isn't broken. I'm not fan of the doctors, so I was avoiding," I answer.

She nods and types out some more things.

"Do you ever feel the urge to self-harm?" she asks.

"No." I shake my head. I mean, I have thought about dying, but I never thought of hurting myself.

"Feel safe at home?"

"Very," I lie.

Okay, that might be a lie, but I couldn't tell her the truth. I mean, I did feel safe until today, and I know she isn't going to believe me when I say my vampire brother wants to drink my blood.

"When was the first day of your last period?"

"Um, July 3." At least I think it was.

"Any chances you might be pregnant?"

"No. I'm still a virgin," I reply. I am so tired of all these questions. I just wish they would get the doctor and send me home already.

"Allergies? And are you on any medications?" she asks.

"I'm allergic to penicillin and hawthorn berries. I'm not on any medications," I answer, looking at Joe. I wonder if she has any idea what hawthorn berries are. I mean, I never knew what they were until a month ago.

"Last question. Your brother is your legal guardian?" she asks.

I sigh. "Joe is my legal guardian. Unfortunately, my parents died a month ago."

Will it get easier to tell people?

"I'm sorry." She gives me a look of pity.

I shrug and don't say anything. I hate the look of pity that people give me. I could probably cope better if they would stop looking at me like that. She wraps the blood pressure cuff around my arm and places a clip on my finger. The inside lights up red. I've never seen this thing before.

"What is this?" I ask, moving my finger up and down.

The blood pressure cuff gets tighter, and I close my eyes. Damn, I hate these things; they always get way too tight. I'm just happy I do not bruise easily. It beeps, and I look up at the numbers. I don't know why I do it; I don't know what any of the numbers mean.

"That looks good," she states. Tasha types the numbers into the computer. I feel like she has been in here forever. When is the doctor going to see me? I just want to be checked out already.

"I have to draw some blood and have you pee in this cup. After that, the doctor will be in to see you." She is finally saying the words I've been wanting to hear.

She ties the tight band around my arm. She uses her index finger to feel around and smiles when she thinks she finds a good vein. She cleans the area with an alcohol swab, pulls the skin down, and pokes the vein. Blood flows into the tube. When she finishes, she tapes a cotton ball to my skin.

"Bathroom is around the corner. Fill the cup about halfway and put it in the little door that is in there," she directs and walks out.

"I personally thought she was never going to get the doctor." I chuckle.

"Just go get it done," Joe states.

I take the cup and head into the bathroom. Sitting down on the toilet, I finally have a little alone time to think. Just when I thought my life was coming together, things get screwed up. Is my life ever going to be normal?

Chapter 11

Four hours later, they finally release me. We waited four hours to find out my nose is severely bruised but not broken. Although the doctor did three x-rays because he could not believe there was no break. The only directions I have are to alternate ibuprofen and Tylenol to help with the pain and use ice for the swelling. They offered something more for pain, but I refused. If there is no break, I will be fine.

It is a very quiet ride home. We pull into the driveway at four in the morning. Exhausted and sore, I'm just ready to pass out in my own bed. It's a good thing we were hunting only thirty miles from home. I get out of the car and walk up to the door. Joe unlocks it, and I follow him in. I turn around to close and lock up, and when I turn back around, I jump backward into the door. John appears right behind me. I'm not quite sure if I jumped because he startled me or because I am afraid of him.

"Is it broken?" he asks.

"No," Joe answers for me.

"Lizzy, I'm so sorry. I tried to control it, I really did," he rushes out.

I don't know what to say right now; I just want to tell him to back up and let me into the house.

"John, it has been a long night. Let's rest, and tomorrow we can sit down and tell Lizzy everything," Joe offers.

"Can we just do it now?" I complain. "I'm exhausted, but I do not think I'm going to sleep until everything is out in the open."

Joe shifts his weight. I know he doesn't want to do this now, but I need to know. John needs to explain his secret life before I can start feeling comfortable again.

"Fine," Joe finally agrees. "Let's go sit down in the living room. John can explain everything, and we can answer any questions you have."

I follow the boys into the living room. They sit down on the chairs while I take a seat on the couch. They both face me, and I feel like I'm in trouble. I glance over at John, and fear and guilt come over me. I look away. Not because of the fear, but because I'm trying to ignore his guilt.

"Lizzy, I don't know where to start," John admits.

I glance back up at him, and he looks scared. "Why not from the beginning?" I suggest.

"At seventeen, I was tired of Dad and Joe telling me what to do, and I thought I was responsible enough to be out on my own. The first year was good. I was living a somewhat-normal life but was still hunting on the side. Then on my eighteenth birthday, some of my new friends threw me this huge party. Like any other stupid, drunk eighteen-year-old, I found this beautiful woman at the party. I thought it would be a one-night stand, that I would never see her again.

"After having the best sex I have ever had, I fell asleep. When I woke up an hour later, I was starving. Except I wasn't hungry for food. I was craving something I never craved before…human blood. I got up and looked in the mirror, and I didn't recognize myself. I did not remember being bitten during sex. I knew right there I fucked up. My goal was to stay in that room and let myself die. Five minutes later, that girl came back and brought a human with her.

"She knocked him out, so he had no idea what was going on. I tried to refuse to eat him, even though he smelled so good. I could hear every beat of his heart, and the blood gushing through his veins. I grew hungrier with each beat. She took a knife and slit his wrist. I tried to resist, and I counted thirty blood drops before I lost control. I sucked him dry and became the thing I had hunted," he explains.

I don't know what to say. "Those pretty ladies will always get you."

"Cindy, that was her name. She took me under her wing, and we became an item, hunting together. Shortly after I turned nineteen, we were out hunting and I heard a shot. I knew right away that it came from the direction where Cindy was. I ran to make sure she was okay. Except I ran right into the hunter—I mean *literally* ran into him—and we fell to the ground. When I sat up, he had his gun pointing at me. But it was Dad.

"Once he realized it was me, he couldn't pull the trigger. He asked me if we could talk, and I agreed. We walked to the car, and he went to put his gun away. I was shocked by how relaxed he was during the whole situation. What I didn't see was him grabbing the tranquillizer to shoot me. The next thing I remember is waking up in the basement. He told me he would keep me alive if I could learn to live off animal blood.

"It took me six months to even tolerate the taste, and another six months for me to stop craving human blood. After that, I never tried to eat a human again. I decided I was going to hunt my own kind and be part of this family again," John says.

Then he adds, "I deeply regret trying to eat you tonight. I promise you, Lizzy, I'm not craving your blood anymore."

I still don't know what to say. I want to believe him, but it is hard. I wish they had been honest with me from the beginning, and maybe then we wouldn't be in this situation. I would not be so terrified of him.

"I just wish we could figure out why my blood smells so good to vampires," I whisper.

"Yeah, so do I," Joe utters.

"Do you have any questions, Lizzy?" John asks.

"How do you just not crave human blood?" I question.

"If I get too hungry, I will crave it. I just have a lot of willpower to not give in. I never wanted to become a vampire, so I just try to live my life normally. I try to go hunting for an animal every day, most often in the morning. Last thing I want is to be caught by another hunter. Other than tonight, I've never given you any reason to not trust me. If I weren't safe to be around, do you think Joe would let you be around me?" John points out.

I'm sure, after a couple of days, I will start trusting him again.

"John, I want to believe you, but you really scared me today. It might take me a few days to feel comfortable again, but I will get there. I promise I will not avoid you," I admit.

"That's understandable." He frowns.

"I have one more question. If you are a vampire, why do you eat the food I cook?" I ask. "It isn't like you need it."

He smiles. "Honestly, it was just so you didn't get suspicious. Now that you know, I don't know if I will eat it anymore. It is hard on my stomach since I don't really digest food."

I will make sure I don't make as much food next time.

I yawn, and exhaustion takes over my body. I don't know if I will sleep tonight, although I can hardly keep my eyes open now. I need to lie down.

"Well, I don't know about you guys, but I'm ready for bed. I'll see you both in the morning." I stand up.

"Good night," they say in unison.

"Good night," I state, walking away.

I head up the stairs to my bedroom. Closing the door behind me, I lean against it. I take a minute to finally breathe. I spot my pajamas on the bed, and I walk over to them. Then I walk into the bathroom to get ready. I stop at my mirror to look at myself. I look horrible with the bruising under my eyes. What are people going to say when they see me?

I go into the bathroom and sit on the toilet. I am so tired I don't know if I even have the motivation to change into my pj's. I decide I'm not going to and throw them into the corner of my bathroom. I finish up and head to bed. When I lie down, I get a second wind. I'm wide awake again. I hate when this happens. Grabbing my phone, I decide to see if I can figure out what I am.

The first thing I search is just my name. Nothing interesting pops up except for sites with information I would have to pay for. I try to search people who are special to the vampire world, and that just gives me information on supernatural beings. I am getting nowhere with this. I will try one more thing, and if I don't find anything, I'll give up for tonight. Typing into the search box "Vampires that die from biting humans," I feel hopeful and hit the Enter key. It's taking a little longer to load, so maybe I've figured it out. My hopes come crashing down, however, when the words "search not found" pop up on my screen.

It isn't meant for me to know, I decide. I plug my phone in, put it on my bedside table, and roll over. "Lord, if you can hear me, please give me a sign. Tell me, what am I?"

Chapter 12

Another month has passed, and we are getting by. I have trust in John again, and it has put both guys at ease. The only thing that has changed is, when we go out hunting, I carry a small tranquilizer with me, just in case it happens again.

We still do not know what I am, and I've been doing research every day. I cannot find anything vampire related that makes sense. Everything seems fictional. It is making me so frustrated that I can't figure out what I am or why my blood kills vampires. It should not be this hard to figure out.

Tonight we are in a town somewhere in Nevada. Joe dropped me off a couple of miles out of town, and I'm walking the ditch back. I have to make sure I stay a decent distance from the cornfield since that was where the police found the dead bodies and animals. The last thing we need is for my DNA to be at any of the crime scenes.

I am about a mile into my walk when a feeling of uneasiness comes over me. I pull out my gun, to prepare myself. Taking another step forward, I hear a twig snap behind me. I turn around and find my flashlight is shining on an older couple.

"Sweetie, why are you out so late?" the older lady asks. "Haven't you heard there have been murders in this area?"

These are the first older vampires I have met. They look like a typical pair of grandparents. The woman's hair is white, while the man's is silver. If I had to guess, they have to be in their late fifties, early sixties. I wonder if this is an act, their pretending to be concerned grandparents before they attack. There is no way I'm going to let my guard down.

"I've heard. I just don't scare easily. I love walking around late at night. It clears my mind," I state, not lowering my gun.

"Please don't shoot. We will not hurt you," she begs.

Who am I to believe her? She is a vampire. I should shoot now, but something is telling me to wait a second. She steps forward and stops. Her mouth drops, and she stares at me. Why is she looking at me like that? I wonder. Did she just realize how beautiful I am?

"Lizzy?" she asks. "Are you Elizabeth McCann?"

What? How in the hell does she know who I am?

"Maybe. Who is asking?" I counter.

"Oh my, Frank, it is her! It is our little girl!" she cries.

Before I could say anything, she wraps me into a giant hug. This is the most awkward hug I've been in. Who is this crazy lady? Why is she calling me her little girl?

"Who are you?" I ask.

She stops hugging me but doesn't let me go. She keeps a firm grip on my forearms. "You don't know who we are?"

"No, I don't. Should I?" I give her a confused look.

"Oh, honey, I'm Gladys, and this is Frank. We are your grandparents. Is your mother with you?" she asks eagerly.

My grandparents? They kicked my mom out when they found out she was pregnant with me. How would they know what I look like? How do they know my name? Why would my grandparents be vampires? The odds are rare for me to randomly run into my mom's parents while hunting. I decide to play along, just to see what happens.

"How did you recognize me?" I inquire. I need to know how they know who I am.

"Your eyes. You always had the most unique eyes. You are growing into a beautiful young lady," Gladys gushes. "Is your mom here?"

I don't know if I should tell them about Mom, but if they are her parents, they have the right to know.

"No, she died a couple of months ago." I sigh.

"That ass got her killed! Did he quit protecting her?" Frank yells.

"Who?" I question.

"That no-good father of yours," he blurts.

This makes me angry. My dad has always made sure we were good. Who are they to judge? They were the ones who kicked us out.

"Don't you dare talk about my father like that! He did everything he could to make sure my mom and I had everything. Unfortunately, he was murdered a week before Mom was. Besides, Mom said her parents kicked her out when they found out she was pregnant with me. So who are you really?" I growl.

"Kicked her out?" Gladys gasps. "Is that what Alyssa told you to keep you away? Honey, we have so much to tell you! We didn't kick her out. You lived with us until you were about three and a half, then one day she took you and ran. All she did was leave a note saying she had no choice. You were never in danger with us."

It shocks me a little when this vampire said Mom's name. Either she is telling the truth or they did their research about me. I tap into her aura to see what she is feeling. She is feeling a lot of joy with a bit of grief. I don't think she is thinking about hurting me anytime soon. I don't think I'm going to let them know I know they are vampires yet; I'm going to play dumb for a bit.

"So have you been living by yourself, then?" Frank asks.

"No. My brothers have custody of me. They are doing a good job," I answer.

"Good job! Who lets a little girl wander around in the dark by herself? Especially in an area that people have died in recently!" Gladys snickers.

Oh, don't start trying to say that you guys did a better job raising my mom, I think. Otherwise, how else would she have gotten pregnant at sixteen?

"They know I'm out here. They are not too far away. We always take a walk at night, but sometimes I wander off by myself. I am safe," I lie.

"Why do you have a gun?" Frank asks.

"As Gladys pointed out twice now, this isn't a very safe place," I reply, putting it back in my pants.

They need to think I trust them. Personally, I do not know what and who to believe right now. If they are telling the truth, it will be a blessing. Maybe this is how I am going to find out more about myself.

"Lizzy, we live right around the corner. Please come with us. We want to know what you and your mom have been up to all these years. We have thought of you every day," Gladys begs.

Would this be a good idea? I glance over at Frank, and he is smiling at me. I need to know the truth, but what if they are just lying? I don't remember living with them, but how else would they have recognized me? Besides, I can protect myself if they try to do something.

"Lead the way," I accept.

Gladys jumps in excitement and walks past me. I wait for Frank to walk by, but he gestures for me to follow. I do, and he follows behind me. Is this so I do not run away? Are they actually planning to attack me before they get to the house? Not letting my guard down, I allow Gladys to lead me to an old house. It could use new siding and shingles. Frank walks past me to unlock the door. Well, at least I know he isn't going to attack me from behind. Gladys walks inside first, followed by Frank, and cautiously I follow. The inside is beautiful. It has hardwood floors and is well put together. They have a fireplace, with pictures on the mantel.

I walk up to the mantel to snoop at the pictures. One is a wedding photo of Frank and Gladys. Gladys is beautiful in her dress. I can see the resemblance between her and Mom in the photo. The next photo is a high school graduation. Who graduated? Mom said she got her GED. I grab it to take a closer look. Sure enough, it is Mom in the photo. She has a diploma in one hand, and a baby in the other. Wait, that baby is me. Why would she lie to me about not graduating?

I am tired of finding all these lies. I close my eyes to take this in for a moment. When I open my eyes again, I am not in their house anymore; I am at a graduation ceremony. I glance around and see my mom talking to someone. Cautiously, I walk up to her. She is talking to Gladys and Frank. They look so proud of her.

"Where is she? I want her to see that no matter what gets in your way, you can achieve anything!" Mom cheers.

"Honey, she isn't going to remember this. She is only a year old, after all." Gladys smiles, moving the hair out of my mom's face.

"I know that, Mom, but someday I will be able to tell her about this day," Mom states.

"She is right here. Congratulations, Mommy!" I hear behind me.

I turn around, and it is a younger version of Dad. He looks a lot like Joe. And he has someone in his arms. Oh, wait, that is me!

"Jason, you came!" Mom shouts, giving him a hug.

"Well, do you think I would miss this? Besides, it gives me a chance to spend a little quality time with Elizabeth. I hate to tell you this, but she fell asleep during the speech. She didn't see you walk across," Dad explains.

"That's okay," Mom states, taking me.

I wake up and look up at Mom. Her tassel is in my face, so I start playing with it. "Jason, will you take a picture? I want proof that I graduated while raising her!" Mom is beaming.

He nods and grabs the camera from her parents. Dad snaps the photo, and the flash is bright, causing me to close my eyes. When I open them, I am back at my grandparents' again.

That was weird. I've never had that happen before.

I put the photo back and look at the last frame. It is my last year's school photo. Even though Mom had no contact with them, she still sent them my picture.

"Honey, I know you must have a lot of questions for us. Please sit down on the couch. Do you like tea? I'm going to make us some tea," Gladys states, rushing to the kitchen.

"Can I use your bathroom before I sit?" I ask.

"Of course. It's down the hall to the left," Frank replies.

I follow his instructions and find it without any problem. I close the door and pull out my phone. I need to let Joe and John know where I am. I could call them, but I do not want Frank or Gladys to hear what I am going to say. So I decide texting would be the best option.

I ran into my mom's parents while out hunting. I know it's weird. I was always told they kicked my mom out as soon as she became pregnant with me. Turns out that was a lie and I lived with them for a couple of years. My last year's school photo is sitting on the mantel. Anyway, I know this all sounds weird, but I'm at their house right now. Turns out they are vampires. They do not know I know yet, but I do not feel like I'm in any danger. I'm going to send you my location to have you meet me here.

I hit Send and put my phone back in my pocket. Grabbing the doorknob, I stop before I walk out. If they are spying on me, I better flush the toilet, just to make sure they think I used the facility. Pretending to wash my hands, I finally think that is enough play and walk out. No one is outside, spying on me, after all.

I walk back into the living room and find Frank sitting on a recliner.

"Please sit down, honey." He gestures toward the couch.

I sit down on this ugly green couch and am surprised at how comfortable it is. I feel my phone vibrate and know I need to look at it.

"Do you mind if I look at my phone? I just felt it vibrate. I'm sure it is my brothers checking up on me," I explain.

"Yes, of course. They are your guardians. They have every right to know where you are. Maybe we can work out some kind of arrangement to have you stay with us for a bit," he replies.

That is when a feeling of uneasiness comes over me. They are planning something, and it is not in my favor. I pull out my phone and act casual to see Joe's response.

Are you stupid? If they are vampires, why are you with them? I'm, like, ten minutes away. Are you sure you are okay?

I hit Reply and type the message:

They want you to come over to discuss me staying with them sometimes. The problem is, when he said that, a feeling of uneasiness came over me. They are planning something, but I don't think it is right now. Either I'm in trouble or you guys are.

I knew it was too good to be true. There has to be a reason my mom ran away with me and we had no contact that I remember. Now I want to know why.

"Thank you. I didn't want them to worry." I smile, putting my phone away. "I would love to stay with you sometimes, but with school starting up here, I don't know if I will have time."

"Maybe you could come for a weekend or something. We miss you!" Frank states.

"Lizzy, dear, do you want green tea, black tea, or hot chocolate?" Gladys yells from the kitchen.

"Green, please," I answer. "So what do I call you guys?" I mean, I just met them; it would be weird to call them Grandma and Grandpa. Do I just call them Gladys and Frank, or Mr. and Mrs. Jones?

"If you are comfortable, you can call me Papa. That is what you used to call me. I'm sure it would melt Gladys heart to have her hear you call her Grandma again." He frowns. "When your mom took you from us, our hearts broke. We looked for you both for a couple of years. Then one year we got a letter in the mail with no return address. It was your kindergarten picture with a note saying that you both were doing fine. We quit searching, hoping maybe the photo was a sign you guys would come back. It never happened, but each year we would get your photo with an update about your lives. It wasn't much, but we looked forward to it each year."

Gladys walks in with a tray of drinks. "Frank is right. I never knew how I was going to fill the void in my heart. Those letters and pictures helped a lot. I'm so excited we ran into you tonight. It is as if someone sent you directly to us. Except I need to ask, why are you here?"

"I've been really missing Mom lately and knew she grew up in this town. So I asked my brothers if we could take a trip just to see what the town was like. I couldn't sleep tonight, so I decided to go on a late-night walk," I lie.

Gladys hands me the cup, and I put it up to my nose to smell it. I love the smell of green tea, except this time, I smell that there is a special ingredient mixed in it. Are they going to drug me?

"It's a little hot. I'll let it cool a bit," I state, placing it back on the tray.

"Of course, we do not want you to burn yourself." Gladys sits next to me and says, "Can I ask you some questions about your life?"

"Of course." I smile.

"What did your mom end up doing for a living?" she inquires.

"Mom managed a little dress shop. Luckily, when it came to me, Dad dealt with everything, so that helped Mom out a lot financially. Dad paid for my health insurance, school supplies, and gave her extra money for food for the month. Of course, Mom had to buy some stuff, but it never broke her," I reply.

"That was how it was when you lived here. We never had to buy a thing for you, unless we wanted to. Of course we spoiled you," Frank answers. "Boy, to think how different your life would have been if you had grown up knowing us. What did your parents say about us?"

"Mom just told me you kicked her out at sixteen when she got pregnant. She didn't tell me that I lived here, and how good you were to her. No wonder she was a good mom—she had good role models," I say.

"So you do not know any family secrets?" Gladys questions.

I'm not going to tell them everything I found out in the last couple of months. Although maybe if I did, they could tell me what I am. I would like to think they are good vampires like John, but why would they put something in my tea?

"What kind of secrets?" I play dumb. "Obviously, Mom wasn't so keen on telling the truth. Is there anything you would like to tell me?"

Maybe they will come clean about being vampires. If they do, maybe I could trust them a little more.

"Nothing we need to discuss tonight. Drink your tea before it gets cold," Gladys states.

"I think it might still be too hot," I lie. "Tell me about yourself."

"Well, I worked as a businessman. I did everything in my power to make sure Gladys did not have to work and could stay home with our little girl. Alyssa was the light of our lives. Everything was fine, until your father came along," Frank hisses.

I feel like it is a good time to call them out about their secret. "How long have you two been vampires?"

They both look at me in disbelief. It's clear they did not want to tell me. I figure, if they are going to attempt to drug me, I have the right to know the truth.

"What are you talking about?" Frank stands up. "What lies did your mom and dad put in your head?"

I roll my eyes. I hate that they are playing dumb. "You know exactly what I'm talking about. I have the ability to tell if someone is different."

That sets Frank off. Before I could react, he has me pinned down to the couch. Gladys grabs my hair to pull it. This causes me to open my mouth to say "Ow." Except before any words come out, she pours the hot tea into my mouth. I scream when the hot water burns my mouth and pours down my face. I try to spit it out, but I couldn't help but swallow some.

"I've been a vampire before your mother was even in the picture. I think I was fourteen when I was turned. Later, I fell in love with a human who wanted to be a vampire. We got married, and I changed Gladys on our wedding night. Except by some miracle, Gladys got pregnant. We didn't realize it was possible. We decided we wanted to raise our baby right, so we switched to an animal diet.

"The transformation was easier on me than your grand-mother since she was a newborn. Except she never strayed once and always ate animals like a champ. Your mother is human and never knew vampires existed until your father came along. When your mother got pregnant, we welcomed your dad warmly. Alyssa never feared us, until you started getting older. If your father weren't in the picture, our family might still be together," Frank reveals.

"Oh, don't worry, we are not trying to hurt you. We are just putting you to sleep until we talk to your brothers," Gladys states.

I am shocked to hear all this. My mom has known about her parents! Why doesn't it surprise me she chose to lie to me about this too? I feel like my mom and dad hadn't been truthful about anything. Frank climbs off me, and I try to sit up, but I feel woozy. I blink a few times to fight off the sleepy feeling, except it is stronger than I am and I fall asleep.

Chapter 13

I hear commotion and open my eyes. My head is pounding, and the light in the room is bright. I close my eyes again and attempt to grab my head. But I cannot move my left arm; something is keeping it down. I force myself to open my eyes again and see both my hands are tied to a chair. What the hell happened?

"Help!" I attempt to yell.

Really, they gagged me too. How did I not realize this before I yelled? What the hell happened to me? The last thing I remember is running into my grandparents.

Wait, they did this to me!

The memories of last night flood my brain. Here I thought they actually wanted to get to know me. A tear escapes my eye. Now I can only hope Joe and John get here before my so-called grandparents hurt me.

A noise comes from the other room. What is going on in there? I wonder. What are they doing? Okay, I cannot just wait here to find out; I have to get free somehow. I've seen in movies that if you can get the chair to tip over and break, you can break free. I wonder if that really works. I move my feet to push myself back, but my feet are tied to the legs of the chair. Of course, they thought of everything! I use my upper body and attempt to rock. The chair does not budge. Either I'm still weak from whatever they drugged me with or this chair is heavier than it looks.

I glance around the room to see if I am close to anything that I can use to cut myself free. Of course, I am sitting in the middle of the room, near nothing. I notice posters all around the room. This room looks like a teenager's room. Turning my head to look behind me, I see a twin bed, with a toddler bed next to it. This has to be my mom's old room. All my life I wondered what my mother's room looked like when she was my age, and now I'm tied up in the middle of it. I wish I could get up and look around.

The doorknob turns, and I whip my head back to see who is coming in. It isn't like I can fight, but I need to be aware of what is happening. A man I don't recognize walks in. Who is this man? Even though he could be a threat, he is good-looking. I would say he has to be eighteen or so. Guessing, with his skin tone, he is Native American. He has brown eyes and shoulder-length black hair. He walks behind me and bends down to my ear level. Goose bumps pop up on my arms when I feel his breath hit my skin.

"Hi, Elizabeth. My name is Liam, and I'm here to help you. I am a hunter, and I ran into your brothers tonight. We were talking when they received your text, and I offered to come with them just in case they needed help. I'm going to free you, but you need to be quiet. Do you understand?" he whispers.

I nod in agreement. His voice is like a god's to me. Every word he says makes my heart flutter. Why is it that the one time I find someone I think is attractive, I'm a damsel in distress? He cuts the rope around my arms, and I rub each of them before taking the gag out of my mouth. I move my mouth and jaw in every direction to stretch them out. He cuts the rope around my legs, and I instantly stand up but fall right back into the chair. Damn, I'm still weak.

Liam offers his hand and smiles at me. Hesitantly, I grab it, and he pulls me up. I fall forward right into his chest! This isn't embarrassing at all. He wraps his arms around me, and I instantly feel safe.

Taking in his scent, I feel like it is just for me. He smells like pine trees, which is my favorite smell. If I could, I would stay in his arms all day. I glance up at him, and he is smiling down at me. I feel my cheeks turn red. He has a perfect smile. In my eyes, this hottie has no flaws.

"I'm sorry I'm so weak," I whisper. I try to say it flirtatiously, but I don't know if it came out that way.

I realize I am becoming the girl I hate, but I can't help it. I can see myself with this guy. I look at his lips, and I wonder how they would feel on mine. I bet we would make cute babies down the line too.

Okay, Lizzy, now you are getting ahead of yourself, I think. You just met the guy, for crying out loud. You don't even know anything except his name. Liam. And such a perfect name too!

"That is quite all right, beautiful. You stay in my arms as long as you need to. I don't mind at all." He winks.

I could feel myself blushing again, and I look away from his glance. I don't get it. Every day people tell me how beautiful I am, but this time it feels different. I cannot comprehend why a guy who looks like him would think I'm beautiful. All I know is I want to stay in Liam's arms forever.

"Elizabeth, are you okay?" John runs to me.

Well, forever is a lot shorter than I thought it would be. Liam lets go of me, and John comes to look me over.

"I'm okay. A little shaken up, and weak, but I'll survive," I explain.

"Why in the hell did you come here?" Joe yells.

I cross my arms and look away from him. I could feel the worry radiating off him, and I couldn't bear to look at him. I know I disappointed him. "I don't know," I answer.

"Do not give me that answer. You know exactly why you came here. You are not stupid. Well, maybe you are, since you did make the decision to come here without us. Especially if you knew you were in danger," he scolds me.

I don't answer. Instead, I shake my head and close my eyes to stop the tears. I do not want to get into this, not now, not in front of Liam.

"Well, if you guys don't need me anymore, I'm going to leave this awkwardness. Elizabeth, it is nice to meet you. If you need anything, here is my number. Message me anytime," Liam says, handing me a piece of paper.

"Thanks for your help, Liam," Joe states, not taking his eyes off me.

Liam walks out the door, and I feel my heart ache for him. Why am I falling for a guy I know nothing about? I do feel safer with Liam than I do with Joe right now. To be honest, I felt safer with my grandparents than I do with my brothers right now.

"I'm waiting for an answer!" Joe growls again.

I sigh, "I wanted to know."

"Wanted to know what?" John asks softly.

I know I need to answer.

Nervously, I start glancing around the room and tapping my right foot. "I wanted to know more about my family. I thought maybe they could answer my questions. I didn't feel like I was in danger when I first met them. It wasn't until after they offered me a drink that I felt threatened. Besides, they did say they didn't want to hurt me. They said I was just going to go to sleep for a while. So maybe it was never about me in the first place. Maybe it was you guys that were in danger. I'm sorry curiosity got the best of me."

By the end of my explanation, I have tears running down my cheeks. I should have waited for them, but would things have been worse if they were with me? I need to ask them what they were going to do to me. Wait, where are they?

"Whatever, they are dead now. Let's go," Joe directs, heading out the door.

What? You killed them? I want to ask him. I suppose if they threatened the boys, it would make sense. That must have been the commotion I heard outside the door. It doesn't faze me like it should, hearing my grandparents are dead. I guess you cannot miss what you didn't know you had.

"Are you okay?" John asks again.

"Yeah." I wipe my eyes. "I'll be right out. I want to look around for a minute."

He nods before walking out.

I stroll toward my mom's old vanity. There are a lot of pictures hanging all over the mirror. Reaching up, I grab one to get a closer look. It is of a group of cheerleaders. I glance through the faces and spot Mom. I remember her telling me she was a cheerleader before she got pregnant with me. I look back up and see one of her in a dress with some guy in a tux. That must be a formal picture. Instead of looking through them all, I pack them all up; they are coming with me.

I look on the table and find what looks like a diary. I grab it and open it to the middle. I wonder what was going on with her life on this day.

April 9, 1999

Tonight was not like any other night I have ever encountered. Thinking I was just going to sneak out and go to Rachel's party like I do every Friday night, but it ended up turning into one of the worse nights of my life. Instead of making it to the party, I was attacked halfway there. A man pushed me into an alley and pinned me to the ground. I tried fighting, but he was a lot stronger than I was. I tried to scream, but he placed his cold, dry hand over my mouth. I thought I was just going to be raped, but it was something else. His pupils got really small and turned bloodred, and his face turned really old. Older-than-my-parents old. His teeth started to come out of his mouth like fangs. It was almost like I was in a horror movie. He bent down to smell my neck. I closed my eyes, hoping all this would be over soon. Whatever he was going to do to me, just do it already. I never felt my heart race this fast. Even when I did coke, my heart didn't race this fast. But before anything happened, there was a gunshot, and the guy turned to dust all over me. That was the most disgusting thing that I have ever experienced. I got up quickly and brushed the dust off my new dress. As I was dusting him off, another guy came up to me and asked if I was okay. He told me his name was Jason and that the guy who attacked me was a vampire. I feel like he is crazy! Vampires are things that only happen in movies, except it would make sense based on what happened. Jason is old, maybe in

his late twenties or something, and very
attractive. He walked me home and said
he would come back tomorrow and answer
any questions I might have. I cannot wait
to see him tonight. I should wear my black
top with my short skirt.

So April 9 was the first time she met Dad. I wonder if
Rachel was a good friend to Mom or if she was just going to
some party. I know I should head to the car before Joe's head
explodes, but I want to read one more page. I skip a head a
few pages and read:

April 28, 1999

Oh my god, I just found out my parents
are vampires! Which has me so confused.
Wouldn't that mean I'm a vampire too? They
sat me down and tried to explain everything
to me. I still do not understand, but I had
to tell them I did, just to get away for a few
minute, to process everything. Jason was the
one who tipped them off he knew. He was
over one day, telling my dad how he saved
me from being raped, and Jason could tell
my dad was a vampire. I don't know how,
but who am I to question? He is the one
who has been doing this forever. So Mom
and Dad sat Jason and me down to explain
their side of the story. They told me I was
conceived the night my mom turned. Which
I find super weird. First of all, I never want
to hear about my parents having sex, and

second of all, Mom willingly slept with a vampire. Eew. They told me I was completely human. They made a pact that they were going to raise me normal, which they always have. Jason was shocked there were actually good vampires in the world. He promised he would keep their secret. I promised too. Now that I know they know about vampires, I decided to tell them that I wasn't attacked to be raped; I was attacked by a vampire. They thanked Jason for helping me. I don't understand how any of this is possible, but I'll figure it out. One day at a time.

So my mom knew her parents were vampires. You would think that would be an important thing to tell me. Oh, wait, she didn't even tell me vampires even existed! I need to know more, but I know if I don't get going, Joe is going to come drag me out. I'm surprised it hasn't happened yet.

I close the diary, grab everything I want to bring, and hurry out.

"Took you long enough," Joe snarls.

"Joe!" John snaps.

I shake my head and walk toward the car. This night needs to be over with already. I want to get back to the hotel and read Mom's diary again. Before I get in, I adjust the stuff to one arm and open the door.

"What do you have there?"

"Just some of Mom's stuff. I think maybe there could be some answers about my weird life in here." I shrug.

He nods, and I get in the car. I place the stuff next to me and fidget to put the seat belt on. I guess I'm more shaken up than I thought. Finally, I get the buckle in, and when I look back up, Joe is glaring at me. Hello, that isn't creepy at all.

"You're grounded for being stupid," he scolds me.

My mouth drops open in disbelief. "What? That is not fair! It isn't like I planned on meeting my grandparents while I was out hunting tonight. I'm sorry if you think I made a stupid decision, but I disagree. And it isn't like they could kill me by biting me."

"They could have killed you some other way. There are other ways to die, Elizabeth. You are not immortal!" he shouts.

I bow my head in defeat. He is right; I need to be more careful, although I don't think they would have hurt me. I do think they drugged me for a reason, but now I guess we will never know. Joe speeds off, and it frightens me how fast he is going. I'm not going to say anything about the speed, though; otherwise, he might go faster.

"How long am I grounded for?" I ask.

"I'll let you know later. Now, drop it," Joe utters.

I know he is mad at me, but now I'm upset. I don't think it is fair I'm grounded for being curious. "I've never been grounded before. So what are you grounding me from? My phone? Okay, but how am I going to get ahold of you if something happens? From friends? I don't have any. From television? I don't watch much, anyway. I know it was stupid to go, but I do think I'll find some stuff out in my mom's diary."

"Good thing you're grounded, then. You will have plenty of time to read!" Joe snarls.

I roll my eyes. If he were in my shoes, he would have done the same thing; he just does not want to admit it.

I grab the diary and flip through the pages. It is too dark to read, but I need to know more about Mom's past.

I glance up at the radio and see it is one in the morning. I'm so eager to keep reading, even if I have to stay up all night. I'm sure I'm grounded from hunting tomorrow, so I could go to bed early if I pull an all-nighter.

In what feels like a five-minute drive, we arrive at the motel. Joe had to be speeding, because I know it should have taken longer to get here. Before I get out, I gather all my new goodies. I get out of the car and see John waiting for me, but Joe is nowhere to be seen.

"Lizzy, Joe is only being hard on you because you scared him. To be honest, it scares both of us not knowing how to protect you. You act like you're immortal, but you are not. Hell, I'm a vampire, and I'm not immortal either, and that is the biggest stereotype about vampires! You are right, you cannot die from a bite, but what if there are multiple vampires? Sure, one bites you and they die, but others will see the threat and snap your neck or something. We want you safe, but you need to help us help you," John explains.

I hate to admit it, but he is right. I guess I was stupid for trusting my grandparents when I knew they were vampires. I just got so excited when I learned something about my life.

I tell him, "I'm sorry, John."

"I know." He smiles.

He wraps his arm around me, and we walk into the motel. Joe isn't in the main room, but I can hear the shower running. I hope he is in a better mood when he gets out. I decide this is a good chance to read another page. I place everything on the table, grab the diary, and sit on my bed. I flip through the pages until I find where I last read.

April 29, 1999

I skipped school today and did research all day. Jason gave me all the websites that hunters use. Although I never knew any-

thing about vampires, I've learned a lot of stuff about them, and it's nothing like the movies. While I was searching, there have been a few times I thought I should stop and ask my parents something. Then I remember I am mad at them. I found out there has been only three cases where vampires gave birth. Well, of course, that they know of. All claimed that although we are human, there is some negative effects of having vampires as parents. I also read that I will never be able to have kids. It is impossible for us to reproduce. Females never menstruate, which makes sense that I'm sixteen and have never had my period. It devastates me that I'll never have a child of my own. I always thought I would be a great mom.

Wait, if my mom couldn't have children, how am I here? I mean, who would let a sixteen-year-old adopt a baby? I don't understand. Maybe I should keep reading, and maybe I will figure out the answer. I flip the page, and it's been about two months since she wrote something.

June 8, 1999

I do not believe this—I am pregnant! I told Jason, and he freaked out, not because he got me pregnant, but because this baby is in danger. I wish I had known that Jason is what's known as a "true vampire hunter." Which is when someone has killed over two thousand vampires in their lifetime. A true vampire hunter and the offspring of a vampire can conceive a baby girl. The problem is, she will probably die by the age of five from a vampire. I cannot write down what she is, but Jason is on a mission to save this child. Let's hope he can find a way to hide the smell of her blood.

Mom always told me I was her miracle child; I just never knew she meant it literally. I am happy Dad figured out the necklace thing to keep me alive all these years. I just wish I knew what it all meant.

I hear the shower shut off and decide to read one more page before Joe comes out.

June 28, 1999

After talking to everyone, Jason and I decided to raise this child as normally as we can. Mom and Dad were furious at first, but I think they are secretly excited they are going to be grandparents. They are going to let me stay here as long as I need to. I'm going to finish high school and work after school. Jason told me he would spend one week a month with me. He promised to take care of the doctor's bills and will make sure we live as comfortably as we can. Our daughter will be the key to the supernatural world, and he vowed to not stop until he finds a way to save her. Jason says he is going to keep her a secret from his boys. They are only nine and five. He doesn't want them to

think he loves them less. I can understand
that. I just hope he keeps his promise about
coming once a month.

I'm happy Dad did keep his promise about coming one week each month to see us. There was only one month that I remember that he couldn't come. He had some kind of family emergency but didn't go into detail. Wait, Mom said something about me in here. Quickly I re-read the page, and I notice mom said I am the key to the supernatural. What does that mean? I flip the page and see that there was nothing written for almost a year. *Come on, Mom, I need more information about being the key.*

"Hey, John, have you ever heard of the key to the supernatural?" I question.

"No, that doesn't sound familiar. Why?" he answers.

Damn, that means more research for me. Personally, I'm just happy I'm possibly one step closer to knowing what I am.

"My mom just mentioned something about a key of the supernatural. She didn't say anything else about it, so it could be code for something," I lie.

I don't want him to know yet that I might have found something important. Not until I know what it means.

"Time for bed. Whatever you are reading can wait until tomorrow. You want to know how you're grounded? You are not leaving with us for the hunt tomorrow. You will stay here," Joe says, coming out of the bathroom.

"Whatever." I roll my eyes, closing the diary.

He turns off the lights, and I crawl under my blankets.

I'm not going to be able to sleep now. Not wanting to make Joe madder, I decide to lie here and pretend I'm going to sleep, and once they are both snoring, I will start reading again.

Chapter 14

The sound of snoring fills the room, and I couldn't be happier. That is my cue to get up and continue reading. Grabbing the diary, I crawl under my blanket and turn on the flashlight on my phone. Flipping the diary open, I find where I left off. I get comfortable and start to read:

June 15, 2000

Every passing day saddens me a little. Why do I have to be mother of this gorgeous little girl? At first, I thought I was just biased because she is my daughter, but I get complimented on her all the time. Jason told me that since she is very cute, she is in fact the key. He hasn't gotten any closer to finding a way to save her. Though I keep telling him he has time. I know the feeling; I wish I knew a way to help our little girl too. I do research every day after I put Lizzy down for the night. She goes to bed at eight, and I do research from eight to ten. She is such a perfect baby. She started sleeping the whole night at just one week. I cannot have anything happen to her. I don't know what I would do if she died.

There were tearstains on this page. Mom was crying when she wrote this. This is the second time she mentioned that I was the key. I need to do some online research myself to see what the key is. I am going to read one more page, and if that doesn't give me the information I'm looking for, I'll do my own research. Good thing Mom wrote down the websites Dad gave her. I flip to the last page to see if Mom said anything important.

May 25, 2003

> *I notice my parents have grown hungrier. They deny it, but they are going out a lot more than they used to. Jason is going to move Lizzy and me far away so we don't have to worry about their cravings. I think my parents have just been around her too long. I hate to take her away from her grandparents, especially since they have been so supportive. Jason and I believe it will be a great idea to keep this world from her, at least until she is old enough to understand. I have to do what is right for my daughter. I'm just going to leave a note and run.*

That doesn't give me any answers. I know I should wait until tomorrow night to do more research, but curiosity gets the best of me again. Shutting off my flashlight, I sneak out of my bed. I tiptoe to the table and grab the laptop. Before I head back to the bed, I glance at both guys—they are still sound asleep. I take another step, and Joe starts to stir. I freeze. If he wakes up and catches me with the laptop, I'm going to be in more trouble than I am already. He rolls the other way, and I rush back to bed and hide under the blankets.

My heart is racing. For how nervous I am, you would think I was going to be caught with drugs and alcohol. But instead I'm fearing that I'm going to get caught with a laptop. After a few deep breaths, I open the laptop and log in.

I glance at the diary to see what websites were written down. Instead of WWW, it was VVV. No wonder no random person comes across these sites. I type in the first site. I circle the Enter key a few times. This is it! I take a deep breath, close my eyes, and hit Enter. When I open my eyes again, I am disappointed to see it is just a search engine site. I click on the Search box and type in "the key to the supernatural."

I hit Enter, and all these random links pop up. It is a little overwhelming. Which one do I click on first? Why not the first one: "The Key: Myth or Fact?" Words pop up on the screen. *Okay, Lizzy, time to start reading. You need to know what the key is.*

While normal people believe that vampires are a myth, we all know they are real. There are rumors going around this world that no one knows the answers to. We hear stories about werewolves, ghosts, witches, and dare I say it, the key to the supernatural. I cannot say if I believe in ghosts, but I am almost sure I don't believe in the key. I mean, if two vampires have a baby, how does the baby survive? Does it suck blood, or is it human? I believe the parents would end up eating their child. Vampires have no self-control. Is it true that "the key" gives off a special smell at the age of five? That baby would be a goner. Especially if their grand-parents get to them. I think I have a better chance of believing there is only one were-wolf and witch in the world. I have heard two different stories about the key, and that is why I find it fishy—no one has ever seen her before. First of all, I hear the last key was born over one hundred years ago. There is no way a one-hundred-year-old is just walking around, avoiding all vampires with her scent. I don't understand why it is always female too. I hear she is either the most beautiful woman you will see or the ugliest lady you will lay eyes on. I haven't seen any ugly or beautiful one-hundred-year-old walking around. So if you ask me, it is a myth.

That doesn't help at all. The only truth from this article is I'm the most beautiful thing you will lay eyes on.

I hit the Back button. The next article is titled "The Key." That looks like a good one to click on.

The Key

The key is like a story that hunters tell their kids. Whoever started the story was a whack-job. Vampires cannot have babies. Hello, they are not even alive! How in the hell would their reproductive system still be working? I guess I am one that will not believe it until I see it.

I shake my head and hit the Back button again. Maybe I will not find out anything about myself and what I am. I start scrolling through the page until I spot a title that looks promising. "Mysticalkeyextramundane, or Key of the Supernatural." I click on it and hope for the best:

It is true!

Reading through articles, I see people are very skeptical about other supernatural beings. Honestly, I was, too, until I experienced it firsthand. How? you might ask. Well, keep reading and you will find out.

I ran into a hunter in the past; we grew to trust each other, and we exchanged secrets. His eldest son is the werewolf of the world. I know it is weird that I would happen to run into him. At that time, his son was only eleven but already was showing signs. He wanted help figuring out how to keep him from phasing. I told him I would help him only if he would help me figure out a way to save my daughter. My secret is, my daughter is the Mysticalkeyextramundane, otherwise known as the key to the supernatural.

Let me help you figure out what is myth and what is truth. She is the most beautiful young lady I have ever laid eyes on. Her mom was a child of two vampires, who, until I came along, didn't even know vampires existed. Her parents are good vampires. My baby girl has blond hair and has the most attractive turquoise eyes you will ever see. They almost glow in the dark!

She grew to have a fit physique and is like a life-size Barbie doll.

Lucky for me that another hunter figured out how to keep my daughter safe past five. I bought her a cross necklace. We read that if you mix holy water, blood of a vampire, and hair of the werewolf, it can make her blood smell normal. And it will make a vampire die as soon as their teeth pierce through her skin.

Yes, you would think that because we have the key and the werewolf, we can kill all vampires, but there is one problem. We do not have the witch. If somehow we come across her in our hunting, then of course we will end it all.

Just because everyone hears the myths and no one knows they are real does not make them fake. It just means they are rare. I just became very unfortunate to have to worry about the key. If I could go back, I would, not because I don't love my daughter, but because of how much I love her. Wouldn't you do anything to keep your child safe too?

Vampire + werewolf + key + witch = end of vampirism or vampire immortality.

We all know that when a vampire sucks every last drop of the key, they become immortal. If they get a taste of her blood when they are injured, it will heal them. If the vampires get ahold of her, the werewolf, and the witch, they could cast a spell and

*make all vampires immortal. But if the key,
the werewolf, and the witch get together,
they can end all vampires.*

*I lost contact with the person whose
son is the werewolf, and I, unfortunately, do
not know the spell.*

*So the key is real. Good luck tracking
me down to find my daughter. I'm using a
public computer.*

"Oh my god!" I shout, pushing the laptop away from me. My dad wrote this about me.

I must have said that out loud, because it wakes up both Joe and John, who jump out of bed, ready to fight. Oops, I did not mean to yell; I'm just shocked I finally figured out what I am.

"Lizzy, what is it?" John asks.

I don't say anything; instead, I just hand him the laptop and head into the bathroom to process what I just read. I close the door, lock it, and sit on the toilet seat. I rest my elbows on my knees and place my face in my hands. I know I should feel relief that I know what I am, but instead I just feel terrified. I never thought about what kind of danger I could be in. If a vampire somehow sucks me dry, they become immortal? Do I have to be alive for it, or can they snap my neck and then drink me? What if a vampire finds out I am the key? I'm not ready to be dead.

I am also feeling angry. I'm mad that Mom and Dad kept this secret from me. This is important in my life; they should have told me. What if vampires start to hunt me? I would have never known why. How old were they going to let me get until they told me?

I sit up and wipe the tears off my face. I am so frustrated right now that I'm actually crying. I wish my parents were still alive so I could yell at them.

"Lizzy," I hear through the door.

I didn't want to answer, but I know I have to talk to them. I get up and open the door. Joe is standing there, and John is right behind him.

"So I guess I'm the key," I state, faking a smile and crossing my arms.

"Well, I'm happy we now know what you are. I hate to say this, but Dad did tell me a story about a girl who could make vampires immortal. When vampires are near, they would smell this sweet scent. If they drain her dry, they would become immortal. Dad gave hints, but I never pieced it together when we met. If he had told me the key wore a special necklace to keep her scent at bay, then I might have figured it out," Joe replies.

Instead of saying anything, I push past them and sit on my bed. Why would Dad tell him it was a story? Why didn't Dad just tell him the truth right then and there? I am starting to believe my parents were pathological liars.

"My mom always told me I was her miracle baby. According to her diary, now I know why. My mom was a child of two vampires. My grandparents did tell me she was conceived the day that my grandma turned. They started to feed on animal blood when they found out they were expecting. They did everything they could to keep my mom safe. Mom didn't even know about vampires until Dad came around and saved her from one. She was never supposed to be able to conceive a child, unless she met a true vampire hunter. Dad was one, and that was how I came into the picture," I inform them.

"What are you thinking, Lizzy?" John asks.

"I don't know," I answer.

I have so many emotions going on I don't know which is the strongest.

"We need to know. What are you thinking?" he pushes.

I sigh. "Honestly, I'm still just pissed that we keep finding out more secrets. I am sixteen. I want to know how old was old enough to be ready to handle all this. Everything I've read said they were going to wait until I was old enough to understand. Is sixteen still too young? I feel like I have gone through a lot of traumatic things that a normal sixteen-year-old wouldn't have to go through. In the last couple of months you have known me, have I freaked out? I guess I did freak out when I found out John was a vampire, but I feel like that one doesn't count."

"Lizzy, I'm not going to ground you anymore. Even though I still think you were really stupid, we did get answers. I suppose your stupidity was for something," Joe says.

I roll my eyes at him. I'm glad I'm not grounded anymore, although maybe being grounded wouldn't be a bad idea. If I am grounded, then maybe there is a chance my identity wouldn't get out. What am I talking about? I have made it this long. Why do I think now that I know what I am, everyone will know? What if there are people who already know what I am?

I gasp and clap my hands over my mouth.

"What?" Joe asks.

"What if the people who killed my mom know what I am? What if they are still looking for me?" I panic.

"Lizzy, we will keep you safe. I believe if they were still looking for you, they would have found you already. Especially the week you were with Ethan," Joe answers.

I suppose that is true. I should not worry so much. Besides, how are people going to find out where I live? I've moved to a completely different state.

"I just wish my life were back to normal," I complain. "I hate to say this, but I cannot wait to start school in a couple of weeks. It will make me feel somewhat normal."

"Said no kid ever!" John laughs.

"I know, but what can I say? My life has changed so much I might as well get ready for school." I shrug. "Well, I think I'm going to lie back down. I suppose we can talk more later today."

I crawl under my blankets, and the guys go back to their beds. Joe flips off the light, and I turn onto my left side. I do hope I feel normal after starting school.

Chapter 15

Most kids are nervous about starting a new school, except for me. I am just ready for some normal in my life. Today is the first day. I feel calm and relaxed. I don't have to look over my shoulder, and I'm not worried about John showing up and eating me in front of my classmates. At least I can hope not.

I am so excited to start I show up half an hour early. I need to talk to the principal, and I want to make sure I'm not late for my first class. When I walk into the office, the secretary is on the phone, writing something down. She doesn't acknowledge that I'm standing here. She is young, maybe midtwenties. Her orange hair is perfectly wavy, without a strand out of place. I cannot say I approve of her outfit; it's not exactly work appropriate. She is wearing a purple V-neck that is showing a lot of her cleavage.

She hangs up the phone and looks up at me, startled. Maybe I should have knocked so she would have known I was standing here. "Hi, honey, how can I help you?"

"My name is Elizabeth McCann. I'm new to the school," I answer.

"Welcome!" She smiles. "I'm Cleo, the high school secretary. I have your class schedule here, and a map of our school. It is small but still can be confusing at times. If you have any questions, do not hesitate to ask any staff member.

Mr. Salome is expecting you, but he is on the phone now. Please have a seat, and I will let him know you are here."

"Thanks," I reply and sit on the middle chair.

I glance over my class schedule, and the classes do not seem too scary. I have geometry, history, chemistry, study hall, English, and Spanish. The only class that might give me trouble is Spanish. Although I've never struggled in school, and I'm not planning on starting now.

"Ms. McCann, Mr. Salome is ready for you. Just right back there," Cleo announces.

"Thank you," I answer.

I gather my things and walk past her desk into a small hallway. To my right is a closed office door. I knock, and I hear a muffled "Come in" from the other side. I open the door and walk in. Sitting behind the desk is a large middled-aged man. If I had to guess, I would say he weighed over three hundred pounds. He is in a black suit with a red tie. He is balding on top, but what little hair he does have is gray.

"Ms. McCann, please sit down," he offers with a raspy voice. He sounds like he has a cold.

I take a seat and smile.

"So, Ms. McCann, I just want to talk with you for a bit before you start your first day. I was reading your file and see you are originally from Centennial, Wyoming. I bet this town is a little different." He chuckles.

He starts to cough and does not cover his mouth. This man is so gross! Did his mom not teach him manners when he was little?

"A little, but I'm getting used to it. Where I live, the view is beautiful," I reply. "Every day I admire it on my morning run."

He looks down and adjusts his tie. I can feel he is uncomfortable around me, but I do not understand why.

We haven't talked about anything of importance. Maybe he doesn't like talking about running.

"I also read that both your parents have died and your brother Joe is your guardian. I know Joe and John quite well. They were in my office more than any students I have had. Am I going to have the same problem with you?" he asks.

I chuckle this time and move my head slowly from side to side. Why doesn't that surprise me that they were trouble-makers in school? "No, sir. As you could see in my file, I'm a perfect student. Never had detention or been in any trouble in school. Unlike my brothers, the only time you'll see me in your office is today."

"I hope this is true. I would hate to see Joe in my office again on your account. Although he does seem like he has grown up a lot. I talked to him when he brought in all your transcripts and registered you to this school. He seems like he has grown into a fine young man," Mr. Salome states.

I wonder if Joe acted out because he wanted his father's attention. I mean, he makes it sound like Dad did not care about them, and he had to raise John when Dad was gone. Maybe he just needed a little love back then.

"He has been a great guardian. Did you know he didn't even know about me? He didn't even know about me before he took me in. On the day he met me and found out he had a sister, he welcomed me with open arms," I explain.

Okay, that might be pushing it a bit with the open arms, but Mr. Salome doesn't need to know that.

"That is great to hear." He smiles. "Well, I will show you to your first class, if you are ready."

Yes, I'm ready to feel like a normal teenager. "Yes, I am."

He stands, and I follow. We walk out to the hallway, which is bare. I look at my watch, and I'm ten minutes late for my first class. Great, now I'm really going to draw attention to myself when I walk in. He stops, and I almost run into him.

"This is your locker, 114," he points out.

I make a mental note. I'm sure my locker will come in handy sometime today.

We start walking down the long hallway again. I've never been to a high school where every classroom is on one floor. In my old high school, the building was two stories tall.

Finally, we get to a closed door.

"This is your English class. Mrs. Mosby will be your teacher," he explains and knocks on the door.

He opens it, and we walk in. Everyone turns around to look at me. Okay, now I'm a little nervous. Mrs. Mosby smiles at me and walks toward us. The chatter of the students starts, and I tuck my hair behind my ear. *Stop looking at me.*

"Class, this is Elizabeth. I'm expecting you all to give her a warm welcome. It is scary starting at a new school, not knowing anyone," Mr. Salome announces. "Mrs. Mosby, I'll leave it to you. Good luck, Elizabeth."

He walks out, and I just stand here looking like an idiot. Where do I sit?

"Welcome, Elizabeth. Would you like to say something about yourself?" Mrs. Mosby asks.

"I like to be called Lizzy. This summer, I moved here to live with my brothers. You will all find out I'm very socially awkward," I answer.

Some students chuckle. Do they think my answer is funny, or are they laughing at me?

"What brought you out to live with your brothers?" Mrs. Mosby questions. "You don't have to answer, really. I'm just curious."

"My parents died, and my brother has custody of me," I say nonchalantly.

It hurts to say it, but I don't want anyone to see a sign of weakness in my answer.

"I'm sorry, dear. Why don't you take a seat behind Riley there?" she replies nervously. I made her uncomfortable with my answer. "Class, I want you to take turns introducing yourself. That way, Lizzy can put names with faces."

Everyone moans but does it anyway. After the torture of everyone telling me their names, Mrs. Mosby finally starts class. It isn't hard since it is only the first day. We get our book and syllabus.

*****

This day is not going badly at all. I meet new people in each class, and everyone is being nice. In each class, we collect our books and syllabus, and in Spanish we get homework already. I am not looking forward to that class.

It is finally lunchtime, and I am ready. I was in such a rush to leave this morning that I forgot to eat breakfast. I grab my lunch out of my locker and head for an empty table. It has never been my thing to try to make friends, but if they want to approach me, I will welcome them. As I take a bite of my sandwich, a guy sits down across from me. He is wearing a varsity athlete's jacket, so I automatically assume he is a jock.

"Hello," I mumble with a mouthful of food.

He does not speak; instead, he keeps staring at me. I swallow and stare back. Does he want to say something?

"Hello, beautiful," he finally says.

"I wish people would be more creative about how they say hi to me," I state, taking another bite.

He frowns a bit. Obviously, he was not expecting that reply. Most girls love compliments. I don't.

"I'm sorry. Hi, your name is Lizzy, correct?" he questions.

"It is, although I don't have the pleasure of knowing your name," I answer.

"Dean." He smiles, stealing a carrot stick, and I watch him take a bite.

"I don't recall you asking for that," I say, nodding toward it.

"It's okay. Nobody ever says no to me. So I know if I asked, you would have said yes anyway," he states.

Wow, this guy is cocky! I cannot deny that he is good-looking. He has piercing blue eyes and shaggy blond hair. The problem is, he is not my type at all. I am sure he thinks I'll make great arm candy. Except I'm not going to boost his ego any more. His head might explode if I do.

"Well, you see, that is where you are wrong. I'm kind of possessive when it comes to my food. I don't share with anyone. You can keep that carrot stick, but that is all you will get from me!" I snarl.

I take another bite, and he looks like he is in shock that I just said that. It quickly changes to rage, and I can feel the anger radiating off him. I might have just poked the bear.

He leans in closer to me. "As I said before, no one ever says no to me. And you will not be the first."

I burst out laughing in his face. I'm sure pieces of sandwich come out of my mouth. I lean in and get closer to him. We are inches from each other. "You don't scare me. Just go."

Instead of leaving, he grabs my head and pulls me into a kiss. I am appalled this is happening. I take matters in my own hand and bite his bottom lip, hard. He pulls away, and his lip stretches before I let go.

"Don't like it rough?" I state.

"You are a bitch!" he yells, and everyone looks over at us.

"I'm a bitch because I said no but you still tried to kiss me? If that qualifies me as a bitch, then I guess I am!" I snarl.

"You will pay for this," he warns and walks away.

I roll my eyes and take another bite of my sandwich. I am not going to let him ruin my lunch.

I feel my phone go off, and I pull it out. Of course it is a text from John.

How is school?

I text him back:

It is good

I place my phone back in my pocket. He doesn't need to know what just happened. I'm capable of taking care of myself in these situations. I finish my sandwich, and it fills me up. I don't even want my carrots anymore. I pack up everything and head toward the bathroom. After I'm done, I walk out, and someone grabs and pins me to the wall.

"Listen, bitch, you will not make a fool out of me. I know you are new here, but you don't know who I am. Any girl would love to go out with me. You should be honored that I'm choosing you on the first day of school!" Dean barks.

I roll my eyes and push him away from me. "Do you think I care who you are? Do you think I have not dealt with jerks like you before? You are not tough, you only think you are. Deep down you are insecure, and that is why you put on the tough-guy act. If any girl in this school wants to go out with you so badly, then go find them. Because it isn't going to be me."

I walk around him, but he grabs my arm. I am done being nice. I twist his arm, and he lets me go. He starts to take some swings, but I dodge them. I give him a left hook, and I make contact with his face instantly. Blood gushes from his nose.

"You bitch!" he shouts.

"Is *bitch* the only word that is in your vocabulary? Obviously, *no* isn't," I state. "I told you, I have dealt with jerks like you before."

That doesn't go well for me. He swings and, this time, makes contact with my cheek. It stings, but it only pisses me off more. I roundhouse him in the stomach, and he falls to his knees. I take my foot and push him back, and he falls onto his back. I put my foot on his chest and smile down at him.

"Now you are my bitch. I'm a black belt in a few things, and you are not going to beat me. You better start taking no for an answer. If I hear you are giving anyone else a hard time, I will beat you up, again. Like I said before, you don't scare me. Now, get up and act like nothing happened," I demand.

He does as I say. He stands there with blood dripping from his nose and mouth. He wipes it off and turns to walk away.

"Dean and Elizabeth, here, now!" I hear someone yell from behind us. I turn around, and there is Mr. Salome. Great, day 1 and I'm already in trouble. "My office, now!"

We both march past him with our heads down. When we get to his office, he gestures for us to take a seat.

"So care to share what I just witnessed?" Mr. Salome asks.

Neither of us speaks. I look over at Dean, and he is looking down.

"Well, Elizabeth, what I saw was you beating up Dean. Is there a reason for it?" Mr. Salome pushes.

I shrug, but I don't look at him. Instead, I keep my gaze on Dean. I tap into his feelings, and all I could feel is fear.

"I don't know, Dean. Is there a reason that I beat you up?" I question.

He doesn't say anything.

"What? Now you are not all talk? You told me no one ever says no to you. So if that is the case, why don't you tell Mr. Salome what happened? If you are telling the truth to me, maybe you will not get into trouble. Did I bite your lip after you tried kissing me when I told you to leave? Yes. Did I punch you after you swung at me? Of course I did. Was I standing up for myself? You're damn right I was," I reply.

"Dean, is any of this true?" Mr. Salome asks.

"Yes," he whispers.

Wow, he isn't even putting up a fight. I'm surprised. Unless he is afraid I will beat him up after school if he does lie.

"I told you, I'm not like my brothers. I'm not going to start a fight just because I can. I'm happy Dean admitted what he did. I hope you don't suspend either of us, but he needed some of the cockiness kicked out of him," I say.

"Dean Matthew Salome, I cannot believe the rumors are true! I've heard you pressure girls to go out with you, but I didn't want to believe it. Also, no girl has ever turned you in. I just heard gossip." He turns to me. "I'm not condoning your behavior, Ms. McCann, but maybe it's good someone finally stood up for themselves." Then back to Dean. "You are off the football team for one month, one week of detention, and you are grounded for two months!" Mr. Salome scolds Dean.

"But, Dad—"

"No buts. What you did was uncalled for and could get you in trouble in the end. All these girls could press charges on you. Don't you realize that? You need to learn you do not always get what you want," Mr. Salome continues.

"Wait, he is your son?" I say, surprised.

He obviously does not get his looks from his dad.

"Yes, Lizzy," he states. "I'm sorry for what he did to you. We do not tolerate violence in our school, though, so you also have one week of detention. You should have gone to a teacher for help instead of resorting to physical violence."

That makes me mad. "When did I have time to get a teacher? When he kissed me in the lunchroom? Dean made a scene afterward, and no one came over to see what the problem was. The teacher in the lunchroom just stood there and watched. When he attacked me in the hallway for saying no to him? You saw the end of that fight. I didn't have time to find a teacher!" I say. "That would explain why he said I didn't know who he was. He thinks because he is the principal's son, he will not get into trouble." I sigh, then continue, "I will serve your detention, but maybe you shouldn't be in denial about your son."

I walk out the door and glance at my watch. I still have five minutes of lunch left. I walk into the bathroom and pull my phone out to let the guys know I have detention.

First day of school and I already have detention for a week. I'll explain when I get home.

I hit Send and look at my face in the mirror. It is a little puffy where Dean hit me, but I am not concerned. He has a mean right hook, but mine is stronger. Well, I said I wanted a normal life; I guess this is my "normal." Fighting high school boys off me was something I always had to do in the past, though I've never had to physically fight them.

Chapter 16

"Who do you think you are?" someone shouts as I walk to the car.

It is four thirty. Who is still here that wants to know?

I turn around and see a couple of girls standing behind me. They are in cheerleading outfits and glaring at me. If looks could kill, I would be dead. The problem is, they do not intimidate me.

"I think I am Lizzy, but I could be wrong. Did you hear differently?" I answer.

"Don't play smart with us," the redhead states.

"Well, you know my name. Can I ask yours?" I reply.

"I'm Monica, and this is Natasha. And we are going to be your worst nightmares. How could you get Dean kicked off the football team? He is like a god when it comes to playing. Now we are never going to win!" Monica whines.

Monica is tall, with long legs. Her red hair is pulled back into a messy ponytail, and her makeup is smudged a little. I'm going to guess from sweat during practice. Natasha is a little shorter, with long brown hair. I feel like these are two classmates I'm not going to associate with.

"I didn't realize only one person made up a football team. I thought it had to have eleven players, plus some backups," I say to mock them.

"Dean *is* the team. We thought we would just inform you that now the whole school hates you. Your first day at a new school and you manage to piss everyone off. Nice work!" Natasha snarls.

"Oh no, how will I ever survive?" I state sarcastically, rolling my eyes.

"You think you will actually survive with all these enemies?" Natasha asks. "Besides, you are asking for guys to drool over you when you make yourself up like that."

I laugh. "Honey, I don't have to make myself up. This is my natural complexion. Not my fault God gave you a nasty look that you have to cover up with makeup. I'm naturally beautiful—be jealous."

I get in my car and laugh. I cannot believe I just said that. I never want people to be jealous of my looks, but if she is going to blame them for Dean's behavior, she has another thing coming. I glance out my window and see that they are both still standing there. I give them a little wave before I drive off. Okay, this first day of school is not how I planned it. I did not think I would make friends right away, but I also did not think I would make so many enemies.

My drive is only five minutes, and I pull into the driveway. I spot Joe's car and look at the time. They are not supposed to be home for another forty-five minutes. Why are they here? I hope it isn't because of the incident at school. But I know that is why, and I don't want to hear another lecture.

Before heading inside, I pull out my phone and see I have a couple of messages from Liam. We have been texting each other all weekend and have been hitting it off well. Every time I see his name on my phone, I get butterflies in my stomach and my heart skips a beat.

I hope you are having a great day.

How was school, beautiful?

I decide I better reply now before my phone gets taken away.

> *It was all right. Punched a guy, made enemies. It was a good time.*

Putting my phone back in my purse, I decide it is time to get the yelling out of the way. Getting out of the car, I put my backpack over my shoulder and head inside. Once inside, I kick off my shoes, put my book bag on the floor, and grab my phone out of my purse before putting it on the hook. I walk into the living room and find the guys are sitting on the couch, watching television. This is the most normal I have seen them in a while.

"Hi," I say, looking at my phone to see Liam's response.

> *I want details.*

"Yoo-hoo, Lizzy, we are talking to you," John says, getting my attention.

"Sorry. You were saying?" I look up to notice they are standing in front of me.

When did this happen? They were just on the couch. I put my phone in my pocket and give them my attention.

"Detention for beating someone up?" Joe crosses his arms. "You could have been suspended."

Of course, they heard I beat someone up.

"Yeah, but he attacked me first. He first threatened me, kissed me, and then attempted to punch me. I only made contact after he made contact first. I was just standing up for myself. I want him to know, no means no. Now the whole school hates me. It was a great first day," I state.

"Yeah, they told us it was self-defense. I want to know, is that the real reason, or was he something else?" John pushes.

"He was just a horny teenage boy who doesn't like the word *no*. His dad is the principal, so he thought he could get away with anything." I shrug.

My phone vibrates, and without thinking, I pull it out to see Liam text me.

What you doing? Homework?

Nope, just talking to my brothers about what happened today. What about you?

"Who are you texting? You have a goofy smile on your face. In the last few months, I haven't seen you look at your phone so constantly as you have these last couple of days," Joe pries.

I clutch my phone in both hands and pull it to my chest to hide the screen. I am not sure I'm ready to tell them or not. I don't want them to tell me I have to stop talking to him. We have a connection, and I do not want to lose it.

"Can't I have a little privacy?" I whine.

I am hoping they will say yes, but I know that isn't going to happen. Privacy does not exist in this house. I am lucky I can shower without being supervised.

"Lizzy, after this weekend, do you think I'm going to give you privacy? So who are you texting," Joe pushes.

I roll my eyes. What I would like to do is run up to my room and slam the door. Isn't that a normal teen's response? Who am I kidding? I'm not normal, and I will never be normal again.

"Liam. That hunter who helped save me on Friday," I inform him. "Please do not make me stop talking to him. It is nice to have a friend."

Joe nods. "He is a good kid."

Wow, I was expecting more of a fight. "I have homework. Is it all right if I go start it? And I'll start supper in an hour."

"That's fine," John answers.

Why is he answering? It isn't like he is going to eat.

"Yeah, be better than us. Go do your homework," Joe smiles.

I turn around and walk back to the doorway to fetch my book bag. I put it on my shoulder and walk up the stairs to my room. Closing the door behind me, I throw the bag on my bed. I sit next to it and pull out my science book and notebook. I lie down on my stomach and open the book to chapter 1. Before I start to read, I pull out my phone to see if Liam messaged me back yet.

I would like to see you again. Do you think your brothers would allow that? The one was pretty heated on Friday. Will he let you out of his sight?

Hell yeah, I want to see him again too! Now, how to get my brothers to go along with it? I wonder if he could just come on the hunt with us this weekend. I can spend some time with him, and my brothers will be there. I know it isn't an ideal date, but it's the only way I can think of, unless we sneak around. I don't think I will get very far sneaking around.

I walk out of my room and skip down the stairs. When I walk into the living room, Joe and John are watching television again.

"Hey, can Liam come hunting with us this weekend?" I blurt out. I decide I am not going to beat around the bush; I am just going to come out and say it. The worst they can say is no.

John turns to face me with a stupid grin on his face. "Do you like him?"

I blush and look away from him. I do not want to answer that question. Although I probably just gave him an answer with not answering.

"Oh, Joe, Lizzy has a crush. What do you think? Should we let the two see each other again?" John states.

This is my crush. What is he so happy about?

"I'm not asking to go on a date with him. You guys will obviously be hunting too. It would be weird if I asked to go on a date with him and have you guys supervise," I state.

"Why not? He can come," Joe answers.

I squeal and jump up and down. "Thank you, thank you, thank you!"

Running back up the stairs, I can't wait to tell Liam we can see each other. I guess he has to accept the hunting invite first. I grab my phone off the bed and decide to call him instead of text. I dial his number, and with each ring my heart flutters.

"Hello, beautiful. How are you?" his deep voice answers.

His voice makes my knees go weak. I sit down before I fall down. How does he do this? I've never met a guy who makes me feel like this!

"I hope I'm not bothering you." My voice is shaky.

Why does he make me feel nervous? I don't want to say the wrong thing. I'm afraid he might get annoyed with me and stop talking.

A small chuckle comes from the other end. "You are not bothering me, sweetheart. It is nice to hear your voice."

Oh my god, I don't think I can handle this! My face hurts from smiling so big. I'm becoming one of those teenage girls I get annoyed with.

"So I know this is probably not what you had in mind when you said you wanted to see me again, but if you want, my brothers said I can invite you to go hunting with us this weekend. We leave Thursday night and come back Sunday. I know it is weird, but it is the best I can do," I mumble.

Did that even come out in English? I think all the words just mushed into one. Great, now I'm going to have to resay it, and I don't know if I have the courage to.

"I would love to come hunting with the three of you! Especially because it means I get to see you again," he gushes.

I can feel my face turning red again. I'm so happy I don't have to repeat my question. "I would like that. I'll have to give you more details when I know them."

"Sounds good," he replies.

"Not that I want to cut this short, but I have homework I have to get done before I start supper, but I will text you... if that is okay," I state.

"Of course, text me anytime. Good luck with your homework, and I'll see you on Thursday!" he says before hanging up.

I lie back in bed with my phone to my chest. Oh my god, I have a semidate this weekend! What am I going to wear?

Chapter 17

To be the most hated person in school hasn't really affected me that much this week. Both teachers and students glare at me in the hall between classes. They whisper "That is her" when I walk by. There is only one positive note: I have made a couple of new friends because of this. A few girls have thanked me for standing up to Dean; I wouldn't say we are best friends, but we eat lunch together.

It is finally Thursday night, and I'm so excited. Joe has talked to Liam some this week, trying to plan where we will meet. I know this is not a date, but I still have butterflies in my stomach about seeing him again. He should be at the motel any minute, and I do not know if I am dressed properly. Maybe I should not be in sweats, but I also want to be comfortable.

"Are you ready for your date tonight?" John smiles.

"Some date, my brothers are chaperoning," I sigh. "Besides, I never said this was a date. We just want to see each other again."

I yawn and rest my chin on my arms. I'm already lying in bed on my stomach, watching the guys get ready for the hunt tonight. I could take a quick nap, but I'm sure they would not wake me up if I did end up falling asleep. They probably would take Liam and interrogate him, and then I would never see him again.

"So John and I talked about it. Although I still don't know if you will make the right decisions, we are going to let you and Liam go off on your own in the hunt tonight. Liam will be there to make sure you don't wander off with other relatives, and I know you will keep both of you safe if something would come up," Joe informs me.

I sit up quickly at the edge of the bed. Did I just hear that right? They are going to trust me alone with a guy? I could jump up and down right now. "Really?" I say in disbelief.

Maybe I heard them wrong. Maybe I just imagined this whole conversation.

"Yes. I mean, what kind of date would it be if we tagged along?" John replies.

"Thank you." I smile.

"Lizzy, we know we can be hard on you at times, but we do it because we care. We also know, since we have met you, your life has been a little messed up. We do want you to have a somewhat-normal life. Remember, you are the one who asked to go hunting with us. We did not make you. You can quit at any time.

"We know that a normal life means you are going to date. We feel like we should be more protective of you since we are your older brothers, and since you are the key, but we know you have to live your life too. It makes us feel somewhat more comfortable that we are here," Joe explains.

"My luck, I would sneak off and get attacked. It's better if I am just honest from the beginning," I state.

"So what are you going to wear?" John changes the subject.

"What I have on. I'm not dressing up fancy for this. I still have to be able to fight if needed. Remember, I'm cursed with beauty. I don't have to try." I smirk.

John throws a pillow at me, and I start to laugh. That is when there is a knock on the door. I stop and stare at the door. This is it; Liam is about to come in that door. Maybe I should dress up a little more. What if he finds me disgusting and walk right back out the door? Why does he make me feel this way?

Joe gets up and answers it. He welcomes Liam in, and it is like a god walking in. In my eyes, he is perfect.

"Hello, everyone," Liam says, walking in.

"Hi," John answers.

I, on the other hand, could not get words to form. He probably thinks I'm an idiot right now.

"Well, let's not waste precious time. Let's go," Joe directs.

We get up, and Joe and John head out the door. I wait for Liam to leave, but instead he stands in the doorway, staring at me.

"Hello, beautiful," he states.

"Hi," I answer quietly.

"You ready for tonight?" he asks.

I nod. Why am I so nervous?

He chuckles and walks out the door. Is he laughing at me because I'm so nervous, or because he thinks I'm hideous looking? Maybe I should have changed. Well, it is too late now.

The ride is very quiet, except for the radio blasting. Maybe that is why Liam isn't talking to me; maybe the music is too loud. I'm so used to it I just tune it out. I glance over at him, and he is looking out the window. I wonder what he is thinking about right now. Is he regretting coming out with us to this hunt? That would just be my luck.

Joe pulls over to the side of the road, and all of us get out. "Okay, plan is, Liam and Lizzy, you will go that way for two miles and come back. John and I will go the opposite way for an hour and come back. If you find something, kill it. Lizzy, you know the rules," Joe directs.

"Don't get bitten, don't die, and do not go off with strange people. Even if they claim to be family." I grin.

"Yeah, yeah. Do you have everything?" Joe questions.

"Gun, stake, wooden bullets, phone, flashlight, and Liam." I show him everything.

"Can I ask a question?" Liam asks. John nods for him to go ahead. "Why does Lizzy show you where she puts everything? Has she forgotten something before?"

I never thought about how weird it could be for someone who doesn't know our situation.

"I've only started hunting a few months ago. I show them and state everything so just in case I did forget something, they can tell me," I explain.

"Only a few months and you are already able to go on your own?" Liam says in awe.

That statement gives me a weird vibe. I am not in danger, but he is hiding something. I want to push it, but I can't. I don't need him to find out how I know he is up to something. I will just watch him closely for the time being.

"I'm a fast learner. Are you ready?" I push.

Liam nods, and I lead the way down the road. I glance behind me, and Liam is following close. I can feel worry coming from him. Why is he worried? Is it because we are alone? Why wouldn't he be nervous instead of worried? Maybe it's because he found out I have only been hunting a few months, and the first time he met me, I was captured. Maybe he is worried I'll get us in trouble. Either way, if he wants to lead this hunt, he is welcome to.

About a mile in, I walk down into the ditch.

"Look," Liam whispers.

I turn around, and he is pointing in front of him. Straight ahead is a full moon peeking above a hill.

"It's beautiful," I say in awe.

Liam grabs my hand, which takes me by surprise. I glance up at him, and he is looking down at me. "Yes, you are."

I look away and feel my face turn bright red. I know I'm cursed with good looks, but I do not feel beautiful right now. My hair is falling out of my bun, and I'm very hot and sweaty. He pulls me closer to him, and my body is now touching his. I need to stay focused on this hunt, but he is making it really hard. He takes his right hand and pushes the hair out of my face.

"You look absolutely stunning," he gushes out. "The moonlight really brings out your eyes."

He bends down and rests his forehead onto mine. I feel really safe with him. Like nothing could go wrong while I'm in his presence.

"I'm happy you started texting me last weekend. I'm glad your brothers let me come with you this weekend. I'm especially excited that they trust us alone. That means I can do this," he states right before his lips meet mine.

Wrapping my arms around his neck, I pull him closer. It is almost like his lips are made just for mine. I've never felt so much passion for someone before. My hand moves up, and I start to mess up his hair while his hand slips under my shirt. He is touching the small of my back and working his way up. Part of me thinks I should stop him, but another part of me wants him to keep going. He kisses my neck, and a chill runs down my spine. A moan escapes my mouth. His hands are now on my bra. He starts to fiddle with it before we are ripped away from each other.

Crap, my brothers must have caught us! I look up to explain but gasp when I realize it isn't either of them behind me; it is a vampire, who got the upper hand while we were preoccupied with each other. I glance across to Liam and see a female holding him.

"You like your neck kissed, honey?" the vampire hisses in my ear.

We messed up, big-time.

"Leave her alone!" Liam shouts.

He tries to fight free, but she is just a bit stronger.

"Stop moving. You should feel privileged. Not many people get to watch how they are going to die. He is going to eat her while you watch, and then I will eat you!" The lady laughs.

He is going to bite me first, and I'm going to have to come up with a lie on why I don't die. I guess that is the least of my worries; I hope after this vamp dies from biting me, the lady lets go of Liam so I can kill her.

The vampire starts to kiss my neck, so I tilt it so he can have better access. "You know, handsome, I will let you do whatever you want to me. First, I need to know your name," I say seductively.

He stops kissing me, and his constricted red eyes meet mine. It is almost like he is looking in my soul. It creeps me out, but I have to act brave.

"Oh, you do not have to worry about my name, dear," he states, kissing my shoulder. "What I'm about to do to you is going to hurt. You will not be screaming my name out in pleasure."

"Are you going to bite me?" I breathe out.

"Lizzy, what are you doing?" Liam quizzes.

"Shut up," the female demands.

"You smell so yummy," he mumbles and licks my neck.

Oh, yuck. "Oh, honey, that feels right." I fake a moan. "Bite me already, hot stuff, and suck me dry. I am ready."

"Lizzy, why are you taunting him?" Liam whines.

I know he is scared, and after all this, he is going to be even more confused.

"Do you want to feel my lips on your neck again?" the vampire questions.

"Yes, please," I beg.

His rough tongue licks me again before he kisses my neck.

"Okay, Shelly, make sure he is watching," the vamp directs.

"Of course, Owen." She smiles.

She grabs Liam's hair and pulls his head up so he can watch. Owen starts to kiss my neck again, nice and slow. Weirdly, for a vampire, his lips are nice and soft. I close my eyes to prepare for the bite.

"Mother of God!" I scream as his teeth pierce into my skin.

He slurps, then lets go. He coughs a couple of times before he collapses. I glance up and give Shelly a cocky smile. She throws Liam to the ground and stares at me.

"What the hell did you do to my husband? You are going to die, bitch!" She charges at me.

I pull out my gun quickly and shoot her in the heart. She turns to dust only inches from me. If I were any slower, I would have died. She wouldn't just have bitten me; she would have ripped off my head. Realizing I am holding my breath, I exhale and walk over to Liam. I can feel my heart pounding. This is the first time I fully realize I could die in other ways. I am scared, but I do not need Liam to know that. Especially because his emotions are overwhelming me right now.

"Are you okay?" I ask, putting my hand out to help him up.

"Am I okay? I should be asking you that. You were bitten! Oh my god, you are going to die, aren't you? How could you do that? Why did you let him bite you? You saved my life. Why?" he questions.

I know I need to get him to calm down first. "I promise you, Liam, I'm not going to die. This isn't the first time I've been bitten, and it will not be the last. I egged him on because I knew if he bit me, he would die, and it would give me a chance to save you from Shelly." I kneel down next to him.

He looks up at my neck and traces the bite.

"What do you mean you are not going to die?" he asks.

"I can tell you, but you have to promise not to tell anyone. Do you understand?" I state, trying to buy time to come up with a lie.

"What? Are you some kind of superfreak?" he questions.

You could say that, since it is kind of true, I think. "I will only tell if you promise me."

He keeps staring at me like I have grown a second head. I know he is waiting for me to explain, but I need to come up with something believable.

"I need you to say it before I tell you anything," I push.

"I promise," he breathes out.

I grab his hand and gaze directly into his eyes. It hurts me that I already have to lie, but I don't know him well enough to tell him the truth.

"Okay, so when I was little, Dad injected me with something. We do not know what it was, but now my blood is poison to vampires. My brothers were not injected. Unfortunately, my father never told anyone what he injected me with," I explain.

He glances down at the grass.

"What is wrong?" I question.

"What if the injection wears off?" he whispers.

"It won't," I vow.

"I should have protected you. We got caught off guard, and it was my fault. I'm sorry you got bitten," he mutters.

I grab his chin and pull his head up to look at me. His eyes look like he is a scared little boy who needs comforting.

"Liam, I promise you I would do it all over again. Now, we better go find Joe and John. Oh, just an FYI, they are going to chew my ass when we tell them I was bitten," I explain.

I pull out my phone to text them both.

Hey, I killed two. But I need first aid.

I can feel the blood drip down my neck. I pull off my shirt and wrap it around my neck like a scarf. I am wearing a camisole underneath, so I'm not walking around in just a bra. My phone starts to vibrate, and I see a text from Joe.

Seriously?

I shake my head before I respond.

I almost lost Liam. I didn't have a choice. I shot one of them.

I glance at Liam, and he is still sitting on the ground. Come on, can we just get past this already and get going? "Penny for your thoughts?"

"I almost died. You almost died. You are 100 percent sure you are not going to die?" he states.

"One hundred and ten percent." I smile. "Come on, we better get back to the car."

I put my hand out for him, and this time he grabs it. I help him up and give him a glance over. He looks so handsome in this moonlight. Wanting to admire the moon one last time, I look past him. It is higher in the sky. I feel at peace for a brief moment, then I gasp when fear hits me.

"Lizzy, what is it?" Liam panics. "Your eyes are glowing."

I cannot explain it. Looking at him only makes it worse. I start to back up as panic takes over my body. I feel my chest grow tight, and it becomes difficult to breathe. The problem is, I am not scared of Liam; I am terrified. Liam takes a step forward, and I back up a few feet before I run. I do not know why I am running, but I know I have to get away. My life feels like it's in danger right now.

I do not remember ever being able to run this fast, but I feel like I'm running at record speed. I see the car in the distance, and it gives me some relief. Not too far from it, I see my brothers down the road and decide to run to them. If I wait by the car, Liam will catch up to me. As I get closer to them, I notice John is kneeling on the ground. Maybe I feel this way because John is hurt?

"Lizzy, I don't know what is going on. He got a shooting pain and is starting to vamp out for no reason," Joe states when I get to them. "Oh shit, what is going on with your eyes?"

John turns to face me, and I scream and fall to the ground. Nope, John isn't the reason I feel this way. I crawl backward, needing to stay away from John.

"Lizzy!" Liam yells.

I don't know which way to go; both Liam and John terrify me.

"Crap, John, go eat. See if that helps. Do not let Liam see you," Joe demands.

John runs off, and I sit here staring at Joe. I am now hyperventilating. I've never felt so scared in my life.

"Lizzy, what is wrong?" Joe whispers.

I cannot answer him. I don't feel safe with Joe either. What is going on?

"Joe, she got bitten, and now she is acting weird," Liam states, huffing and puffing.

Liam is winded from trying to keep up with me. Joe walks toward me, and I do not know what to do. Joe is in front of me, and Liam is behind. Where am I going to go?

"Stay…away, both…of you," I stammer.

Personally, I am impressed I was able to get those words out. I wrap my arms around my knees, hide my head in the crease of my legs, and start to rock back and forth. I am trying to calm myself, and this is actually helping.

"Lizzy, look at me. Why are your eyes glowing, and what is going on?" Joe pushes.

I glance up, scream, and hide my face again. It is weird; I can see my brother, but my brain isn't registering that it is him.

"Elizabeth, what is it?" he questions.

"I don't know," I mumble. "All I know is I'm feeling safe as long as I don't look at anyone."

An arm comes around me, and the fear intensifies. I stiffen up, quit breathing, and cannot move.

"Let go," I mouth, but nothing comes out. I need to get louder. The person pulls me closer to them, and I somehow roll out of their grip. "Don't touch me!"

This time I scream. I don't look at the person; I just stay in the fetal position. This is too overwhelming. I always look fear in the eye, but now I feel like a weenie. Dad wouldn't be impressed right now if he were still with us.

"Liam, can you go to the car? I need to talk to Lizzy," Joe demands.

"But I want to know what is going on," he argues.

"Just go to the car!" Joe yells. "We will be there in a few minutes."

Hearing Liam's footsteps as he walks away, I notice the fear starting to lessen. I glance up at Joe and realize I still have some fear, but I'm not terrified anymore.

"Lizzy, John starts vamping for no reason, and now your eyes are glowing and you are terrified. What in the hell is going on?" he quizzes.

"I don't know. All I know is looking anyone in the eye makes it worse. Actually, anything Liam did triggers it. If John is vamping for no reason, this is not a reaction to being bitten. I felt perfectly fine at first. Then I looked at the moon, and everything changed. I have never felt so much fear," I explain.

Admitting my fear out loud actually relaxes me. My breathing becomes easier, and my heart doesn't feel like it is going to pop out of my chest. About time; I thought this was never going to end.

"Whatever that was, it finally passed," I say. Then I ask, "So John just started to vamp out?"

I know Joe has said it a few times, but now I'm relaxed enough to comprehend it.

Joe nods. "Yeah, we got your text and we started walking back to the car. Out of the blue, he bends over in pain. When I turn to look at him, his face was already changing. The thing is, he didn't even know he was changing."

"Was he hungry?" I quiz.

He shrugs. "He claims he wasn't. Normally, if he gets hungry, he can feel it. He will tell me he has to eat now and then run off." He sighs. "There is something weird going on here, and I don't like it. Your eyes are not glowing as much now."

"You don't like it? Me either. Do you think I love feeling so terrified to the point I can't breathe? Do you think John is enjoying whatever is going on with him? Joe, we need to figure this out. I lied to Liam about why I don't die from a bite. Now I need to come up with a new lie about what just happened," I complain.

"What did you tell him?" Joe questions.

I sigh. "I told him Dad injected me with something when I was little. We do not know what it was since Dad didn't write it down. I also said you guys were not injected, so we are all stumped. He promised he wouldn't tell anyone. I just hope he keeps that promise."

"That isn't a bad lie. I'm impressed," Joe approves. "We could play that your crazy reaction was from the bite. You will not die. One's emotion just gets high for a few minutes. Then you can play stupid, like you do not remember what happened. When he asks why I seemed concerned, I will tell him I have never seen this emotion before or seen your eyes glow. I didn't connect it right away that it was from the bite. I will tell him not to bring it up because you get mad when people do."

I don't know if it will work, but I guess it is worth a try. "I can do that."

He puts his hand out to help me up. "Good. Now, let's get back to the car. I will get you patched up. Hopefully, John comes back soon."

I grab his hand, and he pulls me up. I dust myself off and head to the car. We need to figure out what is actually going on. I do not want this to happen again. Joe puts his arm around me and gives me a side hug. This is weird; he has never done this before.

"We will figure this out, Lizzy. We always do," he promises.

Personally, I don't think we will ever figure everything out. Just when we finally think we have it figured out, something else pops up. I almost want to give up looking for answers. I mean, what is the point?

We get to the car, and Liam walks up to me. "Lizzy, what was that?"

"What was what?" I frown.

"That freak-out. One minute you were fine, the next you were running away from me," he replies.

"I don't have any idea what you are talking about. One minute you were kissing me, and the next I was with Joe in the fetal position. So I don't know what happened. Did you do something?" I yell.

By the look on his face, I've offended him. I feel bad, but it has to be done.

"Lizzy, we were attacked by vampires. You saved my life," he explains.

"I know that. I'm not fucking stupid. Now, if you do not mind, I'm going to clean my wound." I roll my eyes.

I walk to the trunk, and Joe opens the door for me. Liam doesn't really deserve this. I feel really guilty about having to lie to him.

"Liam, can I talk to you?" Joe states. "Follow me."

I hear their footsteps as they walk away from me. Instead of watching them, I keep pretending to look in the trunk.

"Every time Lizzy gets bitten, one emotion becomes really high for a few seconds. I know I was acting like I didn't know what was going on, but this was a new emotion, and when you try to reason with her, it makes it worse. So we just have to play along until it passes. The problem is, once it passes, she doesn't have any recollection of it. Those ten to fifteen minutes all become a blur to her," Joe lies.

"Really?" Liam questions.

"Yes. It is part of the injection she got. The last time we tried to correct her, it made it worse. She was mad the last time," Joe replies. "It is just best if you do not bring it up."

"Okay," he sighs.

They walk back to me, and I glance up at them.

"Wait, did it happen again?" I ask.

"Yes, Lizzy, it did," Joe answers.

"Damn it!" I kick the dirt. I walk up to Liam and wrap my arms around his neck. "I guess you found out more about me than I was planning to share on the first date. I did tell you why I don't die, right?"

"Yes, you did. Don't worry, it is nice to know this about you. Now I don't have to be worried about you hunting," he says, wrapping his arms around my waist.

I give him a couple of pecks on the lips. I pull away and smile up at him. "I probably should get my neck cleaned up."

Joe is already in front of the car. When I start to walk up to him, I step down on my right foot and a piercing pain shoots up my ankle.

"Mother of God!" I cry and fall to the ground.

"Lizzy, what is it?" Liam panics.

I pull my pant leg up, but there is nothing there. I move my ankle up and down and the pain slowly disappears. What is going on? "I must have stepped wrong."

Standing back up, I feel no pain, like it never happened. What the hell was that?

"Liam, I'm going to clean up Lizzy's wound. Why don't you grab the map and figure out our next destination?" Joe directs.

I walk to the front of the car and sit on the hood. I stare off and admire the darkness in front of me. The moon is still bright, and many stars are shining down on us. If it weren't for the attack and this weird reaction, it would have been a perfect night.

"Lizzy, I know you are scared, but we will figure it out," Joe whispers, and I jump.

Lost in thought, I didn't hear Joe walk up. I roll my eyes but never make direct eye contact. What are we going to figure out? Every time we take one step forward, we end up two steps back. We are never going to get anywhere.

"Joe, look down the road. If we didn't know what we do, this would be so pretty. The problem is, we cannot enjoy the little things. Why? Because right when we are about to relax, we get caught off guard and end up being attacked. I just want one normal day. Is that so much to ask?" I complain.

Joe starts to clean my neck. "Is that what happened? Did you get caught off guard?" He sprays some antibacterial spray, and it burns.

"Yes," I sigh. "I know the last couple of weeks I haven't been making the best choices. I don't know what is wrong with me. I'm sure you heard me tell Liam one minute we were making out, the next minute I was with you. We took advantage of the beautiful night and kissed under the stars."

My head hasn't been in the game lately. I wish I could take a weekend to be normal, except I don't think that would work either. Maybe it was just a bad idea having Liam come with us. I don't need any extra distractions.

"It's okay," Joe states.

Wait, what did he just say? The guy who ripped me a new one just last week for trusting my grandparents. Now he is okay that I got distracted kissing a guy? What is going on with him? "I'm sorry I got distracted."

Is he using reverse psychology on me? Maybe he is just giving up on me. I hope that isn't the case.

"It happens to the best of us," he says, placing a bandage on my neck.

I couldn't help but start to laugh. "Yeah, like you have ever been distracted."

He puts his hand on my shoulder, and I glance over at him. "You have only known me for a couple of months. I've been doing this for a long time. This is still new to you. Unfortunately, the last time I got distracted, the outcome wasn't good. Your freak-out is not from you getting distracted. What happened to you didn't cause John to start vamping out. We do need to know what is causing this, though."

I nod. "Do you think my freak-out and his vamping are connected? I have never felt such strong feelings before. What if Joe cannot control himself and starts to hunt people?"

I am starting to get myself worked up again.

"Joe, it is happening again." I jump off the car.

"Lizzy, you are okay. Just relax," he states.

Before I could respond, I hear a high-pitched noise and cup my hands over my ears. That doesn't tune it out completely, but it does help muffle the noise.

"Do you hear that?" I yell.

"No," Joe says while shaking his head.

I would have never known what he said if he didn't shake his head. The noise is so annoying I want to stick ice picks in my ears to make it stop.

The noise suddenly stops, and I feel my phone vibrate. I pull it out, and it is a text from John.

I need both of you now! Liam has to stay there!

"You don't think—"

I stop.

Did John kill someone? Do we need to figure out what to do with a body now?

"I hope not. Grab the tranquilizer from under the seat. I'll grab a few things from the back," Joe rushes out.

I run and open the back door of the driver's side and am surprised to see Liam. I forgot for a brief second he is still here.

"Liam, I know you are trying to wrap your head around everything. Also, I completely understand if you never want to see me again after this. Right now I need you to listen to me. I'm better now. It was just a weird episode that happens. Joe just sat me down to talk about it. I am sorry I cannot remember what happened. We got a text from John saying he is in trouble. I need you to stay here. Not because we don't trust you, but because if something happens to you, I don't want to be the one who has to tell your dad. We will talk to you when we get back," I explain.

He gives me a dumbfounded look. I know he is trying to understand everything I'm telling him, but neither Joe nor I have time to explain now. I grab the tranquilizer, and before Liam can respond, I close the door on him.

"Joe, what if—"

"No, we are not thinking of that now. No what-ifs. Right now we are just going to go and hope he just needs help with a hunt." He slams the trunk.

Joe is playing with his phone when the loud squealing starts up again. I cover my ears again, but this time it hardly muffles the noise. Joe says something to me, but I can't hear him. I want to know why I can hear this noise and he cannot.

"What?" I yell.

Luckily, silence comes upon me again just as suddenly. Letting go of my ears, I wait for Joe to respond.

"I tracked his phone. Let's go," he repeats.

He sprints into the trees, and I am right on his heels. In the trees, even with the flashlights, we can't see anything in front of us. I am following too closely, and branches that move when Joe passes them hit me in the face. Although it should be the last thing on my mind, I wonder how many scratches I will have after this.

The ear-wrenching noise starts again, but this time we are closer. Even Joe ends up covering his ears this time. At least I know I'm not going crazy now.

"What is that?" Joe questions when it stops.

"I don't know, but that is what I have been hearing," I reply.

Joe doesn't respond; instead, he keeps moving. We run a few more feet before I almost run into him again. Why did he stop? Walking next to him, I see an open area with a bunch of trees cut down. All that is left are the stumps. The moon is shining so brightly it lights up the whole area. I notice something lying on the ground in the middle. Wait, that isn't a *something*. It's John.

Without hesitation, I run past Joe and sprint up to John. He is still in his vampire state, but I don't care. I get down on my knees and see he is not well. He is sweating and looks pale. He is holding his leg, and when I glance down at it, I gasp. A chunk is missing, and half his leg is black.

"John, what happened?" I ask.

"Oh no, Johnny," Joe states.

Joe startles me. I didn't realize he is behind me.

"You know as good as I do what this is. This was why I was vamping out for no reason," John whimpers.

What he said confuses me. How do they know what is causing this? I hope they don't mind filling in the blanks for me. When I glance at his leg again, I think the blackness has spread. That is when I realize he does not have his pants on anymore. I'm sure he took the leg out to see what the damage was. I can't imagine the rubbing of the jeans would feel good on that wound.

"That was why Lizzy was freaking out for no reason too. There is a werewolf here," Joe answers.

"Werewolf?" I say in disbelief. "There is one werewolf in the world, and it is here?"

No one answers; instead, John winces in pain, and it bothers my ears. Well, now I know what the sound is; it is a wounded vampire. I hope I never come across one again. Wait, his leg is black. He is a vampire and was bitten by a werewolf. "Is John dying?"

"Yes," John answers. "That is why I want you guys here. I do not want to die alone. There is no cure for vampires who are bitten by a werewolf," he says, resigned to his fate. "I'm sorry, Lizzy. I'm so happy I got to meet you. You are very special, and Joe will take excellent care of you. He did with me. And, Joey, I don't want you to think you failed me, because you didn't. You did everything, plus some, to take care of me and protect me. I love you."

Tears start to fall from my eyes. John cannot die. Not now. I cannot handle losing another person who is close to me. Not only would this affect me, but Joe would also be miserable without him. It has always been John and Joe versus the world.

Glancing over at Joe, I see there are a couple of tears rolling down his cheek. That only makes me cry harder.

"Don't cry for me. This is my destiny. I became a vampire, so it was only a matter of time before something killed me." John chuckles.

His laugh sounds uncomfortable, and I notice a few tears escaping his eyes too. I don't know if he is crying from the pain or because he is dying. I need to do something. There has to be a way to save him.

"John, I can't handle any more death. There has to be a way!" I sob.

"Oh, Lizzy, there isn't. I'm just glad I don't have to do this alone. Joey, will you shoot me? I don't want to die a slow and painful death," he says.

"What? No!" I fight. "There has to be a way."

How could he ask Joe to shoot him? Does he have any idea how that would affect Joe at all? I lean back on my knees and start to play with my necklace. I look down at my cross and smile.

"My blood!" I gasp.

"What?" they state in unison.

"If John bites me but doesn't suck me dry, it could save him!" I beam.

Joe's face lights up.

"That is something we are not going to find out. Do you realize once I bite you, I will not be able to stop? Your blood was delicious the day I tasted it. I can only imagine how it tastes fresh from the vein!" John hisses.

That scares me a bit. More because after he says that, he starts to lick his lips and begins to salivate. I never realized how much he wanted my blood until now. One positive side if he sucked me dry: I would not have to worry about being a key anymore.

"Well, I guess you are going to find out today, Johnny. I will shoot you with a tranquilizer before you kill her," Joe states.

I am happy Joe likes my idea. Although part of me thinks it is probably the most reckless idea I have had yet.

"No, I will not take any part of—"

John stops and grimaces again.

I'm just happy he is not making the horrible noise anymore.

Glancing down at his leg, I realize I need to act fast. John's leg is almost completely black now. I don't give it a second thought. I put my wrist in front of him, close my eyes, and pull off my necklace.

It happens a lot faster than I expect. His teeth are in my wrist as soon as the necklace comes off. Every muscle quits working, and I fall to the ground. To make matters worse, I begin to feel like my body is on fire. My eyes shoot open as wide as they could go. I feel the tears flood my eyes. I want to scream, but I can't. This is a stupid idea, and I need it to be over, now.

"Lizzy, it is working. Are you okay? Blink once for yes and twice for no," Joe states.

He has some panic in his voice. What is he fearing? Is he fearing he is going to have to shoot John or that I am dying? If he is fearing that I am dying, he would be correct. I want to blink rapidly for "Hell no!" but I am growing weaker by the second. I try to blink twice, but when my eyes close for the first blink, I can't get them back open. Breathing is now becoming difficult too. Is this what death feels like? I want no part of it anytime soon. *Joe, please, just shoot him already!*

It is like he read my mind, because the gun goes off. As soon as John's fangs release my wrist, instant relief goes through my body. I sit up and gasp for the first couple breaths of air. I cough and glance over at Joe, and he looks at me in disbelief.

"What?" I breathe out.

"You're moving." He cocks his head.

I am not supposed to be moving? Did he want John to kill me? Wait, when you get bitten, you are paralyzed for five minutes or so. Then again, nothing about me is normal, so this doesn't surprise me at all.

"Honestly, does it surprise you that I'm not reacting as expected?" I question.

"I do not know what to think right now. We need to get you back to the car to eat the berry," Joe says. "I wasn't thinking and left them there."

He stands up and helps me to my feet. It is weird. I feel perfectly normal. I can breathe again, and I do not feel weak. "Before we go, does it normally feel like your body is on fire when you get bitten?"

"Normally, I feel every muscle getting tight. Sometimes it might feel like pins and needles. Why, did you feel like you were on fire?" He hands me my necklace.

"I've never experienced so much physical pain in my life," I admit. I look down and see John's leg is healed. "I guess if it helped, I would do it all over again. I just hope I never have to."

"How do you feel right now? Are you dizzy?" he interrogates. "That is normally the first sign."

"I feel perfectly normal, except my wrist hurts." I shrug.

"Well, let's head back to get that berry. It will make me feel better," he directs.

Nodding, we head back to the car. Part of me feels bad for leaving John, but I know Joe will come back to him after I'm safe. While following, I latch my necklace back on. Suddenly, I fall to the ground. My legs quit working. I reach down but cannot feel myself touching my legs at all. Have I become paralyzed?

"Um, Joe?" I question.

Weirdly enough, this doesn't scare me. I watch Joe stop and turn. He runs to my side and towers over me.

"What is going on?" he asks.

I shrug. "I don't know. My legs just gave out. Honestly, I cannot feel them. I think I'm paralyzed." I say it so nonchalantly. Now I'm kind of worried about why I am not worried about this.

"Here, let me help you back up. Put your arms around my neck, and on the count of three, you'll try to stand up," Joe directs.

He bends over, and I wrap my arms around his neck. He counts to three and pulls me up. Joe does all the work to get me to my feet. Unfortunately, I cannot put any weight on my legs. If Joe weren't holding me up, I would be back on the ground. All this effort starts to make me feel queasy. A wave a nausea comes over me quickly.

"Joe, put me down." I panic.

He does not have time to react, and I throw up all over him. Instead of dropping me, he lowers me to the ground. Using the little strength I have, I push up with my hands to empty the rest of my stomach contents into the grass. I probably look like a cat coughing up a fur ball. So much is coming up I cannot breathe, and my body is physically shaking. I hardly have any strength to hold myself up. If I become any weaker, I am going to end up face-first in my own puke.

Once I stop, I roll to my side and fall back. I feel so weak I know I'm actively dying. I know in the past I have said death would be good, that I would not have to worry about being the key, but it turns out I'm not ready to die. Not by suffering like this. For someone who talks about death a lot, I find out I'm really not as ready to die as I thought.

"Joe, I don't want to die," I whisper.

"We will get you that berry. You will not die on my watch," he promises.

The problem is, I can hear the doubt in his voice. Is he starting to regret this decision? Because I know I am.

"How?" I question. "I cannot walk, and I'm growing weaker by the second. Joe, I'm dying."

I don't look at Joe; instead, I keep looking at the night sky. Will I feel at peace at any point of this, or am I going to suffer up to the last breath?

"Come on," he says, scooping me up in his arms.

He starts running through the trees, carrying me as if it is no big deal. I can hardly hold my head up anymore. My head is resting on his shoulder, but it is bouncing everywhere. If I do not end up with a broken neck after all this, I will be surprised. The movement of my head is causing me to become nauseous again.

"Joe, I'm going to puke again." I gag.

He does not stop; instead, I vomit all over myself. It is like a volcano erupting from my mouth. When I finish, a burning feeling takes over my body. I feel like someone has lit me on fire again. I start to scream and cry. I want to roll around, but I am too weak to move.

"Lizzy, what is it?" Joe questions.

"Make it stop, Joe, please just make it stop!" I beg.

"Make what stop?" he asks. "Lizzy, talk to me."

"It burns!" I scream.

I squeeze my eyes tight, and the tears flood my cheeks. Joe stops, and I feel him put me down on the grass. Are we to the car already? Maybe I will be saved. The burning feeling makes me want to stop, drop, and roll, just like we learned in elementary school. Since I could not move, I settle on just moaning.

Joes shines the flashlight on me. My eyes are still closed, but I can see the light through my eyelids. "Oh my god, Lizzy, there is blood all over us! Fuck, you are in the final stage already. The car is right over there! I will be right back. Please hold on."

To be honest, I do not know if I am going to make it. So this is what the final stage feels like. I do not think it is fair I'm hitting it so soon after being bitten. The pain intensifies, and I just lie here and scream. I do not care if anyone else around me is annoyed by my screams; it's all I can do.

Finally, after what feels like forever, the pain just stops and everything around me becomes dark.

Chapter 18

A pain in my head awakens me from a deep sleep. It is so bad I swear I can hear it throbbing. Opening my eyes, I look around at my surroundings and am surprised to see I am back at the motel. How did I get here? I sit up slowly, and the pain intensifies. It feels like someone is taking a vise clamp and squeezing my head with it. I try to stand up, and that is a big mistake. Nausea comes over me, and I run to the bathroom. I fall to my knees and start to dry-heave. Every time I heave, it causes the pain in my head to increase. At this moment, I wish I had just died.

Someone pulls my hair out of my face and starts to rub my back. I really do not want to be touched right now, but I do appreciate the help. After some time, the pressure in my head subsides a little. I lean back to sit on my leg and notice John next to me.

"I feel like I have been run over by a bus," I moan.

"Elizabeth, you almost died. When Joe got back to you with the berry, he thought it was too late. It scared both of us. Thankfully, I could hear a faint heartbeat, so I knew you were alive but barely hanging on. When I got to you, you were convulsing and blood was coming out of your mouth. It terrified me to see you that way. Especially because I am the reason. Why did you risk your life for me?" John states.

"You were not there. Joe tranquilized you," I reply, giving him a confused look.

"I came to quicker than planned. When I stood up, I could hear you screaming. I knew I had to find you, and fast. When I got to you, you were lying there alone, but I saw Joe running back toward us. When Joe got to you, you just quit screaming and convulsing. You were so gray, and your body looked so lifeless. Joe asked if he was too late, and I told him not yet but to hurry. He squeezed the berry in your mouth, hoping the juices that slid down your throat would be enough. Your heart stopped, and I told him I didn't think it worked. We stood over your lifeless body, lost. I started to yell at Joe how this was his fault, and then I heard the most amazing thing. Your heart started to beat strong again. We saved you just in time," he explains. "Do you want to know what terrified me the most?"

"You thought I was dead?" I answer.

"Yes, but no. Although I was blaming Joe for your death, deep down I knew I was the reason you died. I don't think I could have lived with that guilt. Not only could I not look at Joe the same, but also I wouldn't be able to look at myself the same. If you had died, our relationship would have never been the same. I'm still pissed he went along with your idea, but I'm happy we are all okay," he admits.

Hearing this makes me realize again that I'm not just their annoying orphaned little sister who got forced onto them; they actually *do* care for me. At the time everything was happening, I just thought I had to save John for Joe's sake. And now I would do it over again, as long as we have the berry close by.

"Wait, I ate the berry with my necklace on?" I panic.

"No. I ripped it off before he put the berry in your mouth. I didn't even notice the scent of your blood. So either I was too concerned about you or when you are dying your blood smells normal," John replies.

John then snarls, "Afterward, we got into a heated argument over all this. I suggested he and Liam should go for a walk. If Joe and I were terrified seeing you like that, I cannot imagine what Liam was thinking. Joe explained everything to Liam, with the best lie he could think of, anyway."

"I'm sorry," I whisper.

The feeling of depression starts to come over me. I know I'm normally depressed lately, but this is more than normal. I get off the floor, walk into the bedroom area, and sit back on the bed. John follows me, and I look down. I realize I am in different clothes than I was when I went hunting.

"How did I change?" I ask.

John sits next to me and gives me a weak smile. "Joe and I had to get you cleaned up. You were covered in blood, and when you were convulsing, you lost control of your bladder."

That is embarrassing. "You should have let me die."

"Because we had to clean you up? You could not help it. We could not just leave you like that. We took you in the bathroom, got you washed, and put you in bed. We did not do it to be perverts. We did not touch anything in the chest area, or the private area. For that, we just switched your underwear but did not look," John explains.

I know he is right, but that is not the only thing I am feeling guilty about. "I feel bad you are mad at Joe for going along with my idea. I am happy it healed you, though, and I would do it all over again. You asked Joe to shoot you. Do you think he would get over the fact he shot his brother when there was a chance we could save you? I couldn't sit there and watch you die either. I have lost too many people in the last couple of months. I couldn't lose you. I would rather die than have you die. You asked me why I did it. It was because I had to do something. If I died in the process, at least Joe would still have his best friend."

I cannot look at John; I'm feeling too many emotions right now. I am angry, sad, and depressed. I want to yell, but I also want to cry.

"Lizzy, why would you say that? Joe and I are close, but it doesn't mean we do not care about you. I never want you to put your life in front of anyone else's. You have a lot to live for," John says, wrapping an arm around me.

"Well, if I die, I wouldn't be the key anymore. Besides, I know both your lives would be easier without me. All I do is make your life worse. I have not always made the most logical decisions. I mean, you guys have had to save me two different weekends now," I choke out.

The tears start to roll down my cheeks.

"Our lives would not be better without you!" he barks.

"Sure it would be. I'm sure your life was a lot simpler before you met me. I mean, living with me has to be hard, especially when I'm on my period. I have this fear one day that I'm going to come home to find you with one of my used tampons in your mouth! Life would be easier for Joe not needing to be responsible for a sixteen-year-old girl. I have no friends, and the guy I like will probably never want to see me again. At school, I'm the weird orphaned girl that everyone hates!" I sob. "Sometimes I wish Joe never showed up. Hell, I wish you would have sucked me dry! I mean, I would be dead and you would be immortal."

Okay, now I'm becoming suicidal. Well, I guess I wouldn't take my own life, but if something would happen to me, I probably wouldn't stop it. I do not understand why I am feeling this way too. It is scary.

"It's the bite talking. It is making you super emotional right now. Do you remember when Joe was angry at the world? Being bitten must make you emotional. It will pass," John says, trying to soothe me.

That would make a lot of sense, but my brain doesn't want to believe it. Right now my depression and anxiety are telling me that my life sucks, I'm a nuisance to my brothers, and they probably wish I were dead. I want to go back to when my mom and dad were alive and I was just a normal teenager.

The door opens, and I jump. I am so lost in my own depression I was not expecting anyone to come in the door. Joe and Liam walk in. I'm sure Liam never wants to see me again.

"You're awake!" Joe gasps.

"Knew you would be disappointed." I sigh.

"What is that supposed to mean?" he questions.

"Means the world would be better if I were dead," I reply.

"A bite makes you angry, and it makes her super depressed and suicidal." John shrugs.

"Should we be concerned?" Liam questions.

"It will pass," John replies.

See? No one is concerned about me. Maybe I should just end it. I should apologize to Liam about all this before he leaves forever. "I'm sorry, Liam, that you had to see all this. When I asked you to go hunting with us, I wasn't expecting to get bitten. I understand if you never want to see me again." I sob.

I wasn't trying to make them feel guilty by crying; I cannot control it. I hate being this emotional. Why couldn't I have woken up angry, like Joe? I place my face in my hands and bawl. I wish my life were normal.

"Lizzy, it's okay. Joe explained to me that you got bitten again while looking for John. I know I was supposed to stay in the car, but when Joe rushed to the car and ran back without saying a word, I decided to follow. I stayed far back so I wouldn't be caught. They were arguing, and on the ground I saw your body. That was when I couldn't stay away any longer. I had to make sure you were not dead. They told me no, but I was wary when I saw you and Joe were covered in blood. Joe carried you to the car, and the ride back to the motel was quiet, but I could feel the tension. They took you in the bathroom, and I sat on the bed, trying to piece things together. I could hear them arguing, but I couldn't make out what they were fighting about.

"Joe came out and told me he had to talk to me. We went for a drive, and he explained everything to me. He explained how you were bitten, again, but lost a lot more blood this time. Joe said they gave you the cure and now you had to sleep it off. He believes that since you were bitten twice, your body did not have time to protect itself like normal, but promised you would be okay. The only thing was, you might be a little moody when you wake up since that is part of the cure."

"So you understand?" I questioned.

"Of course I do," Liam says, coming toward me.

Although he is saying it, I don't believe him. He is probably just so uncomfortable seeing me blubber like a baby he is willing to say anything to make me stop. After tonight, he will probably leave and never talk to me again. I'm on to his game. He wraps his arms around me, but I do not hug back. This is a very awkward hug. I don't want to embrace him, because I know I will become more emotional if I do.

"Liam, it is late. Why don't you head back to your room and we will meet up at noon for lunch?" Joe suggests. "You have a lot to think about."

If he agrees, then I know it is because he is in a hurry to get out of here.

"Yeah, you're right. I'm also beat, so I'm going to try to get some sleep. Lizzy, I will see you tomorrow," he says, kissing my head.

See? I knew he didn't want anything to do with me. That kiss was a kiss for goodbye, forever. I watch him walk out the door; he never turns back. To be honest, I don't know if these feelings are still from the bite or if I am acting like a normal emotional teenager.

"Lizzy, how do you feel?" Joe questions.

"I wish I were dead!" I shout and run into the bathroom.

I slam the door, lean against it, and slide down to the floor. Wrapping my arms around my knees, I bawl into the crease of my leg. I am crying so hard I'm physically shaking, and it is causing my headache to come back. How can I shut this off? Do I ride it out or just end my life? I would never end my life, I decide. I know this will be over soon.

After what feels like years, I stop crying and look up. Wiping my eyes, I begin to feel normal again. My mouth is so dry, my head is pounding, and my eyes hurt, so I guess I'm as normal as I can be right now. I go stand up, but my headache does not like that. I sit back down, but this time on the toilet, and hold my head. I flip off the light and sit in the dark. So much better. Maybe it is time to take something and hydrate myself.

"John or Joe, can you bring me a water? And something for headache, please!" I yell, but my voice is hoarse.

That was a stupid idea; yelling makes the pain intensify.

It isn't long until someone opens the door. The light shines in from the other room, and I squint. Joe walks in and hands me a bottle of water and a bottle of pain reliever. I pop the pills in my mouth. My mouth is dry, and the pills stick to my tongue. The taste is disgusting. Washing them down with the water, I drink the whole bottle.

"Thanks," I sigh.

"Do you regret it?" he asks, sitting on the bathtub.

I give him a puzzled look. "Regret what?"

"Living with us," he answers. "Do you wish I hadn't taken custody? Do you really wish you were dead?"

When did I say I didn't want to live with them? Oh yeah, I told John I wished Joe didn't show up to see why we were calling Dad.

"Do you think I am a spoiled brat?" I whisper.

"No. Why?" He tilts his head.

"That was what you said to me after you were bitten. I'm assuming John told you I wished you never showed up. Now that I'm thinking clearer, my life would have never been normal. Either the guy would have come back to kill me or Ethan would have attacked me, and I wouldn't have known why. No one will adopt a sixteen-year-old orphan. I do think John's life would be easier without me, but I do not want to die. You're stuck with me for two years. After that, I can get out of your hair, if you want me to," I explain.

Joe gets up and chuckles. "But if you leave, who is going to cook for us? I like having a home-cooked meal every day. The only thing I would change out of everything is, I wish Dad had told us about you. Then when I had to take you in, you wouldn't always feel like a burden."

"My turn to put my two cents in," John states, standing in the doorway. "You are wrong about a couple of things. My life would not be easier with you out of my life. I'm a vampire—my life hasn't been easy for a long time! Second thing, you will never come home and see a tampon string sticking out of my mouth. The tampon ruins the taste of the blood."

"I'm sorry, John, I didn't mean to say that," I apologize. "I do feel safe around you."

"Yes, you did," John replies. "The bite made what you were feeling intensify. I'm happy it is out in the open, though."

"Wait," Joe says, giving John a weird look. "What do you mean the tampon ruins the taste?"

John shrugs. "I have a past I'm not proud of."

I couldn't help but laugh. Especially because Joe's face looks like he is disgusted.

"Not to change this awkward conversation," I say, still chuckling, "but what did you tell Liam?"

"Exactly what he told you. You got bitten again, lost a little more blood, needed the cure. You looking like death is what happens after you take the cure. If we are being honest here, I'm not impressed with him right now. You are not going off with him alone anytime soon, and if he doesn't talk to you within the next week, I'm going to have a discussion with him, and you will not be able to see him again!" Joe snarls.

"What did he do?" I question.

"I told him if he wants to keep talking to you, he has to be honest with you and you can make the decision afterward if you still want to see him or not," Joe states.

"Will you tell me?" John asks.

"Later." Joe nods.

Now I'm curious what Liam did to piss Joe off. I kind of want to go over there and demand he tell me. Let's see if he does tell me or if I will have to pull it out of him. I decide I'm tired of being in the bathroom, and my headache has disappeared. I stand up, and exhaustion hits me, hard.

"Well, guys, I'm tired. I'm going back to bed. I will see you in the morning. I'll let you two talk between yourselves." I yawn.

"Sleep well," they both say.

I walk to bed and lie down. I'm so tired I am asleep before my head even touches the pillow.

Chapter 19

Finally, I'm starting to feel like my old self again after John bit me. I was attacked on a Thursday, and it is now Wednesday. I don't know where the other days went. Instead of finishing our hunt, John and Joe decided it would be best if they got me home to rest in my own bed. I was thankful for that. I didn't leave my bed at all this last weekend.

Monday and Tuesday were difficult as I had to go to school. They offered to write me a note, but I didn't want to miss my second week. Maybe I should have taken them up on the offer.

Instead of making friends, I feel like I'm making more enemies. There is only one person who will sit by me at lunch now. The rest of them do not want to be associated with me, so they won't be made fun of or be hated. Katrina chooses to ignore the tormenting and stays by my side. More because she never feels like she has many friends herself. High school is so superficial. She has the biggest heart but is made fun of about her appearance. She doesn't put much effort into her looks. Her curly red hair frizzes and strays everywhere, she wears faded clothing, and she has green eyes. What I love about her is she always has a positive attitude and she never lets our classmates get satisfaction in bullying her.

Kat has been so concerned about why I've been so tired the last two days. She doesn't say anything until yesterday, when I am not perky again. When she asks, I just lie and say

I haven't been sleeping well. I feel like she isn't buying it, but she doesn't push the issue. She tells me she knows something isn't right when I would only take a bite of my sandwich and throw the rest of it away. I just smile and thank her for her concern, but I say I would be fine.

Today, when I wake up, I finally have my normal energy back and go for a run in the morning. After school, I have an interview for a part-time job. I get hired on the spot. I even start tomorrow. The job is nothing fancy. It is at the gas station down the street from our place. The owner, Mike, says he knows my brothers and Dad well and he would be honored to hire another McCann. I don't know what he means by that, but I am just excited to get the job. I think getting this job will make me feel somewhat like a normal teen. The problem is, I don't know how my brothers are going to take the news. I never told them I was applying.

Tonight for supper, I'm making spaghetti, with garlic bread, and a salad. When my mom would have bad news for me, this was what she would make. I have to tell my brothers I cannot go hunting this weekend, so I thought it would be a great meal to break the news over. Ironically, this is one of my favorite meals, although bad news always came with it in the past. I'm actually pretty excited about this meal.

The front door opens while I am draining the noodles. Right on time. My heart starts to race a little. I'm afraid they are going to get mad that I went behind their backs and got a job.

"Hey, how was your day?" John asks, coming into the kitchen.

"It was good. Hey, I made garlic bread. Will the smell kill you?" I question.

STEPHANIE TURNER

I never thought of that possibility until now. I mean, vampires and garlic never get along in the movies, but I don't know about real life.

"No, it will not. Except, shouldn't you have asked that before you made the garlic bread? Are you trying to get back at me for almost killing you?" He smiles.

"I kind of forgot that in the books vampires and garlic do not go along, and I really wanted it. Maybe I secretly wanted to kill you?" I shrug while I chuckle. "Supper will be ready in five minutes. Can you set the table, please?"

"Yeah," he answers.

The plates make noise while he grabs them out of the cabinet. He pushes me out of the way to grab the silverware out of the drawer and heads into the dining room. I like that they decided we would sit at the dining room table so we can get away from social media and the news for an hour a day. Sitting down will make it a lot easier for me to break the news to them. I grab the salad and garlic bread and head to the table.

"Yum! It smells amazing, Lizzy," Joe says, sitting down.

"It better," I answer, heading back to the kitchen.

I grab the pasta and take a deep breath for courage. *It will be okay, Lizzy. The worse thing that can happen is they tell you to quit.*

"So, boys, I did something today that I didn't talk to you about," I say, placing the pot on the table.

"What?" Joe asks, serving salad onto his plate.

"I got a job at the gas station down the street. I know you told me to never worry about money, but I want to earn my own. I hate asking for money for things. If I want a new outfit or something, I just don't feel right asking. I start tomorrow," I explain.

I sit down, and they both are looking at me. Joe takes a bite of his salad, and John hands the bowl to me and asks, "So you are going to be working for Mike?"

"What is your schedule going to be?" Joe says while swallowing food.

I feel like these are legit questions. "I know tomorrow is Thursday, and he said I had to work all weekend. So I'm not going to be able to go hunting with you guys."

Studying them both, I cannot tell what they think of this news. John looks fine, but I cannot tell what Joe is thinking. I tap into his feelings, and I can feel annoyance. Is he annoyed that I got this job behind his back?

"If you want to hunt with us, I can talk to Mike and tell him you need weekends off like I had to. He learned a lot from me when I worked there. He was good friends with Dad, so he knew what we did on weekends," Joe states. "You are old enough to stay home alone, so let's see if you can get through one weekend without almost killing yourself."

That last part sounds a little snarky, but I'm happy he isn't making me quit. I should take him up on that offer, about never having to work weekends. I'm actually surprised he is okay leaving me alone by myself.

"Sounds good. So my hours are from four to ten thirty. I'll bring my gun with me. Now, Joe, I have to ask, what are you annoyed about?" I ask, taking a bite of garlic bread.

He swallows what he has in his mouth and glares at me. "Work was just annoying today. Had a customer order something and claim we delivered the wrong things. I apologized and delivered what was on her order within the next hour. When I got there, I had the same stuff our delivery guys had. She started yelling at me about how we do not know how to do our jobs. I pulled up her order, and her face turned pale quickly. She meant to order the items under it but clicked on the wrong button. Then she tried to blame us for making the website so confusing. She demanded she get the stuff she wanted at no charge. I believe that she did it on purpose, but I listened to her. I gave her the stuff she wanted free of charge, and free delivery," he says. "Now, Lizzy, why are you tapping into my feelings?"

That would be frustrating. I'm just happy it had nothing to do with me getting a job. "I wasn't. Your emotions were just strong enough for me to feel without tapping into them."

"Oh, my bad," Joe mumbles.

"Lizzy, do you have any homework?" John asks.

"Nope. I finished before you got home," I answer.

I scoop some noodles onto my plate and stare at them. I don't know why, but I'm just waiting for the bad news to come, even though I'm the one who made them.

After supper, Joe offers to clean up, and John and I go into the living room. I read a book while he is messing around on his laptop. Reading this love story, I hope the main character ends up with someone else. Her true love doesn't seem right for her. My phone vibrates, and Liam's name pops up. We still talk every day, which makes me happy, except he still hasn't talked to me about whatever Joe is mad about.

How are you today?

I type my response:

I'm good. I start a new job tomorrow. I'm not going to lie, I'm excited about it. What are you up to?

After I reply, I shake my head. What teenager is happy to start a new job?

My phone vibrates again.

Can I call you? I need to talk to you about something.

So this is it. Is he finally going to tell me what Joe is keeping a secret?

Sure.

I hit Send and get up.

"Where you going?" John asks.

I can't go anywhere without being questioned. Maybe I just had to go to the bathroom?

"Liam is going to call me. I would like to talk to him in private." I roll my eyes.

Before John can answer, I walk up the stairs. My phone starts to vibrate, but I wait until I'm upstairs before I answer.

"Hello?" I question.

"Hey, Lizzy, I'm sorry, but I need to tell you something. I'm just going to come out and say it, so please do not interrupt," he starts. "The day that we met was actually my first hunt. I was five when my parents divorced, and I lived with my mom. I knew about vampires, but my mom never wanted me to get into it. Once I turned eighteen, I told my dad I wanted to learn. So he trained me for a couple of months before he thought I was ready to go out. That day, I was out with my dad, and I wandered off from him. I thought I would do better on my own and prove to my father that I could do this.

"When I helped your brothers out, I felt like I was successful. When you asked me to go out with you, I thought, this is it, I was born to be a hunter. I'm eighteen, and my dad doesn't have to come on every hunt with me. Unfortunately, I learned I do not have it all figured out. We got caught, and you saved me. My dad never told me there was a cure after being bitten, so when Joe told me he gave it to you, I was confused.

"Finally I, confessed to him I've never had a successful hunt. He was very angry with me. He told me how lucky I was that I was with you and not some amateur hunter. I have a lot to learn. But you are new too."

I don't think he took a single breath during that whole statement.

This is a lot to take in. Part of me is really angry with him right now. He put us in danger. If he was a mature hunter, maybe we wouldn't have been caught off guard.

"You've never hunted before?" I question.

"Not where I actually killed one," he answers.

I push my hair out of my face. I could feel myself growing angrier. "So when I said I've only been hunting for a few months, you didn't feel the need to say anything? You made me believe you've been hunting for a long time. I'm a natural hunter, so we are lucky."

He should have been honest. I've been mostly honest with him about my hunting abilities. How did he think he can just become this amazing hunter overnight?

"I know I should have said something. I am sorry. My dad isn't impressed either. I neglected to tell him I was going out with you guys. I told him I was going to visit my mother for the weekend. He is happy I came back alive. I did tell him how we were attacked but you saved us," he explains.

For the moment, I do not say anything. I need to process everything he just told me. What else has he lied to me about? I hope he didn't tell anyone my secret. Well, I better pretend to forgive him; that way, I can keep him close.

"Thanks for your honesty."

"I really do like you, Lizzy. I just thought I should be honest about everything. I do not think we should hide anything from each other," he states.

Is he being honest because he feels guilty about lying, or is it because he got caught in his own lie?

"That is a good idea. Let's start fresh with a clean slate," I lie.

We talk for two hours after. During the two hours, he tells me his whole life story. When he said no more secrets, he was not lying. Personally, I do not need to know he wet the bed until he was five. I couldn't tell him all my secrets; I just tell him how I ended up in my brothers' custody.

After all this, I get ready for bed and lie down. Once I fall asleep, it isn't restful. I keep dreaming I am out hunting with Liam and he doesn't know what he is doing. I would wake myself up, but when I fall back to sleep, it would start over. It would be a different scenario, but it would always end the same. With Liam dead.

Chapter 20

Last weekend was great. I really enjoyed having some alone time and away from my brothers. All I did was work, do homework, and watch television. Work went so well I'm already on my own.

This weekend, Joe and John have a hunt only thirty minutes from here. They decided to let me have one more weekend to myself, so they are staying at a hotel. Besides work this weekend, I might see if Liam wants to come down tomorrow. I know it is against their rules, but I'm sure they know it will happen eventually. I'll have to text him when I get off tonight.

I pull into the gas station and grab my name badge from the cup holder. Walking in, I am disappointed to see I'm working with Melissa. She is a great worker; she just never interacts with me. She trained me on my first day, but once she found out my name, she became very distant. I think she might be one of the girls who is mad I got Dean suspended from the team.

After clocking in, I get straight to work. If we have no customers, I start by checking the shelves to see what I need to stock. I grab a clipboard from behind the counter and start taking inventory. The first shelf I check, I notice the candy bars are running low. I write down which ones I need to get from the back and glance down to the next shelf. I feel a tap on my shoulder. I turn my head, and Melissa is standing behind me.

"Hey, Elizabeth, can we talk?" she asks.

"Yeah," I say, putting my clipboard on top of the shelf. What am I forgetting to do? I wonder. She walks away, and I give a puzzled look. I suppose I will follow her. She sits down, and I sit across from her. She isn't looking at me; instead, she is watching her thumbs twirl. What does she have to tell me that is making her nervous?

"I know I've been weird around you. I think it is time for me to explain why." She inhales.

"You can just tell me. I will keep an open mind," I reply.

I can feel the nervousness and grief radiating off her. "So it has nothing to do with you, really. It has to do with your brother Joe. My family and him have a history together."

Joe has never mentioned history with another family. What did he do to them? "What kind of history?"

"Well, I had an older sister who was a year younger then Joe. They dated for over six years." She stops.

Is she really holding a grudge with me because her sister and Joe didn't work out? What did Joe do to her sister? Maybe I should just listen and find out. Then I can explain how I didn't know any of this since I have only known him for a few months.

"Joe asked Kiley to go out of town with him. She was excited since she had always been curious about why he always left on the weekends. If she would ask, he would just say 'family stuff.' She was sure he was hiding something, especially because he would always come back with a new bruise. This was her chance to see what he was hiding. Personally, we all thought she was going to come back engaged. My parents loved Joe, and he always treated me like a little sister. He had so much respect for Kiley and our family," she explains.

Melissa is still not looking at me. Did Joe take Kiley out of town to break up with her? What kind of asshole would do that to someone they care about?

"Saturday night came, and all our phones buzzed. It was a picture of the ring, saying, 'Save the date, October 13, 2016.' We were all thrilled. Except a couple of hours later, our home phone rang. My dad answered and heard the worst news of our lives. It was your dad on the other end. He was calling to inform us that Joe and Kiley were in a car accident. They needed to get to the hospital in Denver right away." She stops and wipes her eyes.

"You don't have to go on," I state, grabbing her hand.

"When we got there, Kiley was already dead. Joe survived with a concussion, broken right arm, and two broken ankles. The day of her funeral, Joe was hysterical. Nobody had seen this side of Joe before. He fell to his knees at her casket and started to sob and yell. He kept on saying how it was all his fault, and if he just had her stay home, she would still be alive.

"After the funeral, he would come over to our house every day to see if my parents needed anything. When they would say no, he would just hang out in her room to reminisce. She might have been twenty-two, but she still lived at home, doing online classes. After a couple of months, he just quit showing up. He also changed, and not in a good way. Now, when he sees me, he pretends he doesn't know me. Kiley's death may have been a few years ago, but it still feels fresh. Now I have to know, What happens at these family events? I know you have to know. I see bruises on you too." She cries.

Why would Melissa think something different happened to Kiley? This is the first time I have heard anything about Kiley. I will have to talk to Joe about her on Sunday when he returns.

I put my hand in her hand, and she finally glances up at me. I give her a weak smile.

"Nothing happens at these family events. My dad's side is really into self-defense and tae kwon do. When we get together, we have tournaments against one another. I've only been doing it for the last couple of months, but I'm happy to report, I am in the winning bracket," I lied.

"Would Kiley have come back with bruises on her? I mean, if she weren't in the car accident?" she pries.

"I don't think so," I answer. "I'm going to be honest, I've only been part of this family for a couple of months, and Joe has never told me anything about Kiley. What I do know about Joe is he is a protector. He would have done anything in his power to keep her safe. I'm sure when he found out she died and he survived, it killed him inside. I know he seems like he is a big tough guy, but inside I think he is a big teddy bear. I'm sure Joe wishes things had ended differently. I'm sure he wishes his life were different too."

I'm sure he would hate that I just called him a big teddy bear, but that is how I see him.

"That would explain why Joe never told me that he has a younger sister." She smiles.

"My dad was a very private person. Joe found out about me after he died." I shrug.

The door opens, and the bell rings to let us know a customer has just walked in. A chill runs down my spine, and I close my eyes. "Melissa, this is going to sound weird, but I need you to get in the cooler. I need you to be safe," I whisper.

"What? Why?" she asks.

"Whoever just entered is a threat. I have a sixth sense for danger, and I can tell when I'm not in a safe spot. Right now, I'm getting that eerie feeling about these people. Please just do as I say. I promise I will be fine," I mumble. "When you walk in, you need to act normal."

She gives me a puzzled look, but I counter with a pleading one. She nods and gets up. "Hey, I'm going to go stock the cooler. Let me know if it gets too busy."

"Sounds good. Stay warm!" I chuckle.

I watch to make sure she gets in the cooler safely before I get up and walk behind the counter. Glancing around the store, I spot two biker men walking around. I slowly grab the gun from my pants and put it under the counter. I hope these two are just passing through. Personally, I do not feel like fighting today.

The bigger guy comes up to check out. He still has his sunglasses on, which I find odd. He has dark hair—I believe he is Native—and is wearing leather. I feel like I know him from somewhere before, but I cannot put my finger on it. He puts down two energy drinks and says, "Some cigs too, sweetheart."

I nod and turn around to grab him some. When I circle back to face him, his glasses are off. I drop the cigarettes, gasp, and jump back. Under his eye is the dog tattoo. This is the man who murdered my mom. How did he find me?

"I see you remember me, honey." He smiles.

I want to run, but my only exit is blocked by his buddy. I grab my gun from under the counter and point it at them. He doesn't step back; instead, he starts laughing. Is he not afraid of dying?

"I'm not what you think I am. Those wooden bullets will not hurt me. In fact, it will just tickle a little. Besides, I do not want to hurt you," he informs me.

"Is that what you told my mom right before you killed her?" I spit back. "Why would I trust you?"

"I will be the first to admit, that got out of hand. I never wanted anyone to get hurt. When I came to your house, I just wanted to talk to you, but she wouldn't let me near you," he answers.

I glare at him, but I don't put the gun down. "What do you want?"

He smiles while he leans in a little. The gun is now pressed right against his chest. "Now, I just want a little blood."

"Sorry, it isn't for sale," I say, cocking the hammer.

"Oh, honey, you do not understand. I am not asking for the blood. I'm taking it, whether you like it or not." He snaps his fingers.

I attempt to fire the gun, but his buddy grabs me from behind before I can shoot him. I drop the gun and start to fight. Luckily, I get the upper hand and flip him over my shoulder, and he lands on the floor. I jump over him and try to get away, except he grabs my leg. I fall face-first onto the tile, and it's a good thing my chin is there to break my fall. Using my arms and other leg, I try to get out of his grip, but he keeps pulling me closer to him. Turning myself onto my butt, I use my free leg and kick him right in the face and knock him out cold. My foot comes loose, and I pull my phone out of my pocket and hit Joe's number on speed dial. The other man goes to grab it, and I throw it across the store before he could. I watch my phone bounce and slide to the other side of the store. I hope that call went through!

"What are you doing, bitch?" the leader yells.

He steps on my fingers, and I let out a cry. He is crushing my fingers with his heavy boots. Desperately, I try to use my other hand to pry my fingers free, but it is no use since he is bigger than me. The pain is so unbearable I'm sure my fingers are broken. Even with all the pain, I know I have to do something. With my free hand, I reach up, grab his crotch, pull down, and twist. It works; he drops to his knees, and my throbbing hand becomes free. I sit up and punch him in the face, but it doesn't seem to faze him. His black eyes glare into mine. Is he looking into my soul right now? Is he going to kill me?

"You fucking bitch!" he yells.

He pushes me over onto my back. My head bounces on the floor, and I try not to think of the pain that comes with it. Before I can react to anything, he sits on top of me. He is so heavy he is squishing my lungs. He has to be a good two hundred pounds heavier than me. I struggle to breathe, but I try to fight by punching him in the stomach. That has no effect on him; he just grabs my arms and pins them over my head. The guy I knocked out comes crawling over to me, and I look over at him. He sticks a needle in my arm, and I try to pull it away. He takes the needle out of my arm and grabs my hair to pull my head to the side to expose my neck. Is this guy a vampire? If he bites me, he is going to die. The other man sitting on top of me might end up killing me. If I do not suffocate first. He sticks another needle in my neck.

"What the fuck!" I scream.

The needle hurts worse than a vampire bite. When he pulls it out, the leader looks down and smiles. "Thank you, sweetie. Don't worry, we are not going to kill you. Also, by tomorrow you will not remember any of this. Bye."

He kisses my forehead and climbs off me. I cup my hand over the injection site and sit up just to watch them walk out the door. I get myself off the floor and run to the cooler. When I open the door, I find Melissa sitting in the corner in the fetal position.

"Are you okay?" she gasps.

"Yeah. A little beat up, but I'll be fine." I smile.

Walking over to her, I put my hand out to help her up. When she gets to her feet, she embraces me in a hug. I don't know what it is for, but it is nice. I cannot help but hug her back. I need to act like I'm not terrified of this situation. I need to stay strong for Melissa.

"I peeked out and saw them attacking you. I wanted to help, but I didn't know what to do. My phone had no service in here, so I couldn't even call the police. I felt so helpless standing in this cooler. How did you know? I mean, they walked in, and you told me to get in the cooler. How did you know they were dangerous without even looking at them?" she questions, letting go of me.

"As I said before, I have a sixth sense when it comes to danger." I shrug.

"I guess it is a good thing to have. Except, why didn't you hide if you knew you were in danger?" Melissa pushes.

I sigh. "Because I knew they had to be after me. I somehow always find danger, or it finds me. I didn't want you to get hurt, so I knew I couldn't hide. I'm good at protecting myself."

She gives me a weak smile. "I'm just happy you are okay. Why don't you go sit down? I'm going to close the store for the moment. Afterward, I'm going to call Mike, the police, and help you clean up your chin. You are bleeding everywhere."

I put my hand up to my chin, and when I pull it away, it is covered in blood. The adrenaline starts to wear off, and I realize I'm in more pain than I thought I was. Part of me does not want to get the police involved, though.

"No, don't call the police. Besides, I'm fine, and they didn't take anything from the store," I say in a rush.

"What? We have to call the police. They assaulted you!" she states.

She does have a point. Besides, he did murder my mom, and who says they will not come back for me again? "You are right. I need to let the police know that one of the guys was involved with the murder of my mom also."

"What?" she gasps.

"Anyway, I better go grab my phone," I reply.

"Then, will you sit down so I can clean up your chin?" she begs.

"Yes, I will." I swallow.

I start to feel weird, but I think it is just anxiety. As I walk toward my phone, my legs start to feel like Jell-O. I stop for a second, close my eyes, and try to regroup. I inhale and exhale slowly a couple of times. When I open my eyes again, everything is blurry. What is going on with me? I bend over to pick up my phone, and I almost fall headfirst. If it weren't for the fact I put my hands out to catch myself, I would have hit my head. Slowly, as I try to stand up straight, the room starts to spin.

"It's okay, Lizzy, you are just worked up. Walk back and sit down at the table," I say to myself out loud.

The first step forward and I trip over my own feet and crash into the shelves. Everything comes tumbling down on top of me. "Way to go, Elizabeth!"

I try to get up, but I cannot. I am too weak, and the room just keeps spinning, and now I'm feeling nauseous.

"Lizzy, are you okay?" Melissa asks, running up to me.

Well, I think it is Melissa; I cannot make out her face.

"I don't know," I admit.

I do not feel as bad as the day John bit me, but this is a very close second. I try to stand up, but I fall right back to the floor. This time I give up and just lie on the cool tile. It feels good on my skin right now. I feel like I'm burning up. I will lie right here and wait for help, I decide.

Chapter 21

Opening my eyes, at first, I don't know where I am. My vision is blurry, and my head is pounding. Blinking a few times helps my eyes refocus. Glancing around, I realize I'm in my own room. How in the hell did I end up here? Did the cops bring me home? Did I even talk to the cops? Wait, why did I have to talk to them again?

I have so many questions, but I don't have any answers. Something I really want to know is why my mouth is so dry. I need a drink of water now. I crawl out of bed, and I am really weak. Slowly I walk out of my room and head down the stairs. Fearing I might fall, I take each step one at a time. When I get to the living room, I am surprised to see Joe and John sitting on the couch. "What are you guys doing back?"

It feels like I swallowed a bunch of cotton. I do not wait for their answer; I head into the kitchen and grab a bottle of water. When I turn back, I jump and almost fall backward. Both Joe and John are right behind me.

"We are happy to see you are awake. Do you not remember calling us yesterday?" John asks.

I take a drink of water and think about it. I shake my head no while I down the whole bottle.

"You were attacked and drugged at work yesterday. You really think we would let you stay home alone after that?" Joe explains, crossing his arms.

I give him a puzzled look. "I was not attacked yesterday."

What do they mean? I remember going to work and needing to talk to the police. Maybe the store was robbed and that was why I needed to talk to them.

"What do you remember of yesterday?" John quizzes.

I try to remember, but nothing major sticks out. "I went to school, and then work. To be honest, yesterday is kind of a blur. I know I needed to talk to the cops about something, but I do not remember why."

"Elizabeth, you were at work and someone came in and attacked you. When we got there, the paramedics were just arriving. John rode to the hospital with you, and I stayed to try to figure out what happened. While you were in the ER, they stitched up your chin and did some blood work. The test results came back that you had drugs in your system. John ensured them you don't do drugs and you had to have been drugged.

"Luckily, the surveillance cameras confirmed John's suspicions. They injected you with something. The doctor wanted to keep you until you woke up, but since there was nothing they could do but monitor you, John signed the papers to let you come home. You do have to talk to the police sometime with your statement. I will take you there in a couple of hours. We have the tape here if you would like to see what happened yesterday," Joe explains. "We are trying to figure out who the guys are and why they targeted you."

I nod, and we walk to the dining room. I sit down, and Joe places his laptop in front of me. Hitting Play, I watch it play out in front of me. It is weird seeing me on the screen but having no recollection of this. Melissa leaves the booth to go into the cooler.

"Why did she leave you?" John asks.

"I don't know," I state. "I think I might have asked her to." It starts coming back to me a little. "I think I felt like they were dangerous."

"So you felt its presence?" Joe quizzes.

Never taking my eyes off the screen, I respond, "Yes, but he was something different. When I pointed my gun at him, he told me the wooden bullet wouldn't kill him."

Each part of this brings back a new memory. In the video I start to fight. This is the first time I have watched myself fight, and I must say, I'm all right.

"I'm not disappointed in your fight technique. If this were a fair fight, you would have won. You never backed down. That is one thing I was worried about when Mel said you were fighting them, that maybe you just gave up," John admits.

I am appalled he thought I would back down from a fight. "I've never lost a fight on purpose."

I'm happy he isn't disappointed in my fighting technique.

The main guy turns to look at the camera, and I gasp when I see his face. I shoot up and knock over the chair I am sitting in. The bang of the chair hitting the floor makes me squeal. The tears start to escape my eyes while fear takes over my body.

"What is it?" Joe pushes, putting his hand on my shoulder.

Glancing down and crossing my arms, I try to comfort myself. I inhale and exhale a few times, but it isn't helping. Dropping to my knees, I just start sobbing into my hands. Seeing that guy and being in the comfort of my own house lets me show my true emotions. He terrifies me.

"Lizzy?" Joe whispers.

Looking up at him, I wipe my eyes. "The bigger man who has me pinned down," I say, sniffling loudly, "he was one of the guys who attacked me when my mom was killed."

"Elizabeth…," John states.

"He told me things got out of hand that day. He never wanted my mom to be killed, she just got in the way. The guy explained that all he wanted to do was talk to me, but my mom wouldn't let him anywhere near me. Which if he wanted to talk to me, then why did he take some of my blood yesterday?" I sob.

John wraps me in a side hug. I grab his arm and cry into his sleeve. This is all becoming too much. I don't know how much more of this I can take.

"Did they say what he was going to do with your blood?" Joe asks.

I pull out of the hug and wipe my eyes. "No," I say, standing back up. "All I wanted to have was a couple of weekends of a normal life. Is that too much to fucking ask for? You know what I had planned this weekend? I was going to work and then call Liam. I was going to see if he would be willing to come see me today. Yes, I know it is against your rules, but what teenager doesn't break the rules at times? I appreciate everything you guys have done for me, don't get me wrong, but I'm tired of always being around you. I just want space."

Okay, I know I might be throwing a fit, but I feel like I have every right to do so. If I had a normal life, I would have been going out on the weekends to get away from my parents; instead, I'm with my brothers all the time because I have few friends.

"We agree, we need space from you too. That is why I called Liam. Him and his dad are doing a hunt not far from here, and his dad agreed to have you tag along. Of course, we are going to be paying for your motel room. I know I said you cannot go hunting with him, but I think with his dad supervising, it will not be bad. They should be here tonight sometime, and you will be with them until Monday," Joe explains.

Glancing up at him all wide-eyed in disbelief, I wonder, Did he really say he was sending me away with the guy I like?

"Really? What about school on Monday?" I question.

"Do not worry about that. I'll take care of it," John states.

I somehow get more energy and start to jump up and down. This is just what I need. "So why exactly are you letting me go with Liam?"

"Do you not want to?" Joe raises an eyebrow.

"No, no, no, I do. I just want to know why!" I put my hands up in panic. I hope he doesn't change his mind.

"I just figured you need to get away without us. Since his dad is a hunter, I figured you cannot get in too much trouble with him." Joe shrugs. "But on a sidenote, are you okay? I mean, a minute ago you were having a meltdown. Will you be okay to go?"

I take a deep breath. "Yeah, I will be."

John nods. "Okay, why don't you go get a little rest? Joe can take you to the station later to get your statement. After, you can come back and get ready to go with Liam."

"That sounds great, except I'm not ready to talk to the police yet. I need to figure out how to tell them without breaking down," I explain.

Before they answer, I turn and walk away. I head back to my room and lie down. Grabbing my phone, I notice I have four messages.

> *Joe*
> *Elizabeth! Why are you not answering my calls? We are on our way back!*

Liam
Hello, beautiful, how are you?

Liam
Joe just called me and told me what hap-
pened. Text me when you wake up.

Unknown number
Hey, I lost my phone sometime today. So this
is my dad's number. We will pick you up
around seven. Cannot wait to see you.
—Liam

I know I should text Liam back, but I don't. Putting my phone back on my bedside table, I wrap myself in a cocoon of safety. I try to nap, but instead I think about everything that has happened in the last twenty-four hours. How did that guy find me here?

Chapter 22

After tossing and turning for an hour, I decide I should just get up and get my statement over with. Joe takes me to the station, and the cops write everything down. I'm happy they now have video evidence of the guy they are looking for. Of course, during the statement, they make me go into details about the morning of the murder. It is hard, but I make it through without crying for once. After about two hours at the station, we are free to head home.

When we get home, I go straight to my room to start packing. I just need to get away from these four walls and my brothers. I know Liam's dad will be with us, but I'm still really happy to see him again.

My phone chimes, and I grab it. It is a message from Liam's phone. He must have finally found it.

> *Hey, can you meet me and my dad? I will send you our location. Dad has a feeling there is a vampire around here. It is only a couple of miles away from your house. Leave your bags and we will pick them up later.*

I do not think Joe and John are going to go for this, but it doesn't hurt to ask.

> *I'll ask, but I cannot guarantee anything.*

I zip up my suitcase and head for my dresser. In the top drawer, under all my socks and underwear is where I keep my hunting supplies. Grabbing everything, I head down the stairs. When I get to the bottom, I am surprised by what I see. The guys are sitting on the couch, watching some kind of sporting event. This is the most normal I have seen them. Normally, they are looking up where their next hunt is going to be.

"Hey, guys, I got a message from Liam. They are only a few miles from here, and they think they found something. Liam is wondering if I can just meet up with them now and come back to get my stuff later. I promise I will be careful and not die," I ask with a smile.

"Where is a few miles from here?" John quizzes.

Well, it isn't an instant no like I thought it would be. John didn't even look at me when he asked; this game really has their attention.

"I can text you the location that he sent me. That way, if something happens, you can find us," I answer.

I screenshot the message and send it to both of them. Both phones chime.

"So can I go?"

I am becoming eager. I just really want to see Liam again.

"Hold up, do you have everything?" Joe finally says, getting up, walking toward me.

Rolling my eyes, I nod. Yes, I'm aware I should be more grateful that they are letting me go, but I am a teenager. It's programmed in me to be annoyed with my guardian. He is next to me, so I turn around and lift my shirt to show my gun. After, I pull up my pant leg to show my stake, and dig in my pocket to pull out the extra wooden bullets. "And my phone is in my pocket. Did I miss anything?"

"Your jacket. It might get cold." Joe smirks.

"Is that a yes?" I ask.

I am becoming more impatient the longer he is taking to answer. Part of me thinks he is just going to say no, and I will throw a fit if he does. I want to see Liam, and I do not want to wait until he is done with the hunt.

"I don't see why not. You gave us the address. Go have fun." Joe smiles.

I really want to give him a hug right now. He has done so much for me, and I don't think I let him know often enough how much I appreciate it. I cannot imagine a life without them anymore.

"Well, I will see you guys later. Thanks again! It isn't that I don't appreciate you, but I need to get away," I explain.

"Lizzy, we are sick of you too!" John chuckles.

"I love you guys," I state.

Wow, that just slips right out. I turn away and want to run out the door. How did I just say that? Now things are going to be awkward when I get back home.

"Lizzy," Joe says.

"Yes?" I answer, not looking at him.

"We love you too," he replies.

"Love you, Lizzy!" John agrees.

I do not think I can smile any bigger.

Heading out the door, I squint straight ahead of me. The sun is still bright, which means I can find them without a flashlight. I pull out my phone and put the location in my GPS. It is only a mile away. I lock my phone and put it in my back pocket.

Walking up the driveway, I decide when I get to the road, I will run to the location. Heading north, I run a good three-fourths of a mile before my phone tells me to turn left. Walking down into the ditch, I duck under a barbed wire fence. I'm not trespassing at all. This field is full of trees. I duck and move branches out of the way. Finally, when I duck under a big birch tree, my GPS says I have reached my destination. It is a big open field, but I do not see anyone. Where are they hiding?

"Liam?" I whisper, looking around.

There is no answer, so I pull out my phone to text him.

> *Where are you? I thought you said you were here?*

I am about to hit Send, but I don't. I can sense I am in danger. I drop my phone and turn around. I'm able to make it half a turn before everything goes black.

Starting to wake up, I feel my head pounding. How was I attacked again? I raise my arm up to my head, but something is stopping me. I go to move the other, but that one isn't budging either. My eyes shoot open, and the light is bright. I have to blink a few times to get my eyes to refocus.

Glancing around, I do not recognize anything. It almost looks like a basement. I look at my arms, and they are chained to the headboard of a bed. I lift my head and notice my legs are chained also. What are Liam and his dad doing to me? I try fighting, but the chains will not budge.

"Lizzy," I hear.

I'm not alone.

I turn my head to the right, and there is someone across the room. He is standing, but his hands are chained above his head, and his feet are shackled to the floor. Taking a closer look, I realize it is John, except he is in his vampire form.

"Lizzy, your necklace is off. You smell delicious!" he hisses, fighting the chains.

"John, do you know where we are?" I ask.

"No. Whoever has us tranquilized me to knock me out. They took your necklace off to attract me to the spot you were sent to. I woke up an hour before you." He fights the chains again. "I'm sorry, I'm trying to resist your blood, but my instincts are stronger than I thought. The longer I'm with you, the more I crave your blood!"

A lump forms in my throat, and I swallow hard. John as a vampire scares me more than anything. I know he is a vampire, but normally I do not think of it much.

"Johnny, I know you can fight it!" I say desperately.

"I'm trying. I want your blood now!" he hisses. "Especially because I know what it tastes like."

I hate hearing John talk about my blood. I know it isn't my brother talking, but it is part of him.

The door opens, and I whip my head straight to see who is walking in. Of course it is my worst fear. My eyes widen when he walks in and sits next to me. It is the same man who attacked me yesterday. I would recognize that tattoo anywhere.

"Oh, good, you are awake." He smiles.

I try to swallow the lump in my throat. "Who are you? What do you want from me?"

I put on a brave face, but my voice is shaking. I'm going to end up dead by the end of this; I just know. Either this guy kills me or John gets loose and eats me.

"Don't worry, I mean no harm toward you. My name is Randy, and you and I are very special. Lizzy, I need your help," he explains.

How does he know my name? What does he mean by we are both special? Why does he think I'm just going to help him after all this?

"If you need my help, why don't you just ask like a normal person? Instead, you kill my mother and attack me twice. What makes you think I'm going to help you now?" I snarl.

John's chains rattle again. I look over at him, and he is in his complete vampire form. It almost petrifies me to look at him. Personally, I do not know who I am more scared of, Randy or John.

"Easy, vamp boy. I do not want to kill you. You are going to help us too. I will give you some blood in a bit." Then he turns to me. "Lizzy, to answer your questions, like I said before, I never meant for your mother to be killed. I came over asking her if I could talk to you. When she asked what I wanted to talk to you about, she freaked out and attacked me first. Out of instinct, my friends and I fought back. We never meant it to go that far. The only reason we attacked you that same day was that you attacked first. I grabbed you and told you I wanted to talk, but instead you headbutted me. I did kill my friend for killing your mom," he explains.

Does he think I'm supposed to help him just because he killed his friend? This guy is mental! "You think I'm going to willingly help you? Then you are crazier than I thought you were!"

Why am I talking back to him? It just gives him more reason to kill me. Maybe I should hear him out, but who knows if he will tell me the truth, anyway?

"Well, I'm not stupid. I know you are not going to help me willingly. That is why I tied you to the bed. You are going to help me, whether you like it or not. I'm not giving you a choice this time. If I tried talking to you, it isn't like you would listen to me, anyway," he states, crawling on top of me.

"What the hell are you doing?" I fight.

The chain keeps me from defending myself. He unbuttons my pants and pulls them down, exposing my bottom half. Screaming, I try moving my body back and forth, but it doesn't help. He holds me down and slams himself inside me. The pain is unbearable; each time he slams into me, I cry out. Finally, after what feels like a lifetime, he crawls off me.

I lie there and cry. Why is this happening to me? How is this helping him? There is no way that if he asked me to do this, I would have let him. Every time I think my life cannot get worse, it proves me wrong. Who did I piss off to deserve this life?

"I'll be back with both of your meals later," he says, walking out.

He leaves but leaves my pants down. Now I'm lying here exposed right in front of my brother. To make things worse, I was raped and there was nothing John and I could do about it.

I do not want to feel anymore. I look over at John. "Will you kill me, please?"

I close my eyes and shut down. I wish Randy would kill me already.

Time passes, and he comes in and tries to make me eat. I just keep my eyes closed and ignore him. It is hard to ignore him when he is on top of me. While he is raping me, I just lie there and let the tears run down my face. Finally, I am able to shut down all the way and not feel anything anymore.

I do not know how much time has passed, but I open my eyes and stretch. I feel like I got the best night's sleep of my life. I sit up and see John still dangling in front of me. He looks like he is becoming weak. I stand up and remember I *was* trapped. How did I get free? I don't care; I just have to go get help.

"Don't worry, Johnny, I'll go get help," I state.

He doesn't look up at me or even acknowledge me. "John?"

I hesitantly walk up to him, and he glances up. He looks straight into my eyes. It is like he is looking right through me. It makes me feel uneasy.

"Elizabeth, please wake up. Whatever you do, don't give up," he whispers and fights the chains.

"I won't give up. I'm right here," I answer.

I am confused. Why would he be telling me to wake up.

I turn around and gasp when I see myself still lying in the bed. Tiptoeing to myself, I realize I look so broken. Am I dead?

"John, am I dead?" I ask, knowing he wouldn't answer.

"Your heart is so faint. Please don't give up." It is like he is answering me.

Well, that is good to know, that I'm still alive—barely, but alive nonetheless. "Don't worry, John, I will get us help."

I walk up to the door and am curious if I can walk through it. I back up to give myself a running start and run straight into the door. I bounce back, and the impact knocks me off my feet and I land on my butt. "Ouch."

It doesn't hurt; I just didn't know what else to say. I stand up and dust myself off. I am walking back toward the door when it suddenly swings open. I jump back so I don't get hit. Randy storms in. I sneak out as I don't want to see what he is going to do to me. It was bad enough having to live through it; I do not need to watch it.

Running up the stairs, I stop at the top. How do I get out of here? Glancing around, I spot a door and hope it is my way out. When I open it, I am relieved to see the outside. It is bright outside, but I cannot feel the sun. It is like I am numb to everything. I'm not going to let that bother me, though. I need to go find help. I run up the driveway and stop. Which way do I go? I've never been out here before. I don't know where I'm at. I close my eyes to see if I can connect to Joe. When I open my eyes, I can feel him. I am surprised that works. And he feels close.

I head east for about a half-mile before my path is blocked by trees. All the trees are dead in this area. This cannot be the right way. I mean, how would he get to his house with all these trees? When I turn to the right, I spot a hidden road. I guess that is one way to make sure your house is never found. I run down the road, and before I know it, I'm out of the trees.

In front of me is a beautiful lake. Forgetting what my mission is for a second, I walk toward the lake. I just want to admire it for a second. Before I get all the way to the shore, something catches my attention. I turn my head to the left, and I see Joe. Excitement comes over me, thinking we are finally safe. My heart sinks when I realize he isn't alone. Liam and another guy are with him. I can only assume that is Liam's dad. They are walking in the wrong direction. Somehow, I need to get Joe to turn around.

I run toward them, and my speed is superfast. Part of me wishes I were this fast in real life. When I catch up to them, they are in a middle of a conversation.

"Are you 100 percent sure it is here, Liam?" Joe grumbles.

"Yes, I remember fishing in that lake," Liam answers.

"Well, we have been searching for twelve hours, and I haven't seen a path yet!" Joe fights.

"Joe!" I shout, knowing he cannot hear me.

I touch his shoulder, and he turns to look at me. I know he cannot see me, but I think he can feel me. "Joe, you need to come this way."

I pull on his arm, and he looks down at it.

"Come on, I know you can feel that. You need to help us," I plead.

He glances back at the two guys but does not say anything. Instead, he starts walking in the right direction. Grabbing his wrist, I lead him to the path. I keep pulling him, but he stops. I turn to see why he has stopped and see his eyes are wide and looking straight ahead.

"Joe, what are you doing?" the older guy asks, following.

I glance behind Joe, and they are both close behind.

"Wait, is that a vampire carrying someone?" Liam questions.

I spin around and see that Liam is correct. I walk closer to the vamp and freeze. It is John, covered in blood. In his arms, dangling lifelessly, is me. "No," I whisper.

"Get your gun ready, Liam," the guy said.

"No!" I shout.

I do not care if John killed me; he doesn't deserve to die.

"No, wait!" Joe says. "Call the police. I'm going to deal with this vampire."

"What?" the guy objects.

"Do what I say. I think the person in his arms is Lizzy. If you shoot him, you might hit her. So go call for help. I will deal with him," Joe directs.

Thank God Joe saves the day. I watch while Joe walks closer to John and me.

"Johnny, say it isn't so," he whispers.

"She is still alive, but barely. This isn't her blood. I killed the motherfucker who did this to us. Take her quickly. I cannot resist her blood much longer. I will be back!" John hisses.

John saved me? I knew he could do it!

As soon as John hands me to Joe, John runs off. This feels like a dream, watching my lifeless body dangle in Joe's arms. I stay next to him. I need to know what is going to happen to my body.

"You just let him go?" Liam questions.

"He saved Lizzy. I had no reason to kill him," Joe answers.

He puts me on the ground and goes into his trunk. I stay with my lifeless body. God, this is weird.

"He was covered in blood. Are you sure it wasn't hers?" Liam questions.

"He didn't say, but Lizzy doesn't look like she has been bitten," Joe says, coming back to me.

He kneels down by me and covers me up with a blanket. He then pulls my necklace out of his pocket and puts it on me. When it latches, a weird feeling hits me. I cannot explain it, but something is happening. I can hear sirens from the distance. Pulling up next to us are two cop cars, an ambulance, and a fire truck. Everyone gets out at the same time and runs over to Joe.

"Her name is Elizabeth McCann. She was kidnapped two days ago. We just found her, but she needs help," Joe says to the paramedics.

It is weird watching them do a workup on me. They put a neck brace on me and put me on a stretcher.

"Sir, why didn't you file a missing person report?" one of the police officers asks.

"Because he thought she was with me." I jump when I hear John's voice. I turn, and he is walking back toward us.

He looks like himself again. The blood has been washed off, and he is in different clothes. I just want to give him a hug, but I can't. Not yet, anyway. I notice some scratches on his arms, and bruises where the chains were holding him.

"Lizzy and I went for a hike, and we told Joe we were going to camp out by the lake for the night. Instead, we were both attacked and held hostage. I was chained to the ceiling, while Lizzy was tied to a bed. I watched as he raped her multiple times a day. Finally, I fought hard enough that the chains broke. I sneaked upstairs to see where he was, and I found him dead in his living room. Something or someone killed him.

"His big picture window was broken. Something must have gotten in and enjoyed themselves a little. I thought about hiding in the basement before whatever snacked on him found me and decided it was still hungry. I found the keys hanging by the basement door, and I grabbed them to free Lizzy. I was running for help, and thankfully, I ran into Joe. I told him to call for help and gave him Lizzy. While I could have waited for help myself, my conscience wouldn't let me leave until I knew for a fact the attacker was dead. Unfortunately, when I got back, that was when I saw his neck was ripped out by whatever attacked him. I will be happy to show you where this all took place. He is still in his living room," John explains.

"Officer Jane and Officer Neil will go with you. I will go to the hospital with them," one of the officers directs.

John leads the officers back into the trees. When I turn around to see what my body is doing, they are loading me up in the ambulance.

"I'm going with. I'm her guardian, and she is only sixteen," Joe says. "Brad, will you drive the car to the hospital?"

The older guy nods. "Will do."

Joe throws the keys to Brad and gets in the back of the ambulance. It isn't long until I am alone. Personally, I need proof that Randy is dead, so I decide to go back to the house. I wonder if I can magically transport myself. I close my eyes and picture the house, and when I open my eyes, I am there. This would have been a nice way to find Joe, but then I wouldn't know how to get him to where he needed to go if I didn't run it myself.

Cautiously, I walk into the living room, and there is Randy, lying in a puddle of blood. Slowly approaching him, I see John ripped out his neck. Hearing voices from a distance makes me realize they are down in the basement. I do not need to see that. I have seen enough, and I want to get back to my body. I close my eyes and focus on my body. When I open my eyes, I'm in a waiting room. Joe is sitting there alone.

"God, I know I have my doubts about you, but if you are there, please help my sister. She never asked for any of this. Please just stay with her. Please," he cries.

I walk up to him. It breaks my heart seeing the tears run down his face. Sitting in the chair next to him, I put a comforting hand on his shoulder. He doesn't acknowledge me; instead, he hides his face in his hands.

"I'm right here, Joe," I whisper.

I lay my head on his shoulder and just listen to him quietly sob.

"Find anything out?" The older guy walks in with Liam.

"They are still running tests. They will let me know when they know something," Joe mumbles. He looks up and wipes his eyes.

"Joe!" someone shouts.

John runs in, and Joe stands and embraces him in a hug. This makes my heart hurt. I want to hug them both and let them know everything will be okay.

"Johnny, I'm so proud of you," Joe admits.

"The way I was feeling is so weird. One minute I wanted to eat her, and the next minute I wanted to kill the guy who was holding us captive. Each time he raped her, I could push back my instincts and became the protective big brother. I felt so useless not being able to protect her from that," John explains. "She was giving up. After he raped her for the first time, she wouldn't fight. She just lay there and took whatever he wanted to do with her. I've never seen her just give up. Her heart was so faint today I knew she was dying. I had to do something. Finally, the last time he crawled on her, I broke the chains, forgot about her blood, and ripped his throat out. I am happy you were close. I could smell you and followed your scent," John explains.

"Wait, what?" the older man questions.

I need to get back to my body to wake up. These two need me, and I need them.

They let go of the hug and sit down.

"I'm happy you saved her. Even though I had fear, deep down I knew you could control yourself," Joe praises John. "Now we just have to wait. They are running tests right now. I told them they couldn't take the necklace off again. So I guess you will be the one who tells me if they listen or not."

I sure hope they listen. I really should go find my body.

"Wait, John, are you a vampire?" Liam asks. "Are you the vampire we saw with Lizzy in your hands?"

I am curious how they are going to lie about this one. I mean, why else would John want to eat me?

"Yes, I am," John admits.

Wait, what? He just casually admits he is a vampire? Why would he do that?

"Liam, you learned that Lizzy is the key to the supernatural world. Now you know that John is a vampire. Are you going to blab that to someone too? It is your fault that Lizzy is here. This all could have been avoided if you had just asked us the questions you had!" Joe snarls.

"So you could lie to me again!" Liam yells.

"Liam, I'm sorry, but I agree, this is your fault," the older guy states. "I wish you had come to me with your questions. I told you, you were not ready for this, but you had to show me you knew otherwise. Now look what happened. Lizzy is in the hospital, and your brother is dead. I'm mad John killed him, but at the same time I cannot blame him. I would have killed someone who did that to my sister too. Now I have a lot to think about. We are going to be under investigation because we are related to the person who did the kidnapping."

So this is Liam's fault. I knew it.

"Wait, how did you find us?" John asks.

"After you ran out, Liam and Brad showed up. After some interrogation, I found out Liam told Randy about Lizzy. Brad has known about Lizzy since she was little. He knew that Randy had to have Lizzy after he found out she was attacked a few days ago. I showed him the video of the attack, and he confirmed that was his son. I didn't know where you were, but once I found Lizzy's necklace, I knew you had to be close. Liam knew where Randy liked to hide out, so that was how we got here," Joe explains.

That's it; I've heard enough. I just hope I remember all this when I wake up. I close my eyes, and when I open them back up, I am standing over my body. I don't even recognize myself. I have wires everywhere along with IVs coming from each arm. I grab my hand, close my eyes, and that is the last thing I remember before everything goes black.

Chapter 23

My eyes pop open, and the room is dark. Did he shut off the lights?

"John?" I try to say, but my throat is so dry no sound comes out.

Not moving, I glance around the room with my eyes. I see a machine with numbers on it. Did Randy take me to the hospital? Wouldn't he be afraid that I would squeal on him for kidnapping me? He did say he didn't want me to die, but this seems stupid, even for him. Unless he is still in the room and is never going to leave my side. If that is the case, I am going to be kidnapped forever.

My heart starts to race, and breathing becomes difficult. Starting to hyperventilate, I feel like I am falling right through the bed. The machine starts to alarm, and the door slams open. I quickly shut my eyes, as I don't want anyone to know I am awake.

"What is going on?" a voice questions. The voice sounds familiar.

"We do not know. Her heart rate shot up, and her respirations have increased," a female answers.

Her voice sounds pretty. She must be my nurse. I hope she will save me from Randy.

"Help her, please." The familiar voice sounds panicked.

"Joe?" I whisper, opening my eyes.

"She is awake!" the lady gasps out.

I see Joe leaning over my bed, and my breathing becomes steadier. I have to be safe if he is here, right? I glance over at the lady, and she is in a bluish-purplish top, with black bottoms. Her black hair is pulled back into a ponytail, with a few strays frizzing. The makeup around her green eyes is smeared, and she looks like she is in her early twenties.

"Honey, I'm your nurse, Allie. Are you having problems breathing?" she asks.

Although Joe is next to me, I still do not feel 100 percent safe. He has gotten to me before; who is to stop him for trying again? Next time, I might not be so lucky.

"Where is he? Don't let him near me. Please, I'm begging you, just keep me safe!" I cry.

"Who? Who do you not want near you?" Allie asks.

"Lizzy, Randy is dead. An animal got to him and killed him. You are lucky you got out alive," Joe answers.

"He is dead?" I breathe out.

I exhale a breath slowly, and relief comes over me. Did I know he was dead? I try to remember, but nothing rings a bell. Are they sure that he is dead? Maybe they only want me to believe he is just to relax me. In reality, is he looking for me again?

"Are you sure?" I ask.

"Yes, Lizzy. The animal ripped out his throat. He cannot hurt you anymore," Joe confirms.

"Elizabeth, do you know where you are?" Allie interrupts, shining a bright light in my eyes.

I squeeze my eyes shut, but she uses her fingers to pry them open. "I know it is bright, but I need to check your pupils. Can you try to keep your eyes open?"

It is difficult, but I manage to open them a bit. "I think I'm in the hospital."

I start to cough; my mouth is so dry. I feel like I swallowed sandpaper. "Can I get some water?"

The last time my mouth felt this dry was after John bit me. Wait…

"John."

"What was that, dear?" Allie questions.

"Where is John? He was captured too! Did the animal get him also?" I panic.

"No, he is fine. He went out to get some food. You do have a few people in the waiting room praying for you. They are all anxiously waiting for you to wake up," Joe explains.

"That is good he is still alive." I smile. "Can I please get some water?"

"Lizzy, I'll get you some. You have been out for two weeks now, so I will have to do a bedside swallow study. If I don't think it is safe for you to drink, you will have to go without until speech therapy sees you. You were severely dehydrated when you came in, and ended up with an infection. You got a cut on your leg from where he had you shackled, and you became septic. Your blood work this morning looks like that is clearing up nicely. You have two more days of antibiotics left. The dehydration is because, your other brother said, you refused to eat or drink after the guy raped you. Which leads me to another thing. I'm supposed to call the police when you wake up. They need to ask you a couple of questions," Allie says before leaving.

Why do they have to call the police? I am not ready to talk to anyone about this yet. A lot has happened; I don't even know what day it is. All I wanted to do was spend a couple of days with Liam, and now here I am in a hospital bed. I do not think it is meant for me to be happy. Wait, Liam has to be the reason I'm in this situation. I mean, he was the one who texted me the location. I cannot believe he has been working with these people the whole time! I'm never going to trust anyone again.

"Lizzy?" Joe asks.

I roll over so I do not have to face him. This situation is all my fault. Joe and John have done so much for me, and this is how I repay them. I'm always getting into some kind of trouble lately. The tears build up in my eyes. If I start crying, I'm never going to stop.

"Lizzy, please do not shut down. Talk to me," he pushes on.

Hearing the concern in his voice makes the tears escape. They are rolling down my cheeks, and I'm trying to stay quiet so he doesn't know I'm crying. He might be concerned now, but I know later he will just be disappointed in me. This is all my fault.

"I'm sorry," I say, sniffling. I close my eyes and wipe the tears away from my cheeks.

"For what?" he asks.

He touches my shoulder, and I pull away from him. Although I could use a hug, I do not want to be touched. Not now. "This is all my fault. I keep putting our family in danger. I fell for a complete stranger, and in return, he hurts us. I should have never trusted him."

Rolling onto my back, I look over at him.

"What are you talking about?" he questions.

Is he really acting dumb? "Liam set me up. He was the one who texted me to come to that location. He has been working with Randy this whole time."

I wipe my eyes again, but the tears keep coming. This was probably how I got dehydrated the first time.

Joe doesn't say anything; instead, he sits on my bed and pulls me into a hug. It takes me by surprise, and I'm not ready to be touched.

"What are you doing? Let go!" I cry.

I start slapping him and trying to push him away, but he squeezes me even tighter. *Please let go,* I think. *Please...*

I finally give up the fight and start to bawl on his shoulder. I wrap my arms around him, and I finally feel safe.

"I'm just happy you are awake and safe. We thought we were going to lose you. When you came in, your blood pressure was shitty, and the infection was attacking your weak body. They told us it was up to you if you wake up. I'm just relieved both you and John are safe now." Joe sniffles.

Is he crying? This makes me feel even worse about what happened. "I'm sorry I'm so stupid."

He pulls away from me and frowns. "You are not stupid. None of this is your fault. You do have every right to be mad at Liam, but it isn't for what you think it is. He wasn't working with him. The guy was his brother, and he didn't know Randy was psycho. Randy stole Liam's phone and texted you that night."

I give Joe a puzzled look. What does he mean that monster was Liam's brother? If that is the case, how did Randy find out Liam was seeing me?

"I know what you are thinking: How did Randy find out Liam knew you? Well, Liam was still confused about the injection. Instead of asking his dad or us, he talked to his big brother about it. He didn't want his dad to think he was not ready to go hunting if he asked the wrong questions. Liam didn't tell him exactly, but Randy asked all the right questions and connected the dots," Joe explains.

"Teaches me to trust anyone," I whisper. I wipe my eyes again. "I'm never going to stop crying."

The nurse comes back into the room, and I give her a weak smile. Wiping my tears, I manage to stop crying for a moment.

"Do you have any pain anywhere?" she asks.

"My pride" is the answer I want to give, but what I say is, "My throat, and I have a small headache."

She hands me the water, and I take a big sip and start to cough. Okay, that was stupid to try to drink quickly. I am just so thirsty. Allie goes to take my cup away, but I move. "I promise it was my own stupidity," I cough out.

She gives me that nurse look. You know, the one when they don't believe you because they know better. After I got my coughing under control, I take a smaller drink and it goes down smoothly.

"See? I can drink." I smile.

"Mhmm." She nods. "I'm going to take your blood pressure. While I was getting your water, I paged the doctor, saying you were awake. He will probably be here soon. He is going to go over some of your test results with you. Also, I called the police, and they are going to send someone out to talk to you."

What if I do not want to talk to the police today? Do I get a choice if I'm ready or not? This happened to me, not them. I wonder what test results the doctor wants to go over. Allie already told me that I'm dehydrated and had an infection. What else would there be? Maybe I have a weird blood type; that wouldn't surprise me.

Allie walks over to the blood pressure machine and hits a button. The cuff on my arm tightens, and it surprises me a little. I didn't realize it is already on my arm. I watch the cuff squeeze the life out of my arm. The machine beeps, and the cuff releases. I do not take my eyes off the cuff; I do not feel safe anymore. The squeezing of the cuff reminds me of being chained down.

"Ninety-five over forty-five. Well, at least it's coming up. It is still not where we want it, but we will get there. Is there anything you need before I leave?" she asks.

"Please take this off," I whisper, staring at the blood pressure cuff.

"Sure, I can do that." She smiles. She takes it off and hangs it over the machine. It doesn't help, but it was worth a try.

"Anything else?" she questions.

"No," I state.

She walks out of the room, but I keep staring at my arm.

"Are you okay?" Joe asks.

"Do you know what the doctor wants to talk to me about?" I ignore his question.

"No idea." He shrugs.

I glance at the clock, and it is one fifteen. "Joe, is it day or night?"

"Day. You've been out for two weeks," he responds.

"How did you find me? How did I survive the animal attack?" I quiz.

I need to know what happened.

"Liam knew the general area where Randy lived. After searching the area for twelve hours, I got this weird feeling about where to look. It was like someone grabbed my hand and pulled me in the right direction.

"There was no animal attack. John attacked and killed him. He said he watched Randy rape you too many times. Finally, the last time made him angry enough to break free from the chains. He said he was so worried about you he couldn't even smell your blood anymore. After killing Randy, he grabbed you and ran," Joe explains.

I knew John could do it. "There were many times I wished he would have broken free and killed me."

"Lizzy—"

"Before you say anything, I didn't want to die. I just assumed we were never going to get free and that Randy was going to keep raping me, and death seemed like the logical answer. When I first shut down, I was still aware of what was going on. I knew when he was on top of me, but there was nothing I could do. The whole time I would just let it happen. Lying there, I would just pray, cry, and wish the misery would end. Sometimes I would pray that you would find us, other times it was for John to kill me. I think that was how I got dehydrated so fast—I couldn't stop crying," I admit.

The last thing I want is for Joe to think I am suicidal. I know he needs to know the truth. I want him to know how I felt during those two days. During that time, I felt so empty I was ready to welcome death. It brings a little joy to my life knowing Randy is dead.

"Lizzy, I should have known something wasn't right. I'm sorry I did not protect you. Instead of giving in to your begging, I should have said no. I needed to meet Liam's dad first. Instead, I trusted they would keep you safe, so I let you go. None of this would have happened if I were an appropriate guardian," Joe confesses.

Is he really blaming himself for this? This was not his fault at all. I just wanted to get out of the house. I should have questioned Liam more before I left.

"Joe, you cannot protect everyone. I know you feel like it is your job, but you cannot. I'm aware I'm your responsibility, but you cannot know everything that will happen to me. Danger seems to find me, and I keep walking right into it. With all this happening, does it remind you about how you couldn't protect Kiley from the car accident?" I respond.

He doesn't say anything; he just looks at me with a confused look on his face.

"Melissa told me about the accident. Anyway, I would have loved if someone had predicted this would happen, but no one could. I do have one question. I know you said Liam told Randy about me, but how did you know he took me?"

How did they know it was Randy right away? It just seems odd Liam admitted he told him and then he was the prime suspect in this situation. Randy could have called someone, and they could have taken me. I mean, I'm happy they guessed right, but how did they know?

"Brad, Liam's dad, is here in the waiting room. I think he can explain the answer better than I can. Do you mind if I go get him?" Joe asks, walking toward the door.

Don't leave me! I think, but I say, "Yeah, go ahead."

He walks out, and I start looking around the room.

Although I know Randy is dead, I still do not feel completely safe. I do not ever want to be left alone again. I regret telling them I'm tired of being around them all the time. I was just a teenager throwing a fit.

It isn't long until Joe comes back with an older Native American gentleman. He has long gray hair and is wearing a brown baseball cap. His eyebrows are very bushy and so out of control it is hard to focus on anything else. He is a little bigger built, but not obese at all. I feel like I have met him before.

"Do you remember me?" he questions.

"Vaguely. You do look familiar, but I don't know why," I answer.

"You were about ten the first time I met you. You look the same, except you look sick and you have grown up some. Still have the same unique eyes, and the most beautiful complexion I have ever seen," he began.

I understand I'm cute, but I hate hearing it from someone who is fifty and old.

"Anyway, my name is Brad. Your dad introduced my son and me to you then. Do you remember that at all?" he states.

I think back. "You and a tall skinny boy came over. I think he was sixteen at that time."

He nods. "Yep. That was my Randy."

I gasp when he said that. Randy did not look like the same boy I met back then. He had to have gained over two hundred pounds since then.

"Your father and I hoped after we introduced you to Randy, you both would hit it off. You see, Randy was the only werewolf in the world. Your father and I hoped that since we had the key and werewolf, it would get us one step closer to finding the witch. The hope was you two would be able to tell us who the witch was.

"The next couple of years, Randy started to grow angrier. I decided that it would be best if we stayed away from you for a bit. At least until you were old enough to understand what was going on. I do not know how he found you again, but I'm sincerely sorry that he murdered your mother. Alyssa was always so sweet when we stopped by. Unfortunately, it is Liam's fault he found you at your brother's house. I'm going to let him explain what he did." Brad turns to look over his shoulder.

Stepping away from the door, Liam shuffles in. He is literally dragging his feet and does not look at me. Seeing him makes me angry. I cannot believe he betrayed me.

"Why did you do it?" I raise my voice and sit up.

Normally, Liam makes my heart skip a beat, but this time it speeds up from anger.

"Wellll…" He drags his words, not making eye contact. This makes me madder.

"Look at me when you speak. You are the reason I'm in this place. You are the reason I was raped. I want to know why! I have the right to know!" I shout.

I have so much rage I could shoot fire out of my eyes. It wouldn't surprise me if that is something that would happen.

"Lizzy, let him talk before you rip his head off." Joe places his hand on my shoulder.

I pull away and keep glaring at Liam. "Look at me when you speak!"

Liam shifts his weight to one leg. Finally, he looks up at me, and I can see fear in his eyes. "So I had problems comprehending why you didn't die yet you almost died at the same time. So I met up with my brother to hint around. I mean, he has been hunting his whole life. He should know something about this. I never knew he was part of the super-natural world.

"So I asked him, hypothetically, if someone could be injected with something that protects them from vampire bites. He told me there was no such thing. Besides, he told me, if there was, didn't I think Mom and Dad would have injected us with it? That made sense, but Joe and John said they were not injected either, so I had to go with a different approach. So I—"

"So you told him everything. Even though I told you it was a family secret," I interrupt.

The machine starts to beep loudly. I turn, and the number 140 is blinking. Allie comes in and goes to the machine to make it stop.

"Elizabeth, are you okay?" she asks.

I do not look at her; my eyes are glued on Liam. "Yeah, I'm fine. Just got a little worked up. They are telling me details on what happened during the time I was kidnapped, and what I missed while I was out."

I know I'm lying, but I am not going to tell her the truth. I do not need him kicked out until after he tells me everything.

"Okay, I know you have a lot going on now. Let me know if you need something to help you relax," she says before she walks out.

"Speak!" I demand as soon as the door latches.

"You don't have anyone that you tell secrets to? Even if you are told not to tell anyone?" he quizzes back at me.

"Really, you are going to play that game with me? To answer your question, it is no. I used to, but she is dead now, thanks to your brother!" I snarl.

Does he really think he did no wrong? Even his dad said it was his fault, but he still doesn't see it. Liam's head is so far up his ass he is in denial. All I do know is he is pissing me off.

"Well, I talked to my brother about a lot of things. He, too, is dead now, thanks to your brother. So I guess we are in the same boat," he snaps.

Oh no, he did not! "Tell me what you told your brother and get out of this room. I never want to see your face again!"

How could he just say that to me? His brother killed my mother *and* attacked and raped me. We are not in the same boat at all. How does he know John killed him, anyway? Did they tell him?

"I didn't even tell him anything. I told him I was just curious. He then started pushing the subject. He asked me if I knew a girl who could get bitten but didn't die. I made the mistake by asking if he knew you. It confused me how else he would know what I was talking about. He told me he was good friends with your mom before she died. He wanted to send you his condolences, so I gave him your address. So yes, it was my fault, but I did nothing wrong," he explains.

Before I could object, he storms out of the room. I am happy to see him go. Never in my life have I had so much anger toward someone. I can't even say I hate Randy this much right now. I am so mad I'm almost seeing red.

"Well, Lizzy, it was nice seeing you again. I do have to go deal with my son and plan a funeral. Oh, I do want you to know, I helped your father figure out the necklace thing. So never take that thing off," Brad says before he leaves.

This is too much to take in at once. I cannot believe that Randy and Liam are brothers. They look nothing alike. I also cannot comprehend that Randy is the same person I met a few years ago. How could I be so dumb and not notice who he was? Maybe he gained weight on purpose so I wouldn't recognize him. Although Randy isn't my favorite person, I do feel bad for Brad; he did lose a son that night.

Lying back in bed, I do not feel angry anymore; I just feel stupid.

"Lizzy," Joe states.

"This is my entire fault," I answer.

I cannot look at him. I close my eyes, trying to let everything sink in.

"How?" he quizzes.

How does he not see this is my fault? Is he in denial right now? Later, when we get home, will he realize everything that has happened is because of my stupidity?

"I'm the one who started talking to Liam. I am the one who asked if he could come hunting with us. I am the one who was bitten and lied. I am the one who was kidnapped, which led to John being captured. If I never started talking to Liam, we would have never been in this mess. If I never came to live with you, neither of you would be in this mess!" I sob.

I am so tired of crying. I went from never crying to crying almost every day these last couple of months. Dad would be so disappointed in me if he were still alive.

Joe sits on my bed and pulls me into another hug. I start bawling so hard I am shaking. The machine starts to alarm again. I hope Allie does not come in, but right on cue, there is a knock on the door. The door opens, and Allie peeks her head in.

"Everything still okay in here?" I hear between sobs.

"Yeah, she just needs a minute," Joe answers.

The machine stops, and a few seconds later, I hear the door latch.

"Elizabeth, none of this is your fault. Teenagers are stupid. You will fall for someone who isn't right for you. John and I trusted him enough to help save you, and you said you talked to him every day since then. If he were dangerous, you would have sensed it. You went on a semisupervised date with a guy you didn't know, which was a responsible thing to do. It just didn't go as planned. He chose not to listen to you. So this is his fault, Lizzy, and I don't want you to feel any other way," Joe explains.

The only part I believe in the statement is that teenagers are stupid. "It's going to take time for me not to blame myself."

There is a chance he has no idea what I said, since I'm crying so hard. I need to forget everything, even if it is just for a minute. I pull away from him and wipe my face.

"Tell me about Kiley," I blurt out.

He was not expecting that to come out of my mouth. I figure it would be a great subject change.

"What…do you mean?" he stammers.

"I know it is random. It's just, you are always trying to take responsibility for everything that happens. It made me think about what Melissa told me that night before I was attacked. What happened?" I pry.

"It isn't important." He stands up and walks away from the bed.

Before I could push the subject more, the door opens. John takes two steps in before he stops and stares at me. "You're awake!"

He drops the bags in his hands, runs up to me, and embraces me into a giant hug. I hug him back, and he is squeezing me so tight I can hardly breathe.

"Thank you for saving me," I whisper.

He pulls away, and now I have tears running down my face. "No, Lizzy, thank you," he counters.

Now I am confused. "Thank you for what?"

He smiles. "For showing me I had the strength I didn't know I had. I knew I had to save you, so I really had to dig deep down and ignore the vampire in me."

"Well, I guess since Randy is dead, neither of us will have to worry about it anymore," I reply.

"You are finally safe." He hugs me again.

With both brothers in my room, I finally feel safe. While John tells me what he witnessed during our time with Randy, there is a knock on the door. Walking in is a Hispanic man wearing a white coat and khaki bottoms. He is bald and has bold brown eyes. I'm going to assume he is my doctor.

"Hello, Elizabeth. I'm happy to see you are awake." His accent is thick. I am going to have to pay attention to what he says. "I'm Dr. Fernandez. Can you squeeze my fingers for me?"

I put my hands around his fingers and give him a good squeeze. "Good. Now, put your arms out and do not let me push them down." I did as I'm told. "Now, push up." What is he doing? And am I passing? "Now, I want you to lift your left leg up from the bed." I did. "Now, your right?" This is getting annoying. What is he checking? "Now, push down like you're pushing on a gas pedal, and now, pull back to your nose. Do you know what year it is?"

"Ah, 2016," I answer.

He shines a light in my eyes, and I try not to squeeze them shut this time. Why do they keep doing this? "What month?"

"September," I answer.

"Do you know why you are in the hospital?" he asks.

"I was kidnapped, raped, and dehydrated, and I got an infection," I reply.

"So your blood work looks a lot better than it did when you first came in. Your infection is clearing up nicely, and your neuro signs are good, so that is good," he explains. "And something else came out in your blood work. You're pregnant. Did you know?"

My mouth drops, and I could hear my heart. Did he just say what I think he said? "I am what?" I question. "This cannot be possible. I have never had sex. The only time was when I was raped, which was only two weeks ago. There is no way I could be pregnant already."

My head is spinning. I had to hear that wrong. This has to be a dream.

"Honey, it isn't possible for the test to come back positive if you just conceived two weeks ago. Especially because we test all women in childbearing age when they first come in. Your test said positive the day you came in. There is no way you would be positive after only three days of conception. Do you need your brothers to leave so we can talk?" Dr. Fernandez asks.

"No, because I'm telling the truth. I was a virgin until then!" I cry.

"Well, I'm going to send in for an ultrasound to be done and see how far along you actually are," he says. "Do you have any questions for me before then?"

"Yes, are you sure you have the right patient's test? I want a new pregnancy test. I think there is a mistake!" I fight back.

"We can order another blood test if you want, but I'm sure it will give the same results," he states.

"Yes, please," I beg.

"How about this? I'll have someone come do an ultrasound. If they cannot find a heartbeat, I will pay for the ultrasound test myself and will come and apologize to you for being wrong. If they do find something, then you are pregnant," he offers.

I do not like that idea, but I don't think he is going to redo the test, so I have to take that offer. I nod, and he leaves the room. Lifting the blankets over my head, I decide to hide. This just keeps getting worse. Just when I thought I was safe from Randy, I find out I might be pregnant with his child. There is no way I am ready to be a mom either. I have too much going on in my life to have to worry about a little werewolf baby. I really hope it is just a false positive.

"Lizzy," John says.

"I can't," I answer.

"You know we are here to help," Joe states.

I come out from under the blanket and stare at them.

"With everything that has gone on in my life these last few months, do you think I'm ready to raise a baby? Just when I think I might be getting a normal life, God says, 'Ha, ha, you can handle this too.' My mom always said, 'He never gives you more than you can handle.' Guess what? I don't know how much more I can take before I break.

"I have never had sex, so I do not know how I could be pregnant already. I mean, you said I was missing for two days and been here for two weeks. That means I'm only two weeks pregnant. There is no way I'm pregnant. I can't do this, I really can't!" I stop and start to hyperventilate. "I cannot breathe."

I start to feel claustrophobic, like the room is closing in on me. My heart is about to come out of my chest. I cannot get a deep breath, and the room is growing dark. This is it; this is how I'm going to die. The alarms are beeping, but I'm not sure where its coming from. People rush into my room, but I cannot hear what they are saying. My ears are plugged, and the only thing I can do is take quick shallow breaths. Something sharp pierces into my arm. I try to pull away, but they have me held down. What feels like a lifetime goes by, then the room grows dark and my eyes finally close.

*****

Opening my eyes, I feel really groggy. I rub them and glance around the room, which is completely dark. I start to freak out again a little. "Hello?"

A bright light flips on, and I shut my eyes quickly. That is too much for my eyes.

"Lizzy, you scared us," Joe says.

I open my eyes, and he is sitting next to me.

"What happened?" I ask.

"You had a panic attack. They gave you something to help you calm down, and it sure worked. You have been sleeping for fourteen hours. I asked if they gave you too much, but they just said that is what the doctor wanted. The police came, but you were out. This time they kept someone here so they could talk to you as soon as you woke up. Do you just want to get it over with?" Joe replies.

I really feel crappy right now. I'm nauseous, and I just want to be left alone. Except I know he is right; I just need to get this over with. "Yeah. And will you grab my nurse too?"

Joe nods and walks out the door. John walks over to me and sits at the end of my bed. "What are you going to tell them?"

"John, I'm going to be sick," I answer.

He hands me a basin, and I start to gag before I throw up a couple of times. What is this stuff? I haven't eaten anything in two weeks.

"I haven't eaten anything. How could I have something in my stomach?" I complain.

"Lizzy, they fed you through a tube up your nose. They just pulled it out while you were out this time around. They are hoping you will be able to eat now that you're awake," he explains.

Well, that makes sense.

"I'm going to tell them you and I were on a hike and then got kidnapped," I reply.

"Really?" he asks, taking my basin away from me.

"Yeah. Is that not a good lie?" I question.

"It is. I told them the same thing. I said you and I went on a hike and were kidnapped. Joe didn't question it until later, because I told him we were going to camp out," he explains. "I just think it is weird you were going to tell them the same thing without us talking first."

"Maybe we have been around each other too long that we are rubbing off on each other." I chuckle.

I feel like I have heard them talking about it before, except I don't know how. No one has said a word to me while

I was awake. Before I could question it, Joe walks back in with an officer.

I give the officer a glance over. He is tall and kind of chunky. Although he has thick black eyebrows, he has no hair on his head. Glancing at his eyes, I notice they are a grayish color. Needing to know if I can trust him, I decide to tap into his emotion before I get started. I focus on him, and the only feeling I get is a stabbing pain in the head.

"Oh, fuck, that hurts. That was a really stupid idea, Lizzy. You are not up to par," I say, grabbing my head.

Luckily, the pain disappears as soon as I quit focusing.

"What did you do?" John asks.

"Nothing," I lie.

"Elizabeth, I'm Officer Sheldon Davis, but you can call me Shelly. I need to ask you a few questions about what happened to you. Is it all right if I talk to you in private? I know you are a minor, but sometimes I find that kids can talk to me more honestly when no one is around," he explains.

I look at him but glance over at Joe. I am terrified of being alone. "No, I don't want to be left alone. Not with someone I do not know. I mean, I know I should trust you, but with all the recent events, I trust no one."

"I understand, but you are safe with me," he confirms.

"I know I am. It just scares me to be alone in a room with a stranger," I admit.

"How about this, Lizzy? We will stand outside the door. If you need us, you yell," John offers.

I sigh but nod in agreement. I don't like this idea, but it is better than nothing.

The door latches, and Sheldon sits down in a chair next to my bed. "Before I ask you my questions, I need to know, do you have any questions for me?"

"Are you going to take me seriously?" I quiz.

I didn't mean to ask that, but it slips out.

"Of course I am. I have a daughter your age. If this happened to her, I would do anything to protect her. That is exactly what I'm going to do with you. I want to protect you but need to ask these questions. Between you and me, off the record, I'm happy the monster is dead," he replies.

He does not look old enough to have a daughter my age. He sure is aging well, unless he was young when she was born. I want to ask, but I figure it would not be appropriate. It also helps me relax when I hear he is happy that Randy is dead. I think I'm ready for this.

"So before being kidnapped, what were you doing?" he interrogates.

He pulls out a small notepad and pen. He is ready to write everything down, and it makes me nervous. What if I say something that doesn't match John's story? I mean, he was right, we didn't talk about this.

"My brother John and I decided to go for a hike. We told Joe we were going to camp out so he wouldn't worry about us not coming back that night. All I remember from the hike is walking through some trees and waking up in a basement. When I woke up, my head was pounding, so I assumed I was knocked out," I explain.

"What about after you woke up?" is the next question.

As I think about it, a chill takes over my body. Thinking about that place gives me the creeps. "I tried to put my hands on my head since it was pounding, but I couldn't. I was chained to the bed. My brother said my name, and I saw he was chained up on the other side of the room. Except he was standing and his arms were chained above his head, and his feet were shackled to the floor. A few seconds later, Randy walked into the room."

I do not want to go on. I am not ready to talk about the rape.

"So you knew the guy who did this to you?" he quizzes.

That isn't the question I was expecting, but it is a simple one. "Yes. About three months ago, he broke into my mom's and my home. I escaped, but unfortunately my mom was murdered. The police back in Centennial, Wyoming, have been looking for him. He found me again a day before the kidnapping, when he attacked me at my job. At that time, he drugged me and took some of my blood. The police in Olathe, Colorado, have been notified about that attack. I'm going to be honest, I'm not sure where I am now. I cannot remember where my brother took me for our hike.

"Before he attacked me at my job, he did tell me he never wanted to hurt me. It was also never his intention to kill my mom, he said, that things just got out of hand. Of course I don't know if I can believe him or not. When I was kidnapped, he kept saying he didn't want me to die and that he needed me. I still do not know why," I reply. "Oh, I recently found out that the guy I liked is Randy's brother. There was no connection with Liam knowing Randy was after me. It was just a fluke."

Officer Shelly writes everything down. "Before he broke into your house, had you met him before?"

I nod. "He didn't look the same, so I didn't recognize him. The last time I saw him, I think I was eleven. My dad was friends with his dad."

"So what happened while he had you captive?" he questions, looking up at me. "I know it is going to be tough, but I need you to answer with as much detail as you can."

I close my eyes and swallow hard. I'm not ready to talk about this, but I know I have to. "Shortly after I woke up, Randy walked into the room and was happy I was awake. He came over to the bed and pulled my pants and underwear down. I tried to fight, but it was useless. He climbed on top of me and raped me. The pain was unbearable. I swear he did that every half-hour. After a while, I just blacked out, and next thing I know I woke up here."

Tears start to stream down my face. This is so hard to talk about. Now I see why people don't go to the police about being raped. Besides, there is nothing they can do now; Randy is dead.

"Do you know anything about the animal attack?" he pries.

Shaking my head, I answer, "No. I just know John and I are lucky to be alive."

"Well, I think that is all I need for now. We will be in touch. Thank you, Elizabeth. Do you have any questions for me before I leave?" he asks while putting away his little notebook.

"No questions, but I have a statement. I am happy Randy is dead. I'm happy he cannot torture me anymore," I admit.

"This is off the record, but me too." He smiles and winks at me.

Officer Shelly leaves the room, and John walks in.

"He is talking to Joe. I need you to answer me honestly: Are you okay?" John asks, sitting next to me.

"Honestly, no," I answer. "It's going to take time for me to heal. Are you?"

He shakes his head. "Can I tell you two things? But I do not want you to panic or tell Joe."

Well, of course I'm going to panic now. "Of course you can."

"Randy dried me out too much. I'm struggling with the smell of human blood. I don't want you to tell Joe, because I don't want him to think he cannot trust me. I promise you, I have not and will not give in to my cravings," John admits.

"John, is there something I can do to help?" I ask.

"I'm just going to be out hunting more. I'm only telling you because I want you to know it has nothing to do with you. I'm not struggling because of your scent. I'm struggling because I was starved," he explains.

"What's the second thing?" I worry.

"I can hear its heartbeat." He nods toward my stomach. "It is strong."

I close my eyes and hide under my blanket. "Why is this happening to me?"

"We will help you, you know that," John assures me. "I need to know, though, are you sure you never had sex before? I mean, Joe and I are not going to be mad if you did, but we might lecture you about safe sex."

"I am sure!" I cry out.

I cannot believe he just asked that. Maybe if I hide under this blanket, none of this will continue to happen.

"What is going on?" Joe questions.

I hear the door close. I really hope it is just us three in the room. I do not want any nurses or doctors to come in and tell me any more bad news. Although I personally do not know what would be worse than finding out I am pregnant with my rapist's child.

"Oh, I was just asking her if she was sure it was Randy's child," John admits.

The door squeaks, and I roll my eyes.

"Hello, Elizabeth, my name is Dr. Bridget Morris. I'm an ob-gyn," she introduces.

"Sorry, Elizabeth is not in right now. Please come back when this nightmare is over," I reply.

Did that work?

"Elizabeth, I know it is scary, but I need to examine you. I talked to Dr. Fernandez, and he said you are convinced you conceived two weeks ago when you were raped. I'm going to see how far along you are, and Rose here will do an ultrasound on you." She turns to my brothers. "Can I ask for you guys to step out during the exam? I'm going to expose her a little," Dr. Morris explains.

I come out from other the blanket just to see the boys walk out. "Dr. Morris, I can promise you, I was still a virgin until I got raped. This baby is not normal."

"Elizabeth, just relax. Let me do the exam, and then we can talk about the conception date," she states.

I sigh, "Fine."

It isn't like she is going to believe me, anyway.

"I am going to do a pelvic exam on you. Normally, I do this in my office with beds with stirrups, but since this is a special case, I came here. Do you think you can bend your knees and drop them to the side? You're not going to like it, since you were violated down there, but I will be gentle," she explains.

I do as I'm told, and that is when I realize I'm not wearing any underwear, and I feel like there is something already up there.

"Um, what is in me down there?" I ask.

"You have a catheter. I'm sure the nurse will be taking that out here soon, since you're awake. It just helped you pee while you were unconscious," she explains.

Wow, my lower half has seen more things in the last two weeks than it has seen in its lifetime.

"Now I'm going to uncover you and check your cervix. It will be uncomfortable, but it will be quick," she explains. "Here goes my finger."

I feel the pressure from her fingers going in. I do not want anyone near there for a long time. "You are doing great," she assures me. "Are you doing okay?"

"Yeah," I whisper.

"Okay, now you are going to feel the speculum go in," she warns.

That hurts, and a flash of Randy slamming himself into me comes to my mind. I close my eyes, and tears start to stream down my cheeks. She really needs to get out of there, now.

"Okay, all done. Everything feels normal down there. Are you okay?"

I shake my head and wipe away the tears. "I'm never going to be okay."

I can tell I am making her uncomfortable, but she tries to be professional. "It wasn't your fault," she states.

Well, it sure feels like this is all my fault.

"I'm going to measure your stomach. I'll cover you from the waist down, but I will need to pull up your gown," she directs.

I pull up my gown myself and gasp when my stomach is exposed. There is already a little bump. It isn't much, but enough for me to see it. There is no way I can be showing already; this has to be in my head. Dr. Morris is saying something to me, but I am not paying attention. My eyes never leave my belly.

"Cold gel," I hear right before I can feel it.

I glance away from my stomach, and Dr. Morris has a little machine in her hand. She places the wand on my stomach and starts moving it around. "Do you hear that?" she questions.

I focus and hear a fast whooshing sound. "Yeah," I answer.

"That is your baby's heartbeat. It is strong and sounds healthy," she confirms.

That does not comfort me at all. It just confirms this is all real.

"Now I'm going to see if I can get some pictures of your baby," Rose states.

She puts some more gel on my belly and starts moving her wand around. I glance up at the screen, and all I see is a circle.

"Here's your little baby," Rose gushes.

As I see the jelly bean on the screen, my heart falls in love but shatters at the same time. I cannot raise this baby. It is half-werewolf; I don't know how to raise one of those. No wonder it is growing so fast—it is half-puppy. I'm not ready to be a mom, but I cannot put it up for adoption either. What if normal people adopt it and then it turns into a puppy? How would they handle that? Also, I live with John; if a werewolf bites him, he could die. Ugh, why does this have to happen to me?

"I'm saying you are about eight to nine weeks and a couple of days," Dr. Morris states.

I shake my head. "I can't be."

"Thanks, Rose. You're free to go," Dr. Morris tells her.

"Good luck, Elizabeth," Rose states and walks out the door.

"How is this happening?" I cry.

"You had sex," Dr. Morris answers.

"I was raped two weeks ago," I counter.

She shakes her head. I know she doesn't believe me. Hell, if I weren't living it, I wouldn't believe me either.

"Elizabeth, is there any way you had sex a while ago and you just blocked it out? Was it bad? Do you feel safe at home? Do your brothers make you uncomfortable?" she questions.

"What? No! I mean, yes, I feel safe at home. This isn't an inbred baby! I need you to believe me, this baby is growing faster than a normal child!" I plead.

She is getting impatient with me. She crosses her arms and starts to tap her foot. I find this very unprofessional. "Okay, humor me. When was the first day of your last menstrual cycle?"

"September 2," I answer.

"Okay, if I was measuring from that and not conception date, you would only be three, almost four weeks pregnant. Now you swear your conception date was two weeks ago, so that would make you about two and a half weeks pregnant from your rape to now. Are you saying your baby is growing a month per week? How about this? To humor you, I will do an ultrasound on Sunday before you discharge. If you are measuring thirteen weeks by then, then I will have to believe you. If you do not, you will have to tell me the truth around when you actually conceived. Does that sound like a deal?" she questions.

"Yes!" I about jump out of bed.

I know she still thinks I am lying, but at least she is going to humor me. I cannot wait to see the look on her face when she finds out I have been right this whole time.

"Okay, I'm going to send your brothers back in. I will see you on Sunday," she says while walking to the door.

I'm sure she is thinking, "How delusional is this chick?" She is probably going to tell her coworkers about me. Until Sunday, when she finds out I have been telling the truth the whole time. When she is gone, I have a minute to myself. I place my hands on my belly and take a deep breath.

"Baby, I want you to know, no matter what, I will always love you. You just were conceived at the wrong time!" I cry.

Tears flood my eyes and run down my cheeks. Deep down I really want to keep it, no matter what is wrong with it, but at the same time, this isn't the right time for me to have a baby. I am unable to raise whatever this is. All I can do now is wait until Sunday and see what the doctor decides to do after she finds out the truth.

Chapter 24

"Oh my god!" Dr. Morris states when she walks in.

"What?" the three of us say in unison.

"I cannot believe it! I was reading the radiology results of her ultrasound earlier. You're measuring at about thirteen weeks now. I don't even have an explanation for this!" She sits on a stool and wheels over to me. "Elizabeth, I owe you an apology. I accused you of being one of those teenagers that lie about not having sex. I just thought you were in denial. I am so sorry. I know you don't live around here, but if I offer to drive down once a week, will you keep me as your ob-gyn? I feel like I need to see you through this pregnancy. Let's be honest, no one is going to believe that you are growing a month a week, anyway!"

She is right; no one is going to believe me. I also do not want too many doctors knowing about me. I do not need them to try to study me. Although I'm debating on ending this pregnancy when I get home, I still need a doctor for that week.

"If you want to," I answer. "To be honest, it is weird how much it has grown. I can see its feet and hands better in this picture than the last."

"Do you feel any different since I last saw you on Wednesday?" she asks.

"I don't feel as nauseous, and my shirt is feeling a little tighter," I answer.

"Well, you are heading into the second trimester here in a couple of days. Sometimes morning sickness eases up. Don't be surprised if you still have some queasy days. Also, I'm going to do some blood work on you. We can find out the sex of the baby with it. Do you want to know?"

I want to know, but at the same time, I don't know if I should. She puts a wand to my stomach, and the whooshing sound starts again.

"Although I am stumped on why your baby is growing so fast, it seems very healthy," she announces. "Oh, did you want to know the gender?"

I sigh. "Can you email me it? I don't know if I want to know. This way, if I get an email saying *gender*, I know I can find out if I want to," I ask.

"Of course we can. Well, I am going to try to do some research on your baby, and I want to see you next Friday. I will have my nurse call you when I know which clinic or hospital I will be at. I'm signing you off, and as long as Dr. Fernandez signs you off, you can go home," she states. "It was nice meeting you, Elizabeth."

She reaches out her hand, and I shake it.

"Joe and John, until next time."

As she walks out of the room, I am relieved I can hopefully go home today. I miss my bed. The guys have been sleeping in chairs, so I'm sure they are ready too.

I sit up on the edge of the bed and realize I have to pee for the fifth time in the last two hours. The drive home is going to be fun, since it is a two-and-a-half-hour drive. I walk into the bathroom, sit down, and I can hear Joe and John talking. I decide I'm going to stay in here a little longer and listen.

"What do you think, John?" Joe asks.

"We are going to be uncles," John answers. "Honestly, I think with time she will be fine. She has gone through a lot in the last three months, and now adding a baby to it. You know we are going to have to help her with the baby. We are going to have to help her get through these next six weeks."

"I have no issue helping with the baby. I am just wondering if we will be able to help her emotionally," Joe counters. "I think she should go see a therapist. The doctor did suggest that to us. I know you were captured too, but she went through a little more. I'm not saying what happened to you wasn't traumatic. I mean, you did watch her get raped multiple times, but—"

"She has gone through a little more in the last couple of months than I have. Besides, if I talk to a therapist, I might slip up and say I'm a vampire. We could ask her what she wants to do. If she feels like she can handle this on her own, then we will not push it, but if she needs the help, we will get it for her," John replies.

I love how concerned they are about me. Hearing enough, I wipe, flush, and walk out. Going to the sink, I see them in the mirror looking at me with pity on their face. I hate when they look at me like that.

"That right there needs to stop! Stop looking at me like I'm broken if you don't want me to think I am. Also, I do not need a therapist. I'm fine," I scold them.

Before they could say anything, the nurse walks in. She smiles at me, and I grin back. I decide I am just going to be in denial and act like everything is okay. Nothing could go wrong with this plan.

"Okay, Lizzy, I have your discharge orders here. I am going to go through them with you, wheel you to the car, and you can finally go home after almost three weeks!" she says.

"Great! I'm ready to sleep in my own bed. I think I also need a shower. It's been about three weeks since I took one!" I dance.

"I bet you are!" She chuckles.

My discharge orders are to take my prenatal vitamins, see Dr. Morris once a week, and watch the cut on my leg to make sure it doesn't get infected again. Although, since it is almost completely healed, they do not think I have anything to worry about. The nurse gets me a wheelchair, and pushes me down to the car. When I'm in, she closes the door and waves as we pull off. I feel bad that I do not know her name, but I hope she and the rest of the nursing staff know how much I appreciate their care for me. I glance at the clock, and it is ten in the morning. Yes! That means I will be home by lunchtime. I'm starving!

The ride home is very quiet. I was expecting Joe and John to bring up therapy again, but they don't. The only time someone says something is when I have to pee. Which is only three times and annoys all of us. I know we all have a lot to say, but no one knows how to say it. I want to try to tap into their emotions, but the last time I tried that, I got that shooting headache, so I'm afraid to try again. This ride is too quiet, and I start to get lost in my own head.

Will I be able to raise a werewolf child? Do I even know how to raise a normal child? I do not have the help like my mom did when she was my age. The father and my parents are all dead. I know Joe and John will help, but what if John gets bitten? I cannot let him die because of this child. I wonder if anywhere around does abortions at thirteen to fifteen weeks. I always promised my mom that if I ever end up like her, I would tell her right away and I would take full responsibility. Except that was if I got knocked up by my boyfriend, not raped. Maybe I will be just fine raising a child. I mean, if I don't do anything, I'm going to be a mom in six weeks. Oh, crap, I could be a mom in six weeks! I guess I'll just drop out of school and get my GED. Say goodbye to med school! Who am I kidding? I am never going to med school with this life.

"Home sweet home," Joe states, pulling into the driveway, pulling me out of my trance.

I glance at the clock, and it is one. We get out of the car and walk inside.

"I'm going to order pizza," Joe states. "Does baby have any request?"

Did he really just ask that? Wait, yes, baby does have some requests. "Garlic cheese bread with extra garlic, extra cheese on the pizza, and egg rolls."

He chuckles. "Egg rolls on a pizza?"

"Appetizer. Duh?" I smile.

"Okay, how about I go pick up the pizza and get you some egg rolls too?" he offers.

"I will love you forever!" I answer. "I am going to go shower while you do that."

Heading up the stairs, I get winded by the time I get to the top step. Oh, this isn't good. I need to start working out again. I strip out of my clothes as soon as the door closes. I stop at the full-length mirror, and I'm disgusted by what I look like. My ankle and wrist are discolored, and looking in my eyes, I look defeated. Not only do I look it, but I also feel it. Walking into the bathroom, I turn on the water and wait for it to warm up. I glance down at my swollen stomach and place my hands on it. I cannot believe this happened three weeks ago. Just when I didn't think my life could get more difficult, boom, this happens.

I step into the shower, the warm water hugging me. I thought this would relax me, but it isn't helping. I just feel so filthy. I grab my loofah, squirt about half the bottle of body-wash on it, and start to scrub every inch of my body that I can reach. After rinsing off, I still feel dirty. I add more soap and start to scrub even harder. I get to my stomach, and it reminds me of everything that has happened in the last couple of weeks, and I feel dirty all over again.

I try scrubbing three more times before I fall to my knees and start sobbing. My life sucks so much I do not see a bright side anymore. This shower is not helping; I need to get out. Pulling myself up, I wrap myself in a towel and walk to my bed. I lie down and bawl into my pillow. I don't even care that water is dripping off me, making my bed wet. To be honest, I do not care about anything at all; I just don't think I can do this life anymore.

There is a knock on my door. I don't answer, but it doesn't stop whoever from coming in.

"Lizzy?" John questions.

I sit up to see him walk in, but look away. Why can't they just leave me alone? All I want is some alone time to process. Why won't they let that happen? The water from my hair keeps dripping down my body. It is making me cold, but at least I know I can still feel something.

He sits next to me and tries to put his hand on my shoulder. I pull away and wipe my eyes. Why do people keep touching me? Just stop. I do not want to be touched by anyone anytime soon.

"Lizzy, we need to talk about what actually happened to us," he whispers.

I do not want to talk about it. Not now, not ever. I just want this to be over with.

"I wish you had killed me," I admit.

I'm not trying to look for sympathy or anything; I'm just being honest. He wants to know how I'm feeling? Fine,

I will be honest. My life needs to be done. Glancing over at him, I notice he isn't even looking at me. He is staring at the floor, fiddling his thumbs.

"If I killed you, how do you think that would make me feel?" he questions. "Especially after I came back to a normal state of mind."

Personally, I do not care what he would think. I'm just sick of everything and tired of feeling this pain.

"Honestly, I do not care. I realize I'm being selfish, but I cannot do this. I just want my mom. I want to yell at her for lying to me all these years. Then I want to cry on her shoulder and ask her why this is happening to me. I want to go back to my normal life, where my biggest concern was who was going to flirt with me today. I do not want to worry about if something is going to happen to me. Just because Randy is dead doesn't mean there will not be someone else. Now on top of that, I have to worry about this child, who will be here in six weeks. I cannot do this. I cannot live this life anymore!" I sob.

"Lizzy…"

He is unable to finish his sentence. Without hesitation, I grab my necklace and yank it off.